WHEN FATE RETURNS

A River Flats Series
Book 1

Sheryl M

A catalogue record for this book is available from the National Library of Australia

Publisher:
Australian Self Publishing Group, Pty. Ltd / Inspiring Publishers
PO Box 159, Calwell, ACT 2905, Australia.
Phone: 61-(0) 2 6291-2904
http://australianselfpublishinggroup.com

National Library of Australia Prepublication Data Service

Author: Sheryl M.

Title: **When Fate Returns**
       A River Flats Series – Book 1

ISBN: 978-1-923250-35-2 (print)
ISBN: 978-1-923250-36-9 (ePub2)

"You did it!"

Chapter 1

Where in this town could you find a decent breakfast? It was either some kind of health food with a superpower attached to it and tasted like carboard or an overpriced piece of toast that wouldn't touch the sides of a real man's gut.

Today he needed a breakfast that would sustain him if he was going to make it through the morning.

Drake Harrison had wanted this day to arrive for years, and now it was here, all he wanted was for it to be over and to get back home. Back to the smell of horses and dirt and, of course, Sophie. She would be missing him by now and not liking Reggie coming by all the time. He was only here for another couple of days, and then he could go home and never think of any of this ever again.

Not long now.

Stopping at the end of the motel entrance, he looked up and down the road. The cursed fog had descended across the city again in a thick tainted blanket. He couldn't see much either way he looked, but he knew from the last two days of walking up the road, that there was nothing decent for breakfast that way. He might as well try down the hill this time.

His boots made a click, click on the cement path as he walked down and around the corner, narrowly missing a large black-and-white dog and its sweaty owner. Both were breathing so hard, it was hard to know who was panting more. Shaking his head, he turned back to his mission of finding a good breakfast. He had only made it another few steps when a great big hairy dog decided to wrap its lead around his legs. Grabbing the cement wall for support before his legs got pulled out from beneath him, he cursed as a little voice tried to help.

"I'm so sorry. Here Snickers, come here. Oh! Will you just sit still, baby."

The woman had no control over the large dog and the large mutt was jumping up and tangling himself and Drake more. If he wasn't careful, he would end up with the bloody thing on top of him, while he was flat on his ass.

In a swift move, Drake grabbed the lead from the woman and growled, "Sit." The dog stopped moving and sat just long enough for him to untangle his legs and one arm from the lead and the fool animal. Why did people in the city always want large dogs? They needed space to run and to be trained correctly. If he trained his horses like they trained their dogs, he would have been out of business years ago.

Handing the lead to the lady, who realised the look on Drake's face was not quite as friendly as she hoped it would be, she took the lead and stalked off, whispering something about the bad man to Snickers. The lump of a dog bounded off none the wiser and looking for the next person to say hi to and wrap up in its lead.

"That dog nearly had you flat on your back this morning."

Hearing the elderly voice, Drake turned with a slight smile on his face. "Yes, it did." His eyes fell on a little old lady leaning heavily on her walking stick, standing near a tall overgrown tree in her yard. Nodding to her, he said, "Morning."

"Morning to you too. You're not from around here, are you?"

"What gave it away? My boots and hat or my balancing skills with my legs tied?" Drake smirked at her.

"Oh, definitely your balancing skills," she teased and smiled back.

"I missed my calling with the circus then," he mused.

The old lady refocused her attention on the tree beside her. Reaching up, she held a small tree branch while she poked her walking stick into the spiky looking branches. She was a small-framed woman and a little uneasy on her feet. She reminded Drake a little of Vicky. He missed Vicky's smile and made a mental note to go and see her once he got back. She would want to hear all about his trip and how things were finally over.

Vicky had become his confidant when it had all gone wrong. She never had to ask what was wrong, she just seemed to know, and in her own way, she would get him to talk about it. At least the amount he felt comfortable with. Vicky meant the world to him, and he missed her in that moment.

Focusing back on the older woman, he realised she was trying to get something out of the tree. "Did you need help with something?"

"That paper boy couldn't aim if his life depended on it. This is the third time this week he has put my paper in this tree. I am sure he thinks I have great climbing skills, the horrible little bugger."

Drake bounded over the small cement wall and walked up behind her. He could see the rolled-up paper and another two, up through the tree. Putting the walking stick down, she moved to the side so he could reach them. He pulled all the papers down for her, getting a sprinkling of water over him from the early morning dew. Shaking it off, he looked around. The yard was well kept, and the house looked to be an old workers' cottage from the 1930's era. The paint was starting to peel and the roof was rusting, but he could tell the home was loved.

"My Daniel and I moved into this house about sixty years ago. His father built it and allowed us to move right in with him. We raised all five of our children right here, and now our grandchildren and the two little great-grandchildren come to visit us, sometimes." She said on a sigh, "Well, it's just me now, but I still feel he is here with me." She had a far-off look in her eyes, with a tear in each.

"It must have been good to find someone to spend your whole life with. You're very lucky to have such a great family."

She came back from the past and smiled. "I guess I am. Do you have little ones? A wife maybe?"

Drake shook his head. "No, I don't. I don't think that is the life for me."

"Oh, you say that now but one day it will just happen, and you'll be left wondering how you ever lived without them. They make life complete, full of love and they fill in your day, making the years go by too fast." With that she took the days paper and turned, tap-clicking her way towards the front door. "You can put those in the bin. I don't like reading yesterday's news. Nothing to gain from living in the past."

Looking down at the rolled-up newspapers in his hands, something tightened in his chest. No, nothing good ever came from looking back at the past he thought, especially when all you wanted to do was forget it.

After today he would, and just like these old newspapers, he would put it in the bin and never think of it again. Now though, he thought as he placed yesterday's news into her wheelie bin, he needed to find some good food and coffee and get this day over with.

Kathryn hated Friday mornings. Every tradie in town must have thought that Fridays were a great day to have morning meetings at the café or get that extra half hour of sleep and miss breakfast, only to call in to take it to go. The mornings always started at 6am with the first ones waiting for the café to open. It made the day go by fast, but it was crazy busy.

Secretly, she loved it. In between serving and making coffee she loved being in the kitchen and helping Suzanna get the kilos of bacon, eggs, sausages and hashbrowns cooked for all of them. Her grandmother always said that real men needed a good breakfast, and a cooked breakfast was the way to fill them up.

Since Kathryn had convinced Suzanna to add breakfast to the menu, along with homemade pies, sausage rolls and large sandwiches for the men to take away with them, the café had tripled in sales and reputation. Suzanna had even hired another two girls to help in the morning rush.

This morning seemed extra busy though, and the coffee machine demanded Kathryn's full attention. She had lost count of the number she had already made and there seemed to be a never-ending list of orders attached to the machine. She just kept making cups and calling out names, smiling at the customers, and starting all over again.

One day, she mused, a café just like this will all be hers. One day, she'll be the one in the kitchen making all the orders and putting her twist on the recipes to make the food better. She'd find her own little spot down near the river and have her own café. No more working for anyone else or having to just survive. Nope, the plan is to have her own home, live by her own rules and run her own café. Only a few more years away if she kept working as much as she could, saving as much as possible. Her hidden tin had about $5,000 in it now. She was going to make her grandmother proud and make their dream a reality – she didn't need anyone's help to get there, she'd been brought up by a strong independent woman and was going to be the same. She just needed to keep going and when the time was right, her life would be all they had dreamed about.

The thought of her grandmother made her smile to herself. Her wonder-woman, and Kathryn was going to make her proud and succeed no matter what.

This looked like the place. The street was lined with tradie's Utes as far as the eye could see and the line of people coming in and out was constant. The outside tables were full and what they were eating, finally looked like it could fill his stomach and then some. The smell of bacon and coffee filled the air and his stomach growled in hungry protest.

Pushing through the door, the noise filled his ears and the smell permeated his nose. It smelt so good and reminded him of Vicky's cooking. Every table was filled with people eating, drinking and talking loudly. The only space left was at the corner near the coffee machine, which had a long line of waiting people near it. Squeezing through, he sat and placed his hat on the chair beside him. He didn't want anyone sitting near him, he liked his space when he ate. Looking around, he saw a couple of girls serving and clearing plates as people came and went.

"Morning. What can I get you? Menu or just a coffee?"

Drake turned to see a pretty blonde with blues eyes standing on the other side of the counter. "Morning. Coffee please. Make it strong with a dash of milk and two sugars, and I will have what he is having," he said, tilting his head towards a stocky man just down the bench from him who was tucking into a large serving of bacon, eggs, sausages, hashbrowns and toast. It looked amazing and exactly what he needed.

"Right then. Will do." She smiled and walked off with his order.

The noise drew his attention back around the room. He was so used to the quiet of the farm. That was comforting, this usually was not. He stayed away from crowds and, for the most part, people. However, the noise this morning was a welcome warm feeling. Making him feel that on this day of all days he wasn't alone, even though he was.

Over the past week since he got the news, a coldness had crept over him, making him feel unsafe and unprotected in his emotions and body. It made no sense. He was tall and solidly built, just like the proverbial great Aussie brick shit-house, as Vicky had told him once. But since the news, he felt small and insignificant within himself, just like he did when he first met her. All he had to do was get through the next few hours and then complete it all tomorrow. Then, he could finally get out of here and leave it all in the past, never having to think of it again, never having to feel any of it again. It would be over.

A cold emptiness crept up his spine and made him shift in his chair. He hated the feeling each time it came upon him. After all this time of living with it, he should have been used to feeling, but he wasn't. This week the emptiness had been his constant companion and when it felt like it was taking control of him, he had to move so that it didn't rule his emotions. Emotions were bad, and his were especially unpredictable. Shaking the feeling away, he focused his attention on the going-ons in the cafe. The kitchen was busy, and the coffee machine was still going like crazy. Rubbing his cold hands, Drake took a deep breath and tried not to think about the events ahead of him that day.

"Strong coffee with a splash of milk and two sugars." The soft voice drew his attention back to reality. Unsuccessful in not thinking about the past, his hands were locked together, knuckles white with the strain of the emotions rolling through him and his effort to control them.

"Ah, yeah. Thanks." Drake took the coffee with a nod and a blind look at the girl who had placed it down in front of him.

"You're welcome. Your food won't be long." Kathryn turned and walked back to the coffee machine. Her chest tightened, restricting her breathing and her heart thundered in her chest. Surly, it couldn't be. She had not seen him in nearly ten years but those eyes! She'd dreamt of those eyes for so long and would surely know if she saw them again.

Sometimes, they had haunted her every waking moment, nearly driving her mad. Looking back at the man now, she was sure, but he didn't seem to recognise her. If it was him, surely, he'd recognise her? She hadn't changed that much she thought as she handed out yet another coffee. She still had mouse brown hair and brown eyes. Surely her face had not changed that much in that time.

After this many years, maybe he wouldn't know her, or maybe worse, didn't want to know her. In all truth, maybe it wasn't him after all. Standing at the coffee machine Kathryn kept her robotic movements of making coffees going. Every now and then she would steal a glance at the man. It had to be him. It just had to be. His face was the same, but older and so much more handsome, with a few days' growth of beard on his jaw. His hair was still as dark as night and those eyes were just the perfect emerald green. It had to be him. Her heart thundered harder in her chest, and something told her deep down that he was Drake Harrison. She wasn't mistaken.

"If you keep staring, he'll notice. You're not as sneaky at it as you think you're being. He is definitely your type, though." Annabelle bumped her in the ribs, making her nearly spill the boiling milk on her hand.

"Shhh!" Kathryn replied, frowning at Annabelle as she poured the scalding milk into yet another takeaway coffee cup. "I think I know him. He looks so familiar." She took another quick glance. "And I don't have a type," she jested sarcastically with a roll of her eyes.

"You probably only know him in your wet dreams," Annabelle whispered and winked.

Trust her friend to be so vulgar in front of the customers. Lucky it was so noisy and no one heard. Given that there were mostly men standing nearby, the words 'wet dreams' would have caught their attention if they had heard.

"It doesn't look like he's a local," Annabelle said, both of them now openly staring at the man as he slowly lifted the coffee cup to his lips and drank. "Unless he's going to a fancy-dress ball in the middle of the morning."

Turning to hand over the wrapped bacon and egg burger to the older man at the counter, with the takeaway coffee Kathryn had just made, Annabelle looked at Kathryn. "Where would you have met someone like him? We'd have known if someone so sexy had been here before."

The bell rang in the kitchen, indicating another order was ready to go.

"Oh, and by the way, you do have a type. Any man with jeans, boots and muscles always has you drooling all over them." Annabelle winked as she pushed away from the counter. She was at the kitchen door when she turned and frowned at Kathryn. "How the hell did you get with Rob then? He is nothing like that. Not even close." Annabelle scrunched up her face. When the bell tinged louder this time, like Suzanne had hit it hard with impatience, Annabelle walked through the swinging door shaking her head.

Kathryn sighed. Annabelle had never liked Rob. She didn't understand that the relationship was nothing serious and had started as a desperate measure when she was booted from her last rental. Her old roommate decided to kick her out because her new boyfriend wanted to move in and he didn't like Kathryn. She'd found herself homeless and without the money for her own apartment. She didn't want to use the money she had saved for her café and when she had run into her old school friend, Rob, at the shops one day and found out he had a spare room, she took it. She wasn't the slightest bit attracted to him in any way.

He'd always made her feel slightly uneasy, but she needed the room and desperate times called for desperate measures. They got along well and, over time, she pushed her feelings of uneasiness to the side.

Telling herself it was all in her head. That it was because Rob was the first male she'd ever lived with.

The friendship only turned into something else after a weak moment on her behalf. It was still nothing in her mind, and with all her working hours and whatever it was he did after work, they hardly saw each other; however, his habit was now becoming an issue. Two weeks ago, when he found one of her secret money boxes and took it, she knew the time had arrived for her to get out. However, for the moment she needed to keep a roof over her head and to stay focused. It just made her even more determined to get herself out of there and into her own place and her own café sooner.

Glancing again at the man sitting at the end of the coffee counter, Kathryn shook her head. It wasn't Drake. He was somewhere hours away living in the dust and mud, and she was here, living in the city and working for her dreams. That was what she needed to focus on. Not the sexy man at the end of the counter. Besides, she hadn't seen him in ten years and what was the chance that he randomly showed up here and in this exact café?

The memories of those times must have been playing on her. They did at this time of year. She couldn't help but think about the past and what had gone wrong. Shaking her head to clear her thoughts, Kathryn focused on her job, which was coffees and more coffees. Keeping her head down and working on her dreams. Nothing was going to stop her. Not even the thoughts of Drake or the man at the end of the counter.

Chapter 2

The foggy morning had turned into a warm and sunny day — until now. It had been raining steadily since Drake had climbed out of his Ute. It had taken more time than he thought to get to the cemetery. The minister was not happy about his lateness, but he didn't care. He didn't want to be there anyway. But here he was, standing in the rain, dressed in black, with rain dripping off his cowboy hat.

The sole mourner at the grave-side burial. Nothing special was being said, nothing special should be said for the monster that was going to rot in the timber box forever. The minister had said his usual blessings for the soul and declared that the occupant inside now lay with God, and how this was now a time for forgiveness and moving on.

Hah. Drake knew it was to hell that this soul would go. Only angels go to lay with God.

His eyes remained focused on the box in the hole. No emotion ran through him, only a coldness in his bones that made him feel hollower than he ever thought possible. Finally, it was over, and he was free. Free to live his life and free to move on and never think of any of it again. But forgiveness was something he couldn't do. That monster had created who he had become and now Drake had to live with that inside of him until he, too, was left to rot in the ground. But he would *never* allow himself to become the monster that lurked inside of him.

Never.

"I'm sorry for your loss, my son," the minister said quietly. He was an old man with thick white hair and a hunch to his spine. He was the minister that all monsters got to tell their secrets to on their death beds, and it was to him they begged and pleaded for forgiveness when they knew they were about to take their last breath. Their fear of where their soul would end up next finally becoming a reality.

Hell. They all knew it, and were desperate to tell the minister their secrets so they might clear their sins and get to heaven instead. But not this monster. This one would spend eternity burning in hell. It was this old minister who would have said the last rights over this monster and heard him pleading for his soul. Why did he get that when she never did? She deserved to have her fears heard and to know for sure that she was safe and going to heaven. Where was this old man of the church when that monster stole her from Drake? Nowhere. That's where.

Drake stared at the minster as white-hot rage swamped his body and nearly took him under. He blinked, and with a last look at the hole, making sure the box was where it needed to be, he turned and strode back to his Ute. He needed to get away from there. Calm himself down. Get control of his emotions. But how?

Leaning on the back of the Ute with his arms outstretched, his focus on the wet bitumen, he sucked in deep breaths. The smell of the rain on the hot blackness under his boots made him gag. He needed to get away, but in this state, it was unsafe for himself and others on the road. Looking across the green grassed area he knew what he needed to do. What he should have done many times since that day, but just couldn't.

The time was now. She would be hurt to know that he'd been here but not seen her. Standing straighter, he watched the backhoe move in and begin to fill the monster's hole with wet dirt. Seeing the timber box being buried deep within the ground was a small closure, but not one he wanted to acknowledge.

His focus on her, his boots sank into the mud and grass as he trekked through this plain part of the cemetery. He passed the names of others buried there, their birth and death dates recorded but nothing else on each cement stone that lay on top of the ground. This part of the cemetery was nothing but a gate way to hell for all those whose bodies were rotting here. No one who had love and kindness in their heart would ever have their names found here.

The rain slowed to a light mist as he stepped onto the gravelled path that led to the other part of the cemetery. Passing through the steel gates that looked like something out of an old gothic movie, he noticed that wisteria had grown over the gate's arch and along the brick fence, creating a cascading purple flowering entrance. The grass was clipped to perfection, and the graves all seemed to have flowers or little angel statues on them. This was the place where the gates of heaven were. All these souls were up there.

And this was the part he had not stepped in for years. Not since that day similar to today. How had it been that long?

He had never been able to bring himself to walk through the gates but now his feet couldn't stop him. He knew the exact spot where they were. He knew what the words said and the dates that were carved into the stone. He knew what the angel who sat there to guard them looked like.

His legs carried him through the rows to the patch where his heart, split in two, was buried with them both. Half with her and half with him. Squatting, Drake removed some of the weeds and dead grass from the headstone. His fingers traced the wet stone where the words were written.

"I'm so sorry I haven't been to see you both... I just couldn't get here." Tears filled his eyes. "That's a lie. I could have but..." His breath caught in his throat. "I just couldn't bring myself to come here and be with you." Big raking sobs burst through. "I failed you... Oh Jesus, I couldn't protect you... and that bloody monster... he... he... took you from me." Falling onto his knees on the wet ground, Drake held his head in his hands and let the sobs wash over him, his body rocking back and forth. "I'm so sorry. I'm so sorry. I'm so sorry."

The rain began to pour down, soaking him right through to his bones. He felt small sitting there crying but he couldn't help it. He didn't care who saw him or what they thought. At that moment he wanted to lay down on their grave and be with them, to never get up again. How could he ever get back up again? He had lived, and they had died. He didn't deserve to be living.

This time there was no one to drag him away. No one to drive him to a warm place and feed him. No one. If there was no one then why would he even bother to get up from here? Couldn't he just stay here with them forever?

The rain poured down harder, with a large clap of thunder. Looking up at the sky, he let the coldness hit his face, he was soaked through and now shaking. His emotions were dragging him down.

Get up, get up, her words whispered to him. She would want him to get up. Gathering all his strength, he kissed the little angel's head and whispered, "Goodbye."

Then he stood, a little shaky, and followed his path back to his Ute. The backhoe had completed its job and had left. His heartbreaking sadness began to turn, and he couldn't fight the grief. Didn't want to fight it.

Slamming the Ute door closed and throwing his hat to the other side as he got in, Drake let the tidal wave roll through him, trying to feel it in a controlled manner, like he'd been told, but it was burning him up. Suddenly he had to try to steady his breathing. The stampede of emotions running through him was threatening to erupt dangerously.

Taking huge gulps of air into his lungs he tried to regain his control. To keep it all locked down and buried. He could feel the tears streaming down his face, wiping at them as anger started to burn, and it was a deep, deep hot burn. It tore through him. A growl and scream mixed with pain and agony tore out of his throat in a primal tortured roar and he smashed his palms into the steering wheel repeatedly.

The more the anger and pain rolled through him the more he pounded the wheel, the more he screamed out. A lifetime of pain was flooding out of him, and he couldn't close the gate. He couldn't breathe. The emotions were too strong. As each one tore through his body again and again, he was pulled deeper and deeper down, into the depths of despair and agony.

He was going to die. He was going to die here in the place where that monster was. Where all monsters were. His chest was hurting, his hands were sweating and suddenly the Ute became too confined.

Swinging the door open with such haste it came swinging back and nearly hit him, Drake stumbled out into the rain. The coldness buffeted his body as he fought to calm down and breathe. The coolness of the air and rain filled his lungs and hit him in the face. A moment of reprieve, before he raced behind the Ute and lost the contents of his big breakfast. Twice.

Standing and looking around he tried to make sense of what was happening. Never had he felt like this before. No, that was a lie. He had once, right after it had happened, while he was waiting for what was to come next.

He had to keep his emotions under control and keep to himself. He had to get back to the farm. To Sophie and the horses. It was done now; it was finally over. A hot sensation raced over him, and he lost the last of the contents in his stomach. This time bringing him to his knees, he clung to the tow bar for dear life while his body tried to permanently purge itself of all emotions.

Eventually, the anger and emotions subsided; Drake hauled himself to a standing position leaning on the back of the Ute tray. Shaky, but standing. He would finish here in the city tomorrow, then get the hell out of this place and never come back.

Across town, Kathryn was wiping down tables after the lunch rush. It had been a busier day then normal and for the most part of it she had been on autopilot. The more she thought on it, the more she was positive it was Drake who'd been in there that morning. She would know those eyes anywhere. They had haunted her dreams for years. Mentally shaking her head, Kathryn picked up the plates from the next table and wiped it over with her cloth. It had to be him.

"You know, if you wipe that any more it will be polished so well, I could do my make up in its reflection," Annabelle said as she walked past her with an armful of dishes heading towards the kitchen. The café was all but empty except for a few people sitting in a corner booth.

Picking up her cloth and an armful of dirty plates, Kathryn followed, rolling her eyes at Annabelle's sarcasm. "At least it's clean," she said, placing the dirty dishes into the sink. Pulling open the dishwasher, she mindlessly began to unpack it.

"You, my girl, have had your head in the clouds ever since that cowboy walked in this morning." Annabelle playfully smacked her on her forehead with a dirty hand.

"Oh yuck," Kathryn said, wiping her dirty cloth across her forehead to remove the water and food bits Annabelle had just put there.

"Oh, now that's disgusting!" Annabelle laughed.

Realising what she had just done, Kathryn threw her offending cloth into the sink.

"See, not thinking. You mucked up three coffee orders this morning and nearly killed a customer at lunch by placing extra nuts on her salad instead of no nuts. Your head isn't here today, babe."

Kathryn stopped what she was doing and leaned against the stainless-steel sink. "I don't know what I'm thinking."

"What is it about that cowboy that has you all shaken up"?

"Nothing." She mindlessly started to stack the plates into the now empty dishwasher. "Just leave it, okay."

"You can't say that to me and think I will leave it."

Kathryn sighed, knowing Annabelle was right. She had fast become Kathryn's closest friend since they started working with each other six months ago. They loved to go to the thrift shops and buys lots of clothes together and she was the only person, apart from her grandmother, that Kathryn felt she could truly trust in this life.

She'd told Annabelle lots of things, and Annabelle had told her things that she really didn't want to hear. Like about her and Johnny's sex life and all the costumes and toys they have and when they use them, but if she blushed then Annabelle would tell her even more.

She loved her friend. It was nice to have one again that she felt that close to. Annabelle had coaxed her out of her shell a little and even got her a second job at the pub. Life was so much fun with Annabelle around.

"I know." Kathryn stopped stacking the plates. "I used to know this guy that had eyes the same colour as the cowboy, as you call him, this morning. I haven't seen him for a long time and the cowboy just remined me so much of him, how I miss him and what we had. He just brought back a lot of memories, that's all."

Annabelle touched her shoulder. "If it's meant to be it will be, and if it wasn't him this morning at least he gave us something to drool over for the day. You never know, he might come back in the morning, and I can question him for you."

"No! Just leave it." Even though Annabelle had that look in her eye meaning that was the last thing she was going to do, Kathryn let it go. It was no good arguing with her. When she got her teeth into something, Annabelle was like a dog with a bone.

Besides, Kathryn didn't want to think about the cowboy anymore. He was gone, and she had bigger things to think about. She had her dreams and, looking up at the clock, if she didn't hurry up, she'd be late for her shift at the pub and miss the money needed for those dreams.

"Are you working tonight?" Annabelle asked as she dumped another full load of dirty dishes into the sink that Kathryn had just emptied.

"Really?" Kathryn huffed as she looked at the dishes. The pile seemed never ending. "Yep. I start at 4pm for the prep." It was 2.30 and she had to be out of the café by 3.30. "I have to get moving, otherwise I'll be late again and Billy and Ronnie won't like it." Leaping into action with a newfound energy, Kathryn sped up her movements.

"You work too hard. You need to have some fun." Annabelle grabbed the bin and headed for the back door. "You're going to burn out and miss the best years of your life."

"They will be the best years of my life. Only another few years and I should have enough saved, then you can come work for me!" Kathryn called after her with a smile, but Annabelle's answer was with the slam of the door as she headed toward the big bin outside.

Chapter 3

Kathryn really enjoyed her second job too. The Grand old hotel had been standing for over a hundred years and was still as grand and magnificent as the first day it had opened. Billy's family had owned the old girl since that first day, and the family had taken such good care of the place, it gleamed.

About three years ago, the kitchen had an upgrade worthy of a five-star restaurant in France or New York and the restaurant was constantly booked out a month in advance, sometimes two in summer.

Best of all, Billy had taken Kathryn under his wing and shown her how to do things so that when she got her café, she would have all the business knowledge and skills needed to make it a roaring success. Ronnie had increased her food knowledge and culinary skills, 'worthy of head chef' he'd told her one day. So now, in both a business and food sense, she had all the knowledge she required. She'd promised them both that they'd be first through her doors when she had her grand opening. They had become her cheer squad and were always encouraging her when she felt down and out about it not happening as fast as she wanted.

She was in the middle of plating up a steak and salad for a counter meal when Annabelle came crashing through the kitchen doors at the back of the pub. "Kathryn, Kathryn!"

Kathryn moved the plate to the serving counter and rang the bell for the wait staff to take it to the customer, then smiling, she turned to her excited friend. Annabelle was ready to party by the looks of it. She had on a little red floaty dress with matching red high heels, which matched her bright red lipstick. She was stunning.

Reaching Kathryn's side, she asked "Are you done yet?" She obviously wanted Kathryn to join her for a night out on the town.

Kathryn didn't want to. Her legs ached from being on them for over fourteen hours and she was tired. All she wanted to do was go home and sleep before her morning shift at the café. "I'm not going out with you tonight, Annabelle," she stated as clearly and firmly as she could. Too firm and Annabelle would get upset, but too light and she wouldn't listen. "I have to work in the morning, and so do you, Belle. Just leave me to go home and sleep. Pleeease."

Ignoring her pleas, Annabelle, full of sweetness and fluttering her eyelids, turned to Ronnie the head chef. "She is done for tonight, hey?"

Shaking his head with a smile, he answered, "How can I say no to you, honey?"

Internally, Kathryn groaned. Of course, he'd say that. Ronnie had a soft spot for Annabelle. All men seemed to have a soft spot for her. With her long blonde hair, blue eyes and lushest full red lips all she had to do was turn on her charm and she could lead them around by the nose.

Kathryn frowned. All but Johnny that is. But that was for the best otherwise he wouldn't have a say in anything, and Annabelle probably wouldn't want him. Her friend constantly told her how she loved the challenge of Johnny and using her sexual powers over him. They were a match made in heaven.

Taking Ronnie's yes, Annabelle grabbed Kathryn and removed her apron and smoothed down her hair as best she could. "Well, I guess you will have to do. Oh, wait," she said, pulling some awful smelling cherry lip gloss from her little clip bag.

"Oh, really Annabelle." Kathryn scrunched up her face. "I already smell like the kitchen and my chef's clothes are dirty. I'm not dressed to go out. Do you think that a smear of lip gloss will make all the difference?"

"You never know who you will meet. So yes. Now be quiet while I put some on you." Annabelle applied a thick coat to Kathryn's lips.

"Yuck. That stuff stinks and tastes horrible."

"Yes, but the boys love to kiss it off."

"I'm not going to be kissing any boys tonight, I'm going home to my bed. Alone!" She glanced across to Ronnie for some help but he just shrugged. No help at all.

"Not tonight, my friend." Annabelle grabbed her hand and pulled her half-walking, half-running. "Come on. Quick."

"Annabelle. Stop. Why quick?" But before Annabelle could answer or Kathryn could protest any more, they entered the loud crush of people in the bar area. Friday nights drew a massive crowd. Most came directly from work for after work drinks and stayed for dinner. Many were leaving now, but to every person that left, three others walked in, ready for a night of drinking, dancing, fun and laughter to celebrate the end of another working week.

Tonight was no exception. The place was packed and loud. You could hardly move but Annabelle pulled Kathryn by the arm through the crowd. Pressing through groups of men and women and working her way to the other side of the bar.

"Annabelle. Stop. What is going on?... Annabelle. Please just stop!" Kathryn tried to pull back against Annabelle's grip, but nothing slowed her friend's determined path. She finally stopped at the bar and, with all her might, pulled Kathryn forward with such momentum that she stumbled past her friend, catching herself before nearly landing into the bar and the mountain of darkly clothed muscle sitting next to it.

"Hi, my friend thinks she knows you. Do you remember her?" she heard Annabelle yell over the noise to him.

Kathryn found herself looking into those emerald eyes and wanting to kick Annabelle so hard. She could have just said and let her make her own choice. Not thrown her right at him like this.

He was dressed in a dark shirt and jeans. His face had stubbly growth on it, which did little to hide the chiselled structure of his jaw. He was devastating to her senses. Even more so now she was standing so close to him they nearly touched. The last time she saw him, he had been ten years younger and handsome as hell — and looking at him now had her stomach fluttering. It was Drake. She was certain of it.

Would he remember her? If not, she would just die of embarrassment and melt into the old floorboards. Annabelle was going to pay for this.

Slowly, Drake closed his eyes. He didn't need this tonight. His emotions were raw and all he wanted to do was go back to the motel room and sleep. He only had to finalise things tomorrow and then he could go home. He had come here tonight to have a quiet meal and beer then go back to his room, but the restaurant was full and overflowing, so he had to settle for his steak and salad at the bar. Ordered forty-five minutes ago, he was starting to regret his choice. His mood didn't allow for this. So far, he had rejected a woman who was trying to win a bet with her friends and now this one was using the worst pick-up line in history to try and set her friend up with him.

Why did girls do that? It was tactless and embarrassing. This is why he never went out, even at home he never went to the pub unless it was for someone special. There were very few people he would do that for, and he liked it that way. He stayed to himself and that suited him fine. Drake opened his eyes and looked firstly at the blonde who had spoken and then at her friend, who was dressed in a dirty chef's outfit.

It took him a moment for his mind to work. He hadn't seen her for nearly ten years and now here she was, standing in front of him. She had not changed much at all, other than to become a truly beautiful woman. Her eyes were the same chocolate brown, with long eyelashes that gave them a seductive look. For so long, he had not thought about her, not wanting his mind wandering to places it had no right to be — But here she stood. Right before him.

"Kathryn?" His voice was barely audible over the hum of the crowd.

She smiled shyly and nodded. He rose to his feet and pulled the chair out beside him for her to sit.

"My work here is done. See you in the morning." Annabelle winked at Kathryn and with a big grin only true friends would know the meaning of, said, "Enjoy." She disappeared into the crowd.

"How have you been?" Kathryn asked.

He was still staring at her, his mind unable to believe it was her and that she was here, sitting next to him. What were the chances in this city that they would ever meet again? "Okay, and you?"

"Okay. Busy." She looked awkward, as if she didn't know what to say. Understandable. They had a past together, but he had left, and not contacted her again, not even once to say why.

"Are you still on the farm?" she asked.

It broke the spell and he nodded, taking another sip of his beer as his meal was placed in front of him. "Yep. I will never leave. It's my life." He gave a small smile and looked around at the bar, then back to her. "Would you like a drink?"

"That would be great. A lemonade, please."

Drake waved at the beefy bald man behind the bar, who walked over and smiled at Kathryn.

"Ronnie let you off early tonight?"

"Annabelle found my friend here and came and got me. Ronnie said it was okay. It is, isn't it?" Kathryn looked a little concerned, but the beefy man just smiled as he poured her a lemonade.

"Ronnie has never denied a pretty face so why would he now?" He winked and placed the tall glass on the bar beside her.

Billy looked at Drake, asking if he wanted another, but he shook his head. He wasn't a big drinker. He only had one or two after a hard day's work in summer. Watching the big man walk off, Drake gave Kathryn a puzzled look as he cut into his meal.

"I work here in the kitchens on weekends. That was my last meal for the night." She nodded at his meal then started to talk about her work here and all she had learned.

It felt so easy to be talking with her again, now the initial awkwardness had vanished between them. It was like the past ten years had never happened, like it was only yesterday that they had last spoken.

For the first time in the last week, Drake felt himself relax a little listening to Kathryn talk about the pub, its history, the owners, and the café where she and the little blonde, Annabelle, worked. He was happy that she had made a life she loved here and was working towards her goals. She had this vibrance about her when she talked about food and recipes. She just glowed.

The time passed quickly as they talked. The noise of the crowd became a low drum in the background of their conversation. She even managed to make him laugh a couple of times. It wasn't until Annabelle rushed up to them that he glanced at his watch and realised it had become quite late. Mind you, Annabelle seemed to be always in a hurry Drake thought as she rushed into their conversation.

"Kathryn." The blonde gave Kathryn a side glance and nodded to the front door. "It's time to go. *Now.*" There was an unspoken word between them.

Kathryn stood and tried to look over the crowd in the direction Annabelle had nodded. Then, after drinking down the last of her lemonade, she smiled at Drake. "I have to go, but will you stop by the café in the morning for breakfast? I'll make sure you have one of my specialities."

He stood ready to walk her out, but she shook her head.

"It's fine, Johnny and Annabelle will see me out. I'll see you tomorrow." She smiled when he nodded again, then wove her way into the crowd.

Pushing through the front doors, Kathryn followed Annabelle as she wound her way through the people seated outside on the pavement around tables and chairs, drinking and talking. A group burst out laughing as Annabelle and she walked by.

Kathryn then noticed the group of men standing on the footpath a little further down from the pub entrance. Johnny stood in front of Rob talking, his mates flanked him to block Rob's path into the pub. Kathryn felt sick. Rob must have been coming to see her and they had stopped him. If he'd seen her with Drake, he would have caused a big scene.

Rob didn't like it if she spoke to men he didn't know. He always said they wanted to root her and that he was only protecting her from them. He'd have tried to accuse Drake of that, and it would have created a big fight with Rob later. She hated fighting with him. It was better to just go along with him now — until she moved out.

Annabelle touched her arm as they neared the group. "See, I told you I'd find her for you, so you didn't need to go in. She was cleaning tables." Annabelle raised her eyebrows, a fake smile plastered on her face.

Kathryn caught on real fast, knowing Annabelle and Johnny had just saved her from one of Rob's bad moods. He was always in them lately. He never used to come and walk her home but over the last month he had, and if she was not out by the time he arrived, whether her shift was finished or not, he would demand she leave right that second with him.

Tonight, he looked ready to fight anything that got in his way, but Johnny had kept him distracted while Annabelle found her. Billy didn't like Rob either, so having him cause a problem in the pub was something they all tried to avoid. This job meant the world to Kathryn, and so did the respect of Billy and Ronnie. They all thought they knew what was happening behind closed doors with her and Rob, but it was far from the truth. For her, anyway.

Kathryn smiled at Johnny as she moved past to Rob's side. "I'm sorry. I lost track of time. We can go now." She took Rob's arm and looked both ways before she stepped out onto the road and headed for home.

"I'll see you at work in the morning," Annabelle called after her. "Don't forget you promised to help me in the afternoon after we finish."

Waving back, Kathryn answered, "I remember."

Once out of sight of the others, Rob grabbed her arm and squeezed it so tight she winced in pain and let out a little cry. She tried to break free of his grip, but he was strong.

"What were you really up to in there?" he demanded.

"Working." She tried to hide the tears in her eyes. "That's all, I promise." He squeezed again. "Ouch, you're hurting me. Let me go!" She tried again to break his grip, but he squeezed her harder and pulled her into his body.

"Don't bloody lie to me," he said through gritted teeth, his temper about to blow. "You were whoring yourself out again!" Forcefully pushing her away from him, he continued to walk. "You're such a slut."

Kathryn stayed as close to the road as she could as they walked home. She needed to not provoke him any further and once home she could lock herself in her room. He'd leave after she fed him. He always did.

Lately, he had become increasingly physical with her. She could see in his walk and the nervous state of his body that he had been smoking drugs again. She just had to keep calm until he left. The more he smoked the horrible substance the more intense and physical he was. Luckily so far, he had not forced himself on her. But tonight, as she walked along with him, she wasn't so sure that she wasn't in danger. He was scaring her. More than ever. She needed to get away from him — and fast.

Chapter 4

The next morning as she lay in her bed, the door bolted and a chair jammed behind it, Kathryn listened to the birds singing and knew she couldn't stay any longer in the apartment with Rob. She needed to get out. If she used all her saved money for her café, she could possibly get a one-room apartment and maybe some furniture from the thrift shop, then she could be free. She would go and see a real-estate on Monday. Maybe she could stay with Annabelle until then. Sleep on her couch. Hopefully, it wouldn't take long to find an apartment.

It was still early, and she had not heard Rob come back from where he went after she fed him last night. Thinking back to last night, Kathryn felt her stomach drop and she began to feel sick. He had stood in the kitchen with no pants on and pulled himself off while he watched her prepare his meal. When she realised what he was doing, she was horrified and fearful that he would rape her. He didn't, but she was not going to stay any longer. She wasn't safe here. After she finished work, she would pack up and leave.

Climbing out of bed and checking to ensure she was alone in the apartment, Kathryn made herself a coffee and went to sit at the little wooden table and chairs on the tiny balcony of the apartment. The sun was rising over the city and the noise of cars driving past in the street had begun again for the day. The sounds never really stopped, but this was the start of a new day and as more people woke and moved around, the city started to come alive.

Taking a sip of her coffee and a deep breath, she calmed herself. It was the first real breath she had taken since Annabelle had come and taken her away from Drake. Thinking of him now, a smile lit her face.

It had been so good to see and talk to him again. He was so sexy and made her stomach flutter, but it was more than that. He listened to her every word, and she felt safe with him. Always had. She felt she could tell him anything and he would be understanding. Hopefully, he'd come to the café this morning to see her.

Leaping up from her spot and downing her coffee, Kathryn showered and after taking extra care with her hair and clothes, went to work. She would deal with her situation with Rob after work.

Kathryn arrived at work half an hour earlier than her usual start time to find the café packed and Annabelle and Suzanna were the only two on. They were struggling to keep up. Kathryn took over the coffee machine from Annabelle and slowly they clawed their way back to organised chaos.

"Are you okay?" Annabelle whispered in Kathryn's ear as she collected another order of coffees from next to the machine.

"Yes." Kathryn leaned over and whispered in Annabelle's ear, "But can I stay with you and Jonny for the next few nights till I find somewhere else to live? I can't stay with Rob anymore." She didn't need anyone else knowing her business and felt ashamed that she'd put herself in this position in the first place. She had been so blinded by her dreams that she didn't see Rob as a risk until it was too late.

"Of course. But remember Johnny's mother is moving in for the next month or two on Tuesday after her surgery so I won't have room after that, sorry."

Calling out another takeaway coffee order Kathryn smiled her thanks. "I'll have a place by then, I hope."

Rain falling and the lights blinding him, Drake could hear her yelling, telling him to leave. "Leave now!" she screamed. He ran yelling for her and then there was blackness and nothing.

Drake bolted upright in a cold sweat, screaming for her. He was confused and dazed as sleep returned to its darkness and his mind located where he was. Shifting in the tangled sheets, he turned and swung his legs over the side of the bed. Pulling open the curtains a little, he rubbed a hand over his face to scrape away the last dregs of the nightmare and watched the dawn arrive. His sheets were cold and wet, and he had yet to fully stop shaking.

He always woke after a nightmare with the shakes, but over this last week, they had been there constantly. The little tremors were unnoticeable to others, but he could see it when he held his hands up. The emotions of the week were really starting to affect him.

Only today to go, and he was done. He could go home and never come back.

The first rays of the sun splintered the sky and fell on the window. A new day to finally have it all finished with. After this morning's appointment he would go, leaving it all behind him. Vicki had told him that he had to let it all go and never think of it again, that living in the past was never a good thing. He thought on her words now.

The past had caught up with him last night when Kathryn stepped back into his life. A distracting surprise. Their conversation had flowed so easily, like it always had, and her calming effect on him had made the day's earlier events easier to overcome as he went to sleep.

He had actually slept well until the nightmare crept into his dreams. Thoughts of Kathryn had been on his mind instead of the torment that usually accosted him as he drifted off. He'd welcomed the thoughts of her, letting his mind recall some of their memories together, but not all. She was still as beautiful as ever.

Thinking about her now his stomach growled, and he smiled to himself. He had promised to see her, and he would keep his promise. It was a lesson he had learned and valued years before and he never went back on a promise once made.

Stretching his legs, he decided a shower and a shave would be best before he walked down to the café to see her. Smiling, he stood and headed for the bathroom. By the time he was ready, the café would be open and she would be there.

Drake entered the busy café about an hour later and found Kathryn immediately. She was at the coffee machine. Her hair was tied up in a high ponytail with a few stray strands framing her face. She looked very beautiful.

Kathryn smiled up at him when he pulled up a seat near the coffee machine.

"Morning! Would you like a coffee?" she asked, smiling so widely that his heart beat a little faster.

"Morning, yes please. How did the rest of your night go?"

A shadow crossed her face before she answered, "Okay, and yours?"

"Yep, okay." He looked around the room, thinking it was very busy for a Saturday. He'd hoped it would be quieter so that they could talk a little, but it was hopeless. Small talk was all they could manage. It annoyed him. He'd be leaving this afternoon and would never see her again — he doubted that she would ever venture as far as his farm. It was a full day's drive and was nothing like the city. Thank goodness.

Handing him his coffee she smiled a little oddly at him. "Here you go. It's one just for you."

He could smell it before he tasted it. She had remembered. His face lit up more.

Caramel? It was his favourite and she had added it to his coffee. Looking up at her he raised an eyebrow. "Really. You put caramel in my coffee?"

"Try it." When he looked sceptical, she added, "Trust me, you will like it."

When he hesitated, she laughed. Taking a smell again, he slowly raised the cup to his lips. It was bitter like coffee, but sweet like caramel, yet not overly so. The perfect balance and he loved it. She gave him a 'told-you-so' smile.

Annabelle arrived with his breakfast — which he hadn't ordered. He figured it had arrived curtesy of Kathryn. A big breakfast too, of bacon, eggs, hashbrowns, fried tomatoes, toast and scrambled eggs. Just Like the ones he used to eat with her years earlier. Smiling at both women, he said his thanks and started to eat. Their conversation simple and pleasant.

Annabelle arrived to clear away his plate as soon as he had finished. "Did Kathryn tell you that it's her birthday today?

Kathryn shot a glare at Annabelle, her face heating with embarrassment.

Drake looked to her and smiled. "Happy birthday. Sorry, I never knew when it was. How are you going to celebrate?"

Annabelle cut in before Kathryn could say anything. "We were meant to be going for a picnic and some shopping at the thrift shop, but now I can't make it." Annabelle winked at Kathryn.

Drake hid his smile. Annabelle was as cunning as a fox.

"So, she will be all alone today now," Anabelle stated sadly, taking a tray from another girl as she started to walk backwards towards the kitchen. Cheekily, she asked, "Maybe if you're not too busy you could take her in my place?" Then she disappeared behind the swinging door.

Drake watched the kitchen door close, then turned to Kathryn. "Were you really going on a picnic this afternoon?"

Nodding, she started to work on yet another coffee order. "It's okay, don't feel you have to. I'm a big girl and can take care of myself."

He hated spending his birthdays alone, but it was for the best that he did. He didn't want Kathryn to spend hers alone, he could meet her for a picnic lunch and then be off. "If you want, I would like to join you. But only if you like."

Kathryn's face lit up. "Thank you. That would be nice. I finish around noon, is that okay?"

"Perfect. I will see you then." He pushed back his chair and stood. With a smile, he went on his way.

Her shift over and a few nervous and excited butterflies in her stomach, Kathryn walked out of the café and turned right. Into a solid brick wall of muscle. His quick thinking had his arms around her, stopping her falling backwards off his body. "Oufff. Sorry," she said as she looked up and into Drake's emerald eyes. His strength surrounded her and so did his scent. He smelt so good.

"My pleasure," he said with a slight smile and slowly removed his arms from around her waist, ensuring that she was steady on her feet. "Are you ready to go?" He stepped back, holding up a small brown bag. "I have a gift for you. It's not much though, as I didn't have enough time."

Drake being there was a gift already, but she couldn't help the excitement of getting a present. When she was growing up her grandmother hadn't had much money, so thrift shop clothes were often her birthday presents. That and a walk along the river with ice-cream at night. It was her favourite thing to do on her birthday, sitting on a blanket watching the sun set, while eating ice-cream for dinner.

He gave her the bag, watching as she weighed it in her hand first, smiling and enjoying the moment. Scrunching her face up playfully as she tried to think what it could be. Giving up, she opened the bag and let out a squeal. It was a fresh peach. Being the start of the season, they were so expensive to buy, but he'd remembered how much she loved them and bought her one for her birthday. Removing the peach from the bag, Kathryn put it to her nose, smelling its delicate, sweet perfume. Her eyes closing as she took it all in.

Placing the fruit carefully back into the bag, she couldn't wipe the smile off her face. It felt good to genuinely smile again with Drake. Butterflies fluttering in her stomach, she picked up the picnic basket she had put down to take his gift. "Are you ready to go?"

"Lead the way," he replied and stepped around her so that he could walk next to the road. Taking the basket, he carried it for her.

Her arm in his, they ambled down the street past a few boutique clothing stores, towards the park. Kathryn talked about the park they were going to and how she loved to come and sit there, sometimes for hours, just to be with nature and have time to herself. Her, the ducks and the trees. Drake listened attentively.

The entrance to the park had a beautiful old climbing rose bush growing over the top of it. The branches rolling and twisting over the rock and timber frame, providing a perfumed welcome to the lush green flow of grass beyond. Walking under the archway entry, Kathryn led the way to the right that led onto another path.

It snaked around past a lush overgrowth of trees, ferns and fallen logs, reminding him of what it was like to walk through a rainforest. The temperature dropped a little and a swirl of breeze surrounded him as they walked on and over a little bridge with water flowing under it and around some rocks to a waterfall you could hear just around the corner. It was like a walking meditation, and you didn't have a choice but to relax and take a deep calming breath.

Stepping off the bridge and walking towards the sound of water falling, Kathryn dropped her arm from his as the path narrowed from overgrown hedges. Leading the way, she took each stone step slowly, running her hand along the leaves of the hedge, smiling at the feeling as she went. She had been quiet since they had entered this part of the garden and looking at her closely, he realised she was simply enjoying each and every moment.

Each touch of the leaves and branches gentle and tender, a real connection to what she was feeling both emotionally and physically. A touch of pure joy and pleasure to feel what each touch sensation was.

Watching her, Drake's eyes moved down her body to the slow sway of her hips as she ascended the steps. Her short summer dress and boots showed off her toned legs and butt. She had a very nice body. Drake couldn't help himself as he watched her move up the path right in front of him. He knew he shouldn't be watching her like that, or thinking about her body, but he couldn't stop. Shaking his head, he knew the reasons why he shouldn't be looking at her like that.

Glancing up at the sky and trees above, he nearly tripped on the steps. Catching himself, he decided to focus on his feet instead of her or the sky.

On reaching the top step, Kathryn stopped to look out at the park before her. The view flowed out to the large grassed areas and the pond beyond where ducks were swimming and a few people had set out their picnics near the banks.

"I love this park," she murmured. "It's my favourite place to be outside of the kitchen. Walking and touching nature ... grounds me back to myself."

Turning back to look at Drake, she said, "It's such a beautiful view, isn't it?"

Drake stepped so that he was one step below her, and their eyes were level. She could smell the soap he'd used that morning and see the chips of darker green in his eyes. She had never noticed that before. Neither spoke for a moment as her heart thundered in her chest. They seemed to be locked there in that moment, staring into each other's eyes. The world began to melt away.

Drake moved first, breaking the stare and looking out over the view. She studied his profile and tried to remember to breathe.

"Yes, it is," he answered, a coy, shy smile on his face as he glanced back at her. "Very beautiful."

Kathryn's cheeks coloured and flushed before she turned back, continuing on the waterfall path, it led through to the 'valley of the roses'. The smell was intoxicating as they meandered along. It appeared as though Kathryn couldn't help herself and stopped to smell her favourites. Drake was following slowly, watching her intently as she bent and smelt each rose, delicately taking each one in between her fingers and lifting it to her nose.

It was somehow seductive to see her touch each one so delicately and enjoy the passion of the smell. He found that he simply couldn't look away from her. The sun was shining down and when she lifted her head to look at him, it created a halo around her. His heart thumped in his chest. She was stunning, and he was drawn to her like never before.

Smiling, she slowly made her way the few steps back towards him. He couldn't move his eyes from her. She was only inches away from him when she took his hand and placed something cool and silky in it.

Looking down, he saw a white rose nestled in his palm. Her hand was warm and soft against his toughened, calloused one.

He studied the rose with its white silk petals, the little green sepals supporting and protecting each delicate petal, and the thorns on the stem dug slightly into his skin. Drake took the image in as memories flowed back. Slowly raising his head, he met her eyes with a smirk on his face. She had remembered — and it was quite clear in her dancing eyes that she was teasing him.

She wasn't going to get off that easy; he knew how to get her off balance. Closing his hand that held the rose, gently around her wrist, he brought the flower to his nose and inhaled the intoxicating smell, which always reminded him of her and their days sitting on the front steps together, a large, old white rose bush right beside them. The bush had been so highly perfumed that it had imprinted the smell of any rose in his brain and always took him back to her and those steps. Once, she'd caught him late at night in the garden smelling all of them. He had been so embarrassed that he wouldn't look at her at breakfast the next morning. He had left that day, without a proper goodbye. Now she was here teasing him again.

Her eyes held his and danced as he took in the scent, daring her to pull her hand away. The only sign of her being shocked by his actions was the subtle widening of her eyes, although she seemed determined to outwardly give the impression of being unphased. The corners of his lips lifted.

Kathryn watched Drake's eyes close slowly as he bowed his head to breathe the scent in deeper. Her heart was beating hard in her chest as the heat from his hand crawled its way up her skin and into her veins. The sensation both excited and scared her. Her other hand itched to touch him, but she held it tight, locked beside her. She needed to move away from him before she did something stupid like move closer to his body.

His head lifted and she saw the playfulness in his eyes. He had deliberately tried to unsettle her! Standing strong so as not to show him just how successful he had been at unnerving her; she eased her hand out of his, allowing him to keep the flower, and moved to find a spot for their picnic as she fought to get her senses back under control.

Laying out the rug and food, Kathryn focused on her task and not on him. He had a way of making her heart beat a little faster, and her body feel slightly off balance and floaty. She needed to keep her wits about her.

Sitting watching a mother duck and her ducklings glide across the water, all serene on top but paddling like crazy under the water, Drake leaned back on his elbow, his legs stretched out in front of him. What the ducks were doing was how he felt inside as he watched her set out the picnic. Watching her with the roses and then holding her hand while he smelled the one she had given him, had affected him. He was trying to understand it but his brain wouldn't let him. All he knew was that she was beautiful, always had been, but something had changed today.

Picking at the food, they enjoyed friendly banter and general conversation. Cutting him a slice of her birthday peach, he bit into it. The sweet, sticky juice flowed down his throat and triggered his memories.

Whenever he would come and visit, he would always bring a box filled to the top with peaches or oranges, or whatever was in season and growing in abundance on the trees in the orchid. Kathryn had delighted in the fruit each time, taking one immediately from the box in his arms before he could bring it inside the house.

Drake watched her now as she brought the sweet tasting fruit to her lips and touched it there for a second before slowly crunching it between her teeth. She savoured it as she chewed slowly, a bit of juice escaping from the corner of her mouth to dribble down her chin. She wiped it off with a giggle, the sound making him smile too.

She put passion into everything she did without effort and it was intoxicating to watch. He found he wanted to be part of it, to experience what she did, how she felt in those moments. She did it so easy and with such expression, he could get lost in just watching her enjoy each beauitful moment. The thought made him shift his position and sit up to look out at the water again. That was dangerous terrain he had let his mind stray to. It wasn't safe at all.

"How's your grandfather?" she asked quietly.

"He passed away a few years back. Heart failure." His grandfather had been his rock after it had all happened, and unfortunately, the stroke he'd had a couple of years before his heart gave way, had been a big one. It had taken months of rehabilitation for his grandfather to get his speech back and the ability to walk again. He was down but not out — once he got home, he was out in the ring daily, giving lots of orders.

It was in those last years that he had really pushed Drake to hone his natural skills and ability with the horses to ensure that Drake knew how to keep the farm and horse training all going after he was gone.

The night before he passed, his grandfather had taken him to Reggie's for tea, and it was that night Drake had met Sophie. She had been with him ever since, until he travelled to the city, that was. He'd leaned on her for support the day he had found his grandfather sitting hunched over on his stump near the training ring. He had been watching the sunrise that morning and had slipped away peacefully when his heart finally failed.

"I'm sorry to hear that." Kathryn picked up a piece of grass that had fallen into her lap and twirled it between her fingers. "Grandma passed away about the same time." Her voice filled with sadness and the words hung in the air before she sat up taller and sucked in some air.

"But she wouldn't want me feeling sad for myself." She tossed the blade of grass to the side and looked at Drake with a firm smile planted on her face. "She would come down here and kick my butt for it, saying that being sad for her was a big load of hogwash and that I have bigger things to worry about than missing her. She was always saying silly things like that." Kathryn's fake smile faded as she watched a magpie land just in front of them, pick up a bug and fly off.

Her grandmother had raised her from a toddler when her mother had been unable to. She and her grandmother had been the best of friends. Kathryn couldn't remember ever fighting with her, just her loving arms always ready to give a big hug and a kiss to the top of her head. Thinking of her now, especially today on her birthday, made Kathryn feel like she would never feel that safe in someone's arms again. She yearned to feel safe and protected again, especially after last night. She had to get herself somewhere safe and work harder to accomplish her dreams. But now wasn't the time to dwell on that. Not today. Not at this time. She was enjoying her day too much.

"She was a truly beautiful woman and loved you with all she had. Everyone could see that," Drake said and gave what sounded like a half laugh. "Do you remember that clip under my ears I got when I accidentally burped at the table?" He rubbed the back of his head and smiled. "I'm sure I still have her handprint there."

Kathryn giggled as she remembered. Her grandmother had been appalled by the burp. Manners were viewed as religious as going to church every Sunday.

"Are you still wanting your café near the river?" Drake asked, the banter seeming to have broken down the sadness of before. "It was her dream as much as yours, if I remember correctly."

"Yeah. its why I'm working at both the café and the pub as much as Suzanna and Billy will let me. I nearly had enough money, but things happen, so I'll need to start again." Kathryn knew she would have to use all she had saved to get away from Rob, but her grandmother would be fine with that.

She would say 'everything happens for a reason, and do what you must, it will all work out in the end. Probably in a way you never thought it would.' She had said it many times over the years and it was normally true. Things had always been very, very tight financially, but the love she and her grandmother had shared was a constant, and everything always did work out for them. They always had what they needed: clothes, food, warm blankets and a solid roof over their heads. Nothing was abundant, except for her grandmother's love. In the end, that was all that mattered.

"Why do you need to start again?"

"Oh, it's nothing. Just life is full of surprises. Some good, some bad, and some are here to teach us valuable lessons, I guess. That's all." Her evasive answer made him frown but she ignored it. She was not about to tell Drake her problems. He couldn't help, anyway. She'd be out of Rob's apartment and on Annabelle's couch in a few hours. No need to divulge it all to him. It was her problem, and she was going to fix it.

"Are you going to serve your famous hot chocolate in your café?" Drake asked, feeling that Kathryn seemed to have grown tense with her thoughts. The little frown between her eyebrows was dimming her vibrancy. He didn't like seeing her smile gone from her beautiful face.

"It's not famous, but Annabelle loves it. Some girls love eating a tub of ice-cream after a fight with their boyfriends, Annabelle loves my hot chocolate and a good girly chat. So, I guess its famous for keeping her and Jonny together." She smirked. "You loved it too, once. However, I don't think that Eskimos will be coming all the way from the south pole to have it." She bumped into his shoulder playfully. It had been a running, encouraging joke between them.

"What. Say it isn't so," he mocked and pretended he was wounded. Holding his hand to his heart, he fell back onto the picnic rug. "Oh, such devastation to my heart. How will I ever recover without the Eskimos coming to your café for your famous hot chocolate?"

Laughing, Kathryn tried to playfully hit him but he caught her wrist and pulled her down on top of his chest. Her fingers near his neck, she tickled him. He twisted and turned and before she knew it, she was flat on her back pinned to the ground. The length of his body pressed to the length of hers, his one leg pinning her hip and holding her still. His one hand pinning both her hands above her head.

She froze for a second, her mind racing, thinking it was Rob who had her before Drake tickled her ribs. The spot only he knew she was sensitive, bringing her back to the moment with him. She tried to get her hands free, but his grip was rock solid. She was giggling and laughing, twisting, and moving.

Then something changed and crackled between them; they both stilled. Part of her hair had fallen out of its tie and was across her face. Blocking her view. She knew he was close, could feel his breath on her chin.

His fingers lifted from her side and slowly moved the hair from her eyes, revealing his darkened green eyes locked to hers. Three heartbeats passed before his eyes moved to where his fingers were gently tangled in the silky strand of her hair. He followed his fingers with his eyes as they tracked down to the corner of her eye and lingered before moving ever so slowly again, down her cheekbone to the fullness of her bottom lip.

Her heart was racing, and her breathing faltered as his eyes touched her lips. It was like a hot brand to her fine skin. All she wanted in the whole world at that moment, was for him to lean in and kiss her. Her eyes flicked to his lips and she ran her tongue over her own now dry ones.

Drake watched as her tongue moistened her lips, his male instincts following the trail of her movement as he leaned in ever so slowly. He watched her eyes drift closed as he neared, their breaths mingling. He was so close she could taste him already.

Drake pulled back and sat up, looking back over to the water as he cleared his throat and rubbed his hand over his face.

Chapter 5

The wet weather set in that afternoon and soaked the city as Drake arrived at the pub to wait for Kathryn. To pass the time while he waited, he'd ordered a beer and a meal but now it was later than he thought she would be, and he began to worry she wasn't coming.

She'd told him she had the night off but had a job to do that afternoon and would meet him that night for a goodbye drink. It now looked like she was not going to show.

He had hurt her by not being able to control his emotions and letting himself breathe her in for that one moment. He had so wanted to kiss her. To taste her. He had always been drawn to her but his actions that afternoon was a slip-up and should never have happened, no matter what he wanted to do.

In a few hours, he'd leave and never see her again. It was better and safer this way. He would keep his distance from her and go back to his life. The risk was too high. But he wanted to say goodbye and wish her luck with her café.

The pub was loud and full of partygoers all eager to enjoy themselves. The noise was deafening and intruded on him and his thoughts, making him shift uncomfortably in his chair as he continued to wait for her, his agitation growing deep within.

The crush of people made him feel enclosed and suffocated. Drinking down the last of his beer, with a final glance at the door to the restaurant just to make sure she wasn't coming through that way, he began moving between the crowd, toward the entrance door. She was not coming, and he should exit before his emotions got out of hand and he lost control.

The rain had stopped and the smell of it against the hot bitumen filled his nose. He struggled to not gag at its intensity. He hated that smell, above all else. He would rather load horse manure all day and be smelling that, than one second of the hot wet bitumen he was smelling now. His mind tried to flicker back but he fought to keep it focused on the here and now. Already on edge, he didn't need those thoughts adding to his already volatile mood. The sound of his boots on the wet pavement rang in his ears as he walked back up the hill towards his motel room. This time tomorrow night he would be close to home.

Home. Secure and away from everyone. Finally able to move on, just him and Sophie.

"You little whore! Where the hell do you think you're going? I won't ask again!"

The shouts had his ears pricking and his steps slowing. All the hairs on the back of his neck stood up.

"Oh, you think you're leaving me. After all that I've done for you? You think you can just pack up and leave me? I don't bloody think so. You're mine. Now get your fat ass back in there and make me some bloody food to eat, I'm starving."

The sound of garbage bins falling over and a woman crying out in pain stopped Drake in his tracks.

"Get up. You're not hurt. Stop fucking around and get up before I make you wish you were not on the ground, woman!"

A breathless moment passed before Drake heard the sickening thud of a kick to the woman's body. A coldness rushed over him. He was drained of every thought and emotion. His feet moved silently down the darkened alleyway toward the back of the block of units. He heard movement and the woman's moans of pain as she was trying to stand up, he guessed. Strong woman. She knew she had to get up before she suffered another blow.

"There, see. You could get up. Now get back inside and get me some food."

Drake was nearly to the end of the alley.

"No. Get your hands off me and let me go!" the woman shrieked back, her voice sounding strangled and hoarse, like she had been screaming for long periods of time.

"Oh, you little bitch. You'll pay for that."

Drake had made it to the end of the alley and cautiously moved to look around the corner.

"No, get off me! Stop that!" He heard grunts and muffled noises. She was fighting back. "Let me go. Now!" The woman snarled through gritted teeth.

A sickly sound of a head hitting brick reached Drake's ears as he peeked around the corner and saw a man dressed in black, his hand falling from his victim's face as her body slid to the ground, unmoving. Drake moved silently and fast, just like he used to do. The instinct came back without a thought.

The black devil swung around to kick his victim again, but Drake's big hand engulfed his throat and drove him back forcefully, with a deathly hit to the brick wall that had the bastard's eyes widening with shock and surprise — and then terror as he saw the beast of a man who had hold of him right before the wind was knocked completely out of his body. The devil dropped to the ground, down the wall, hard.

All of Drake's well locked up demons came out and his temper took full hold, raging with anger and hatred as he picked up the devil's body and slammed him into the wall again. He smashed hit after hit into the devil's gut and head until the man couldn't stand and slumped to the ground with a bloodied mouth and a puffy, split black eye.

Somehow, the man was still conscious. He looked up at Drake and snickered. "She is mine, and you can't take her." Then he rolled onto his back on the ground.

Breathing hard and shaking violently, Drake stood for a moment, fighting the demon inside who wanted to kill the bastard. To rid the world of him. He looked down at him lying on the ground with thoughts about wrapping his hands around the bastard's throat and squeezing until the life had left the body and other torturous ways to make this monster suffer for what he had done to the woman.

Then reality stepped in and pushed the dark side of him back to the corner it lived in. Taking deep breaths, Drake took a step back and tried to understand what had just happened, when he heard the woman moan. He lost all thoughts about the black devil and looked around to find her. He needed to get her to safety and away from this evil.

Finding her, he froze. He knew the dress and boots; she had been wearing them all afternoon in the park with him. Red hot anger filled him along with a deep burn of protectiveness. His guts rolled but he kept his mind on what needed to be done.

Kneeling ever so gently beside her, he looked over the lifeless, beaten body. Her dress was ripped nearly off. Her legs and arms were scratched and bleeding like she had been attacked by a cat. Carefully, he brushed aside her hair. His hands shook wildly, and he fought hard to control himself. He knew what he was going to find as he brushed the hair from her face but wished to God that it was not her — but it was.

He knew it was Kathryn the moment he saw her dress and boots. His guts clenched and his throat was tight. She was not moving, her face already swelling, the bruises starting to colour. With what little light he could see by the moon, she was seriously hurt.

Shaking wildly with every emotion he could possibly feel, fear leading the charge, he gently touched her pulse. He couldn't breathe. Did not want to breathe. Flashes and voices screamed into his head, and he tried to focus and push them aside as the memories mixed with reality.

Closing his eyes, he whispered his second ever prayer and hope to God that this one was answered. The earth stopped moving. She was alive. Drake let out a breath of air and relief. The world started to spin rapidly. Moving closer toward her he cupped her head ever so gently in his hands and turned her to look at him.

"Kathryn. Kathryn. Wake up. It's me, Drake. Please. Please wake up. I need to get you out of here. I need to get you to safety. I've got you. You're safe with me. I won't let anyone ever hurt you again." He was rambling and not making any sense.

He continued talking to her as he studied her face looking for any sign that she could hear him. His voice came out strained and hurting, full of emotion and absolute fear and anger. She must wake up. He needed her to wake up. He'd never be able to live with himself if she died and he wasn't able to save her either.

Moving even closer, Drake moved his arm under her legs and positioned himself to gently cradle her head against his shoulder so he could lift her. A movement behind him made him turn his head, just as a foot glanced by his face, sending him sprawling beside Kathryn.

He realised what the devil was about to do: send a boot directly into his ribs. Just before it reached its target, Drake managed to grab the foot and twist. The devil landed heavily on the ground at his feet. Scrambling up, Drake was ready for the flurry of fists that came his way as the black devil sprang up with what seemed like unlimited energy and went for him again.

Deflecting and ducking, Drake managed to dodge the punches. The devil had no idea what he was doing, there was something off with him. This was nothing like any fight Drake had ever fought before — this bloke had no fear. No understanding that Drake outsized him in height, weight and skill. The bloke was a raging, feral animal, trying to bite, kick, punch, scratch and leap onto Drake.

Circling and deflecting was all Drake could do until he got a chance to knock the bastard out. Taking a moment, as he circled around again, he caught sight of Kathryn's still body against the wall. She needed urgent help. He had to get her to a hospital.

The devil took that moment of lack in concentration to throw a solid right hook. Seeing it at the right moment and ducking, Drake came back up, countering with his own hook. This time, he smashed the bastard squarely in the jaw, laying him out cold against the other wall.

Not giving him a second look, Drake raced to Kathryn and kneeling again, moved his arm under her legs. He wasn't sure what was up with the bastard that had attacked her, but he didn't want to risk fighting him again and delaying getting Kathryn to safety. She moved ever so slightly; her eyes started to flutter open. Moving his hands from where he was about to lift her, he instead cradled her head in his hands to help her focus on him.

"Kathryn, Kathryn. Can you hear me? It's me, Drake. I've got you. Can you hear me? I need to lift you so I can get you to safety." She was moaning in such pain that his heart squeezed tightly.

Her eyes flashed open and she pulled away, starting to scream, hitting his hands away as she frantically tried to crawl away. He moved back and tried to calm her, repeating her name and his, but she couldn't hear him and was too terrified and confused to see him properly. He grabbed her hand and pulled her back toward him forcefully and tried to firmly tell her, "Kathryn, it's me Drake, please listen."

She kicked out at him, narrowly missing his groin.

He pulled her hard back against him and held her tightly wrapped in his arms. "It's okay Kathryn, it's me, Drake. I've got you. You're safe, I've got you."

She fought him to let her go as she sobbed and screamed. "Let me go! Nooo. Let me go! Let me go!"

Drake was losing his grip on her and on his emotions. With swift action he pulled her into his lap with all his strength and held her, one arm locked around her waist, plastering her to his body as he used the other to pull her face gently around so that she could see him fully and stop frantically swinging her head around.

"Kathryn, stop. Look at me. It's Drake." He whispered into her face, from right up close. He could feel her heart beating wildly in her chest, and her eyes were blinking madly trying to focus through her pain and confusion.

It took a few long and tight heartbeats, but eventually her struggling and fighting slowed. She held his gaze for a moment before a sob ripped through her. Then Kathryn twisted and fell against him, her arms wrapping tightly around his neck. She was gripping onto him for life.

He knew he was her life in that moment. He was the only thing between her and death, and she wasn't going to let go. She was trying to hold him tighter and pushing her body closer against him for safety and protection.

Drake held her as tightly as he dared so as not to hurt her anymore. He beathed a sigh of relief. She was going to be okay. He had her. He had saved her. Stroking her hair ever so gently, he just held her for a moment, breathing her in. He couldn't stay here long, she needed help, but he needed to hold her.

Pulling back slightly so he could remove his jacket, he wrapped it around her shoulders and pulled her torn dress over her. Placing an arm under her legs and another one tenderly around her ribs, he stood with her in his arms. She felt so small as she draped her arms around his neck and held tight.

Drake looked back at the devil lying against the other wall. Deep down, he knew this time he had beaten the monster and that he had saved Kathryn. His mind flickered and in a teeny corner of his heart, he hoped that he had made her proud from up there, that he had been able to do it this time. That she was looking down at him, smiling. Maybe they both were. He would never forgive himself for what he did to her though. That was his to live with forever.

Walking back down the alley with Kathryn safely in his arms, he could see the police lights flashing. Relief washed over him. They would be able to call an ambulance for help and arrest the bastard. He quickened his steps.

"Help, please help. She needs to get to the hospital!" he called as two police officers raced around the corner and toward him up the alley. The woman officer instantly reached out to check Kathryn's pulse. The bear of a policeman held Drake with a stare. Drake could read the expression in his eyes: did he do this to her?

Ignoring the questioning gaze, Drake looked to the police woman and pleaded, "Please call her an ambulance." He glanced down at Kathryn, making sure she was still breathing. She was drifting in and out of consciousness.

"Miss, are you alright? What is your name? What happened?" The woman officer gently shook Kathryn as she moaned and mumbled.

"Rob came home. Found me leaving." Kathryn slurred her words; her head was becoming heavier on Drake's shoulder. "Drake saved me." Kathryn drifted back into the unconscious.

The policewoman looked to Drake with a questioning look in her eye. "Who are you?"

"Drake Harrison. I'm a friend of Kathryn's." Quickly piecing together Kathryn's story, Drake added, "A bloke, I guess is Rob, is sprawled out back up there. I had to knock him out to save her." Drake turned and nodded back up the alley so they could go and find Rob for themselves. He was not in the wrong here, and he would not let them stop him getting help for Kathryn any longer.

The policewoman looked at her colleague and tilted her head up the alley. She was going to stop Drake going any further until she knew that he was no threat to Kathryn.

Drake's temper dug in.

It all happened in less than a breath. Kathryn's head moved gently as Drake lifted her higher onto his shoulder, just as the whip-like crack sounded and wind passed his face. Drake blinked and looked down at Kathryn as her head exploded in blood, splatters hitting him in the face.

She fell limp in his arms, her head falling back over his arm and her arms slipped from around his neck. Everything moved in slow motion. He dropped to his knees, screaming her name and holding her head to his heart. A warm stickiness filled his hands and ran down his arm.

"Kathryn! God, NO! Kathryn!" He rested his forehead on hers, tears streaming down his face. Looking up with tear-blurred vision, there was chaos around him.

The policewoman was staring back up the alley and talking rapidly on her radio. She had an arm around him as he shielded Kathryn. The next moment she was pulling him up by his arm and running with him towards the street. Kathryn's lifeless body was locked tight to his chest. He turned left and was pushed into a brick fence in front of a house. A roaring filled his ears, and he could hear nothing but his heart pounding in his head.

It seemed like hours before the ambulance came. His arms had gone numb from holding Kathryn and his shirt was sticky and soaked with her blood. The policewomen had bandaged her head, but Drake couldn't remember her doing so.

He couldn't think. Couldn't speak. Couldn't move. He couldn't work out what was real and happening now or what were horrible memories flicking into his mind. He was floating above his body, but yet he was sinking into the depths of hell for what he had done.

"Hey mate, we can take her now?" A soft masculine voice started to pierce through the depths of blackness and fog, but he couldn't work out who it was or where it was coming from.

"Mate. I've got her, you can let her go now. I need to help her."

Drake blinked and shook his head as he looked down at Kathryn. She was pale and still lifeless in his arms. A hand was resting on his upper arm. He followed it up to a face he didn't know. They seemed to be talking to him, but he couldn't work out their words. Then they were moving him forwards. Slowly, reality screamed back to him. He pulled Kathryn closer to his body as he climbed into the ambulance, locking her in his arms. While she was there in his arms, she was safe. He could protect her.

The ambo was tugging on his shirt sleeve. "Mate, you can put her down now. She'll be safe in here. We need to check her out and stop the bleeding."

Drake looked from the ambo to Kathryn, confused but then nodded and placed her as gently and as slowly as he could onto the stretcher. She moaned in pain. He cursed; he should have been gentler. She was suffering and he'd added to it. The two ambulance personnel leapt into action caring for her. Drake moved to get out of their way when a female ambulance officer stopped him. She had been standing at the doors at the back of the van.

"Have you been hit, sir?' She reached out to stop Drake from moving.

Looking down at his shirt dazedly; he shook his head. It was all Kathryn's blood. The smell, warmth and stickiness started to turn his stomach. He needed air.

"Right then, sit down. We need to get her to the hospital, fast." The doors slammed shut in his face, stopping him from leaving the ambulance and making him swallow his nausea down.

The van lurched forward and sped through the streets, the sirens blaring into Drake's head. The vehicle was rocking with the speed and motion of the race to the hospital. Drake watched in silence as they worked on Kathryn. They rebandaged her head and checked her for other injuries. She was now under a blanket and had been given pain relief. Her moaning had not stopped, and she was beginning to hallucinate — calling for her mother and grandmother to not leave her and crying out for Rob to stop.

The ambulance officers tried to calm her, but she was getting worse and thrashing around more. Drake's heart was breaking at everything she had gone through. If only she had told him that day that she was in an abusive relationship he would have helped her leave safely, he would have protected her. He wouldn't have let this happen.

"Drake! Drake!" she screamed and thrashed about more.

He leaped forward and gently held her head still. Cooing to her, "I'm here. You're safe, nothing is going to happen to you now. I'm here."

Slowly, she ceased thrashing around as his whispers and nearness penetrated her thoughts and illusions. He held her hand and continued to console her until she seemed to slip into an unconscious state again. Sucking in a deep breath, he sat back.

"Good job, Mate. You must mean a hell of a lot to her. She calmed straight away with your voice."

Drake just nodded and looked back to Kathryn's pale face. She meant a lot to him, he realised. He would protect her and help her get better, no matter how long it took.

Chapter 6

The doors to the ambulance flew open so hard that they rocked the vehicle and Drake grabbed the edge of his seat. Instantly, there was a flurry of activity and people at the back of the ambulance. Everyone seemed to be talking at once and moving around quickly as Kathryn's stretcher was pulled from its place and wheeled into the building as fast as they could go without running.

Drake was told to follow and asked a million questions he didn't know the answer to or how to explain. He was sat in a chair, thrown a towel to wipe his face and hands clean of Kathryn's blood and then a cup of hot sweet tea was placed into his hands. He was told to drink it and stay where he was. The doctors would come out and talk to him once they had Kathryn stable and there was news to tell him.

Drake rubbed a hand over his face and leaned his elbows onto his knees, hanging his head, he stared into the cup of dark, steaming hot liquid gripped between his hands. Taking in slow deep breaths, he tried to clear his mind of the past and only go over what the hell had just happened. Nothing made any sense. Bits and pieces were clear, but mostly it was just flashes. Placing the tea on the ground, his hands were shaking so violently he stared at them.

The stickiness and coldness of his blood-soaked shirt touching his skin seemed to be sinking deep into his body. He needed to be rid of it. Now. Standing, Drake pulled and tore the shirt out of his jeans with such force the stupid thing ripped apart.

"Fuck it all!" he cursed.

"Here, mate. You'll need this." The ambulance officer who had been tending to Kathryn came striding up to him with a blue hospital scrub shirt in his outstretched hands.

Taking it with his thanks, Drake pulled off what was left of his blood-soaked one and threw it to the ground, then pulled on the new one.

"I thought you might need this too." The ambo handed him a chocolate bar and a black coffee that looked as though a spoon would stand up in it. "It tastes horrible but will help settle your guts. The chocolate will take the taste away."

"Thanks," Drake answered quietly.

"You deserve it. You did an awesome job holding Kathryn and keeping her calm tonight. She would have been in a lot worse state, if not dead, if it wasn't for you. She'll recover quickly after a few days, once they calm her and give her some pain meds."

"I hope so." Drake didn't know what to say. If only he had got to her sooner. If only he hadn't stopped with the police in the alley, he should have run with her out of the alley. He should have killed the bastard when he had the chance. His guilt was eating him up inside.

"Look. You can't go back and change the past; just know you did all you could at the time. I don't think many men, none I know anyways, would've been able to fight off a bloke, then carry her out and hold her till we arrived. You did a great job. You'll feel it tomorrow, though." The ambo's radio came to life and called him to a car accident. Shaking Drake's hand and slapping him on the back, he called out to his partner, who was walking down the hall towards them. "Ben, let's roll. We've got another."

They both nodded to Drake as they left him.

Drake watched them go. He didn't know how they could do their job. Facing all that life and death and dealing with crazies all day and night. He couldn't do it, but by God, he was glad they had been there for Kathryn.

Taking a sip of the coffee he screwed up his face. Yep, it tasted horrible, but he persevered and got the stuff down. The ambo was right, the coffee and the chocolate did help. Having something in his gut helped with the nausea he had been battling and stopped his hands from shaking as much.

It seemed like a lifetime before anyone came to see him. He had passed the time by alternating between pacing and sitting and at one point, he had even drifted off to sleep. It was only minutes, but it had revived him. He was about to start to pace again when the doctor came out.

"Are you the man they brought in with Kathryn White?"

"Yes, I am."

"Are you family?"

"No."

"We need to talk to her family, I'm sorry. Do you know who we should call?"

"She only ever had her grandmother, and she has passed away."

"Then who are you?"

"I'm her friend. How is she?" Drake didn't like being interrogated. He had done nothing to hurt Kathryn. Just not been able to protect her. The stabbing guilt sliced at his stomach. Ignoring it, he watched the doctor look him up and down, weighing up whether it was safe for her to give out Kathryn's details.

After a few moments she must have thought it was. "Miss White suffered a graze to her head from the bullet. It required stitches. She also suffered a trauma to the back of her head, which we'll need to monitor, two cracked ribs and lots of cuts and bruises to her face and body. We are going to admit her to the hospital for a few days, maybe a week. Other than that, she is lucky to be alive. You saved her life."

Relief washed through Drake. She was going to be okay and heal. Physically, at least. He slowly nodded at the doctor before he cleared his throat and asked what she had yet to say.

"Kathryn's dress was ripped, and she had lots of bruises and scratches lower on her torso and legs ..." he cleared his throat again. This was horrible, even talking about this with the doctor. He was only Kathryn's friend, but he was worried that she had been raped. She had been so terrified that he was going to attack her when she first came back into consciousness. The thought that bastard had forced himself onto her... his nausea and temper rose again. He had to sit down. For Kathryn's sake, he had to stay calm.

The doctor pulled up a chair next to him and sat while she looked over her notes.

"It doesn't appear so." She said quietly "Her underwear was intact, and the grab marks and bruises don't go high enough for it to look the way you are asking about."

Drake sat back and rolled his head and neck. The tension was burning and locking it up. "Thank you," he whispered.

"She'll be moved up to the ward once we have a bed available. She is under some strong meds now and may not wake 'til tomorrow. You can sit with her until she is moved, if you like."

"Thank you. Yes."

"I will let the nurse know and she'll come and get you. A doctor will call in and see Miss White tomorrow once she is on the ward." With that, the doctor left.

Drake got up and started to pace again. The energy building inside him was making him restless.

Fifteen minutes later, the nurse came and found Drake. Following her past a seemingly endless row of curtained off rooms, they finally stopped at one opposite the nurse's station. The nurse pulled open the light blue curtain a little, to allow Drake entrance. Ducking his head under her arm, stepping into the room, he murmured his thanks.

What he saw would haunt his dreams for the rest of his life. Kathryn was laying on the bed, her head wrapped in a fresh bandage, her face swollen and discoloured so badly that it was distorting her beautiful features. She was covered under white blankets, which made her appear pale and small. She had drips and monitors hooked to her and they made an eerie sound that echoed in the room. He stood at the curtained doorway, his feet unable to move him any further forward. She looked so weak and helpless.

The nurse placed a reassuring hand on his back and gently pushed him into the room. "She is sleeping with the help of the pain medication. She is comfortable." She leaned in and whispered, "She'll know you're here. Hold her hand and tell her. Talk to her." She gave him a firmer push and this time his feet responded. "I will come and check on her a little later." With that she dropped the curtain and left.

Drake was left in the room with only the sound of the monitors and the dull drone of the workings of the emergency ward beyond it to keep him company. He wasn't quite sure what to do, so he stood there, staring at her blankly.

The nurse came back in with a blanket for him. After he took it and still did not move closer to Kathryn, she pulled the chair up to the side of the bed and told him to sit. He did as he was told without taking his eyes from Kathryn.

"What's your name?"

"Umm ... Drake." He looked to the nurse and then back to Kathryn. Flashes of when his grandfather had been in hospital came back to him. He had been hooked up to monitors too, but the room always had someone in it. Vicki, Reggie or other friends; his grandfather had never been alone. Nor had he been. His grandfather's friends had filled the room with warmth and camaraderie, but here, the room just seemed cold, and he had no idea what to do.

Kathryn always started the conversation because he was too shy around her. He would be polite, but she would start the conversation and usually made a joke to make him smile and relax. What was he going to say now? Was he expected to talk about the weather and how the city was still going on even though she was here in this hospital bed because he had failed her?

How could he make it up to her? How was he to explain that he was too late to save her? Too late to stop what had happened. That if he'd kept his hands to himself that afternoon, then maybe she would have told him about being in a domestic violence situation and let him help her. What the hell was he meant to say to her?

"She will be fine. Right now, all she needs to do is rest and know you're here." The nurse touched his shoulder to reassure him before she disappeared again.

Drake watched Kathryn's chest rise and fall with each breath. Her hands lay on the white blanket, all scratched up with blood and dirt under the nails. Reaching out, Drake touched a finger to her wrist. She didn't move. Her hand was warm against his ice cold one, and a streak of her warmth slithered into his veins. It felt good.

Taking her hand delicately in his, he studied it. Hers was small and petite in his big one. He placed his other hand over the top. She had long slender fingers and beautiful nails. The few that were not broken or soiled, that is. The nails were not long but not bitten either. Lifting it, he studied her hand, turning it over in his large one and then holding it up so her hand and fingers lay up against his. He measured it against his own, how it fit to his perfectly. Smaller yes, but it fit. He could hold it easily. Not too big and not too small. Just perfect together.

With a brief smile, Drake looked back at her face and carefully laid her hand back down beside her, but not letting go. He watched her sleep.

Chapter 7

The fog was thick, and it was very cold. Nothing moved, her heart was pounding hard as clothes moved and danced around the room to avoid her. She was grabbing for them and each item she grabbed kept crawling out of her grip and dancing again. She had to pack quickly; it would be back soon. She grabbed the dancing dress and coat and threw it in the bag, it will have to do. Holding the door open just enough to see into the lounge room — it was all clear.

Stepping out, she fell down the cliff and a rope pulled tight around her neck as she slammed back into solid rock, her head smashing into the rock wall and sending searing pain and blackening her eyesight even more than the thickness of the night. The blackest-of-black animal pulled her down to the cold riverbed, ripping and tearing at her clothing, she had to fight and get away, she kept lashing out and striking at the animal. A direct hit and she could run. Again and again, she tried. Her foot collided with it.

Pushing through the trees and down the rock walled path she ran, but it was too late. The animal had her and was throwing her around. She hit the wall again and felt nothing. She couldn't speak, couldn't move. She didn't know where the beast was or where she was. There was complete blackness.

"Kathryn, Kathryn!" She could hear her name being called but could do nothing about it. Then a flicker of light appeared in front of her and as it grew larger, the voices got louder and louder. It was her mother and grandmother. They were beautiful and calling for her to come home with them, to stand up and walk. Kathryn tried to call out and tell them she couldn't walk but her voice wouldn't work. Her mother

and grandmother turned and left her there in the dark with the black monster.

She could feel its breath on her. She had to get away. It touched her leg and she tried to move but could only manage to move her head. Then it called her name. It knew her name! Run, run, run now!

Summoning all her energy she tried to run, she found her voice and was screaming for help, but it had her. She needed someone to help her. To find her. No, she could do this herself, she needed to fight. Kathryn punched and scratched and screamed as loud as she could, but it had her. She couldn't move. She laid her head on its chest and felt its heart solid and beating fast. She was going to die. It touched and shook her with a growl. It clawed at her head. Pain split her head open and then there was nothing.

Drake startled awake to the sound of screaming. Leaping to his feet, it took him a moment to realise where he was. Three nurses were in the curtained room as he stood blinking into recognition and remembrance. Kathryn was thrashing around and screaming in a nightmare. She was calling for her mother and grandmother. The nurses were trying to calm her down, but nothing was working. They called for the doctor to get a sedative. The room was in chaos and panic.

Not knowing what made him do it, Drake pushed his way to Kathryn's side and held her as tight as he could. Not like the nurses were doing, but in a protective and secure way. His body pressed to hers, he cooed her and told her she was safe, that he had her and she was okay. After a few panicked heartbeats, she calmed. He held her until he knew she was settled, then he sat on the bed and held her hand, stroking her hair as the nurses checked her head and monitors.

"Where did you learn to do that?" one nurse asked. She was an older nurse with greying hair and a stern look about her. She reminded him of Mrs Murdoch, his English teacher at school. Kind, but don't mess with her. They had got on well and she had helped him find a love of reading, especially old western books.

"My grandfather." Drake starred at Kathryn. "He was a good man."

"As are you, young man." She patted his shoulder "I'll get you a coffee. She'll be moved to the ward very soon."

As she walked out, Drake whispered to himself, "I wish I was a good man." Softly, he stroked Kathryn's head again. His grandfather had done the same to him every time he had been in the mists of his demons. It was all he could do to help when Drake would see her face and hear her screams in his dreams. His grandfather would hold him until he knew the gun had gone off and the blood had flowed from her lifeless body. Until he was back from the black wet road, hollow and shaking at what he had done.

An hour later Drake found himself following Kathryn's bed through a rabbit warren of halls and wards, in elevators and down cold corridors. It was nearly dawn and the hospital was beginning to awaken.

The Wardsman was polite as he talked to the nurse and tried to involve Drake in their conversation, but Drake was distracted, trying to figure out their location within the hospital and how the hell he was going to find his way back out of this place. How anybody found their way around was amazing. He bet that somewhere in these dark halls and corridors, there was a lost patient who had been wondering alone for years.

Finally, they burst through a set of heavy double doors and onto a ward. It was still dark with only low-level hall lights for the nurses to find their way around. Passing darkened rooms, with young and old sleeping in their beds, curtains drawn to keep the imposing new dawn out for as long as possible, Drake continued to follow Kathryn's bed.

Walking further along to an open area he found himself at the nurse's station. The desks made a square horseshoe with only one way in and one way out and were covered in papers stacked high with empty coffee cups dotted between them. At the back was a glassed-in office and inside it was a large nurse, who looked up at their arrival. She made her way out of her office and through the station to Kathryn's bedside.

Speaking to the nurse who had accompanied them from the emergency ward, they swapped notes and medical details, then the large nurse looked at the Wardy and said, "We want her right near us please, Luke. Room 12." Next, she looked Drake up and down. "You're her friend, I take it?" She had authority and was making it known to him.

"I am." He held out his hand for her to shake. "Drake"

Instead, she looked at it and said, "Well. We will see," and walked off to follow Luke into room 12.

Drake watched her go, not sure how to take the rejection of his offer of friendship or the fact that she just implied that he may have been the one to do this to Kathryn. Frowning, he moved after her.

The emergency nurse walked past him, saying back over her shoulder, "Ruth will look after Kathryn. She's stern, but very kind. Good luck to you both." She continued her path back to the emergency.

Kathryn's room was just like all the others. White walls, dark curtains pulled closed, a tv on the wall in the corner, a small table with two chairs for guests and a fake timber bedside table, now positioned against the wall, beside Kathryn's bed. On the other side of her bed was another door, which he assumed was Kathryn's private bathroom. Drake stood just inside the room near the door and watched while Ruth and Luke locked the bed into position and set the monitors in place.

Ruth pointed to another chair just along the wall from where he stood. "For you, if you want to sit next to her bed." She walked out, Luke following.

Drake walked slowly to the chair and moved it to Kathryn's side. Taking her hand, he watched the sun rise through the gaps in the curtains.

He had been dozing when the rustling of material and feet trying to move through the room quietly drew his attention and he opened one eye. Yet another nurse, come to check Kathryn's vitals. He sat up and stretched.

The nurse looked up from her watch and whispered, "Sorry, I didn't mean to wake you. Just doing my first round for the day."

"I wasn't really sleeping. How is she?" He leaned his hand over and gently touched Kathryn's least bruised cheek, thinking that she had a little more colour to her skin.

"She's doing well. She should sleep for the rest of the morning. You, however, look like you could use a shower and some breakfast. If you want to go and come back a little later, I'll make sure she knows you were here and will be back." The nurse looked to Kathryn before looking back to him. "That is, if she wakes before you're back. Which I doubt."

A young nurse, she looked to be the same age as Kathryn. With blonde hair and chocolate eyes, the nurse looked full of life and was caring by the way she was tenderly looking over Kathryn.

Drake felt he could trust her. "She's been having nightmares and hallucinations since it happened. I just hold her and tell her I am here."

"If she wakes or has another one, I'll do the same and will let the other nurses know too. It will be alright."

The thought of a shower and some food did sound good, but something deep inside of him didn't want to leave her. To keep her safe and protect her, he needed to be here with her. Drake didn't move from his chair.

"She will be fine here. I promise. You can ring us once you get home to make sure, if you like. My name is Lucy, and this is medical ward five." The nurse gave the impression that he needed to go.

Taking the hint, Drake stood and caressed Kathryn's hand, leaning down to whisper that he would be back soon. He promised.

He nodded to Lucy before walking out of the room and down the hallway towards the double doors. Now all he had to do was find his way out of the hospital and to the taxis.

The elevator outside the double timber doors of the ward was taking forever, but finally it arrived and when the doors opened, out stepped the ambulance offer who had helped Kathryn last night.

"Great, I finally found ya, mate. I have your jacket, you left it in our ambulance."

"Oh. Thanks," Drake took the jacket from him. "How did you know it was mine?" Noticing it had Kathryn's blood all over it, he rolled it up into a ball and tucked it under his arm.

"It had your wallet and motel room key in it. Thought you might need it. Can I walk out with you?" The ambo was such a friendly bloke and very cheerful for someone who'd just worked a full night shift. He seemed to have too much energy for this time of the morning.

"Yeah, that would be good. I have no idea how to get out of here." Drake smiled at him and received a cheeky one back.

"I know how you feel. When my wife had our first one, I got lost after dropping her off at the maternity ward entrance and parking the car, nearly missed all the fun of the birth. She would've never let me live that down." He chatted away about his family and his latest fishing trip, all the while leading Drake out of the hospital and to the taxi rank.

It wasn't until Drake had stopped at the side of a taxi that the ambo stopped chatting and turned the subject to the real reason he had led Drake out of the hospital.

"You know mate, she wouldn't be alive if it wasn't for you. By the sounds of it, that bloke was high on something. The wounds he inflected were more animal than human. Not your normal domestic violence scene, either. The fact he had a gun meant he was out to do more damage than just to her for the night. You saved her, and I'm proud to have met you." He held out his hand for Drake to shake, which he did, and nearly got his arm shook off.

"You take care, and keep her safe now." He pulled out a fifty dollar note and handed it to the taxi driver. "Take him back to his room and keep the change." To Drake, he said, "This one's on me."

Drake watched the ambo walk back into the hospital, hands in pockets, whistling, before he climbed into the taxi.

Chapter 8

Throwing his wallet and keys onto the little plastic timber side table near the door, Drake turned and shut his motel room door, pulling the bolt across the latch. He leaned his head against it and allowed the coolness of the plain off-white door to seep into his forehead. Eyes closed, he just stood and breathed, the door taking his weight.

Nothing. He felt absolutely nothing — and relished in it. The shock of the night would catch him in a minute, but for now there was nothing. He hauled in a shaky deeper breath; wrong move, it hit him.

Moving fast, around the bed and into the small bathroom, he only just managed to lift the toilet lid before he regurgitated everything that was in his guts. Nausea washed over him again and again, until there was nothing left, but still his body tried to expel more.

Slumping from his knees to his butt he sat on the cold tiled floor, his back against the wall, arm resting on his knee, staring at the crack in the tiles behind the toilet. His body shook and throbbed from the exertion. His heart pounding painfully against his rib cage. He tried to swallow his bile down, but it won the war and hit again, having him dry retching with excruciating pain because nothing was left. Absolutely nothing was left, physically or emotionally. He was done.

Slamming down the toilet lid he sat back against the cold wall, resting his head back and stretching out one of his long legs. Sighting Kathryn's blood on his boots, his stomach rolled and a cold sweat broke out and prickled his skin. Images of that night mixed with the night before, flashed through his mind as he continued to stare at his boots.

Get them off. Get them off now!

Jamming the toe of his other boot into the heel, he pushed and kicked at the solid leather boot until it came off. The other one was quick to follow. Reaching forward, he picked them up and threw them across the room. They flew over the bed and hit the wall on the far side with a loud thud, then slid down out of sight.

Standing, he tore the hospital shirt off and ripped at his jean's buttons all at once, he needed to get out of them all and now. They were suffocating and restricting him. Hands shaking, his body sweating and naked, he turned on the shower and stepped in.

The ice-cold water took his breath away, along with the need to feel anything but the icy temperature. He stood there with water running over him from the top of his head, down his back, over his thighs and to the floor, eventually flowing down the drain, taking a part of him with it. The cold made his shaking worse, but he stood there and took it, it beat feeling anything else. He never wanted to feel anything again.

By the time his hands had turned blue and he had lost all feeling in his toes, his body was shaking violently from the cold. With fumbling fingers, he turned on the hot water and let his body start to warm. Gradually, he stopped shaking, but the feelings returned.

He couldn't get away from the torment. Couldn't feel clean enough. Couldn't rid his body of her blood; it wouldn't wash down the drain. Breathing heavily and panicked by the need to be rid of their blood, Drake picked up the wash sponge and soap and scrubbed and scrubbed at his body until his skin stung and was red raw.

He still couldn't get clean enough. Washing his face again, a sob caught then another and another. Sobs rose up from the deepest parts of his body and took over, dragging him under, over and over again as wave after wave of grief and pain, hatred and heartbreak crashed and rolled and heaved throughout his soul.

Dropping to his knees, he curled up on the floor of the shower in the foetal position. His relentless sobs were painful, cutting at his throat and piercing his heart and mind. He could hear her cries and smell the wet bitumen; he could hear the gun shot and blackness that surrounded him afterwards. The flashlights and yelling for help, her screams and her lifeless body replayed over and over in his head like a never-ending movie reel.

Anger took over. He dug his nails into his palms to stop from punching out at the glass surrounding the shower. Instead, he kicked at the tiles revelling in the pain ricocheting up his calves with each blow. His anger was at its peak, and uncontrolled.

He was at his most dangerous.

After a while, the strength of his anger subsided and he lay there as water continued to rain down over him. Fear began to take over: as it always did. It froze him in sheer terror and took him to places he never wanted to go. Closing his eyes, he let his body do what it needed. He didn't care anymore. They were coming to get him anyway; they could take him now for all he cared. He just wanted this nightmare to end.

Drake didn't know how long he had lain there with water falling over him. The water had turned cold, bringing him back to reality. His emotions were now back in place — until next time. He stumbled to his feet and turned the shower off. His hands were scuffed and his knuckles were swollen. His legs ached and he had a few bruises and cuts on other parts of his body. It was satisfying knowing that Rob, wherever he was, was in a worse state this morning. He had met his match in Drake and wouldn't be hurting Kathryn ever again.

Drake smiled viciously as he pulled on his jeans. He had taken a small pleasure in beating the hell out of Rob. Now though, he felt sick at the thought. What normal person would take pleasure from that? But he already knew it — a monster — and his actions proved it.

Sitting on the bed, shirtless and bare foot, he hung his head in his hands. He didn't want to be like this anymore. He didn't want to be one of them anymore. He needed to stay away from people and get away from this place. Go back to his farm and the safety and isolation it provided.

At least there he couldn't hurt anyone. He could fight his demons. He could contain them. He had managed this long; he could do it again.

Standing, he let out a primal roar of frustration and rage as he paced the floor, raking his hands through his hair.

"This is why Kathryn has to stay away!" he yelled at the ceiling, to whom he didn't know, maybe God for putting her in his path this way.

"She will get hurt. I will hurt her; you know this so why would you do this to me? To her? Why?" he yelled and sat back down on the bed, flopping on his back, glaring up at the ceiling. "You're a sick bastard, you know that?" he growled in disgust, putting his arm across his eyes.

He would make sure Kathryn had everything she needed and was healing, then he would say goodbye and leave, returning to the safety of the farm. A sharp pain seared his chest, but he ignored it. That horrible little thing that everyone called a heart, had curled up and died years ago with her that night. This pain was nothing but a reminder to stay away from Kathryn, and everyone else.

He would have to fight to keep the monster locked away, and he could only do that if she stayed away. He closed his eyes on the pain of how he would walk back into that hospital, cold and heartless like he truly was, and tell her goodbye forever in her biggest moment of need.

He truly was a monster.

The heavy rain hitting the motel room window drew Drake from his black sleep a few hours later. He was tired and sore but try as he might, he couldn't get back to sleep. Turning to his side he looked at his boots flung on the floor, the blood still on them. They needed to be cleaned. Taking a deep breath, he pushed up onto the side of the bed and sat.

On the bedside table lay the rose Kathryn had given him the day before. That it was only yesterday seemed strange. Yesterday, she had been smiling and laughing with him, so vibrant and full of life. A few hours later she was fighting for her life.

Drake reached out and gently touched one of the petals. It was silky to his fingertips and the feeling made him think of her hair. He had touched it yesterday when it had fallen across her face, and when she had looked at him with eyes of liquid chocolate, something inside had pulled him towards her.

At times, the way she looked at him made him sure she could read his thoughts. She had always seemed able to do it, but yesterday, his thoughts were purely primal male when he'd held her pinned beneath his body and he knew she had wanted him to kiss her. Her lips had been so close he could nearly feel them on his, but remembering himself, he had pulled away, steeled himself against that need. He wouldn't allow anyone to get close, especially her. She was safer that way — and so was he.

Picking up the boots, he walked to the bathroom and scrubbed her blood off as quickly as possible, watching it wash down the sink. His stomach turned, he needed coffee and fresh air.

An hour later Drake found himself walking through the hospital. The food he'd chosen at the hospital's cafeteria was horrible, and the coffee tasted like it had been brewed twenty years ago. But it slid down his throat as he walked along the corridors.

The soggy sandwich gave his stomach something else to think about instead of putting him through the motions of pain it seemed to like doing since his arrival in the city.

The corridors of the hospital were all painted a sickly, dated minty green with brown handrails leading the way along. The carpets were stained in patches and the smell of stale disinfectant filled the air all the way to medical ward five.

The big heavy wooden doors were now locked back open, and the rooms were flooded with light, even though the day was bleak and rainy. The light made the spaces more bearable to be in.

Some patients had visitors and as he walked past, they watched him warily. He figured he must look frightful. He was dressed all in black and hadn't shaved. His eyes were swollen and red from his emotions and sleeplessness. Not the right appearance to come visit a friend, but he didn't care. He was here now and once he'd checked on Kathryn, he would say his goodbyes and leave this place for good.

At the nurse's station, Ruth looked up and saw him coming. "I didn't think we would see you till later this afternoon. She's still sleeping."

Her words released some of the tension in Drake's shoulders he hadn't realised was there. He smiled at her and briefly touched eyes with the other two nurses sitting at the station before he entered Kathryn's room quietly. The room was in darkness and the monitors still beeped their rhythm. Going to the side of her bed, he softly stroked her cheek. She was pale, and the bruises had become darker and more raised, but she was sleeping peacefully.

He pulled the seat he'd sat on earlier that morning to the side of the bed and stretched out his legs in front of him, crossing them at the ankle. He would sit and wait until she woke — and then say goodbye. Taking a sip of his coffee, he let it burn down his throat.

Lucy, the young nurse from that morning, walked in with another older nurse. It was change of shift. He must have drifted off. Pulling his legs in, he stretched and then leaned his elbows onto his knees, observing the two women. They spoke softly while looking over Kathryn's chart. Drake tried to hear what was said but it was all in hushed tones.

Lucy eventually glanced up and nodded towards him. The older nurse followed her gaze and looked him up and down, assessing him with a critical view before looking back to the notes in the folder. Then the two nurses moved out of the room.

Lucy put her head back around the door. "I'll see you in the morning. Gail will be looking after Kathryn for the evening shift."

Drake nodded politely and stood to stretch his legs, walking to the curtained windows. She would not see him ever again. Pulling aside the curtain to look out at the rain falling across the city, he knew he would never be back.

It wasn't safe for anyone.

Chapter 9

She was dead, she had to be. She could hardly feel her body, and everything was dark around her. All she could smell was sickly disinfectant and a faint, familiar, masculine smell. Her head hurt and something was wrapped around it. Her eyes refused to open and hurt like she had gravel in them.

Where was she? Forcing her eyes open she tried to focus. The room was dark, except for the small rectangular glass panel allowing light to penetrate the room from the other side. The walls seemed bare and there was an irritating beeping noise from beside her. Turning to look at what it was, she caught sight of the dark figure standing near the window. Her heart thumped wildly.

Blinking slowly, she stared at him. His hand still holding the curtain, his eyes were locked on to hers, but he didn't move. A dark shadow standing there unshaven and dressed all in black. His black hair was tousled as if he'd run his hand through it many times. The only splash of colour to him was the emerald of his eyes, and they were watching her, unmoving.

Blinking again, she tried to focus to see him better. She tried to move, to sit up, but pain tore through her body. She couldn't remember anything or figure out where she was or how Drake came to be in the room with her. All she knew was that she hurt all over and was so glad he was there.

Kathryn tried smiling up at him, but the side of her mouth re-split open and she tasted blood. Letting her tongue move over her lips and then inside her mouth, she felt the cuts and the swollen split on her bottom lip. She closed her eyes against the pain. Slowly opening them, again, she saw Drake still had not moved, nor made a sound. She became uncertain whether he was real or not. She couldn't make out anything.

Trying to speak was impossible. All that came out was a painful rasp. Her throat was so dry. Slowly, painfully she tried to move her head to look for water but she couldn't see out of one eye properly and the other was still blurry in spots. She needed water.

"Are you okay?" Drake asked in a rasped voice.

"Water. Please." Even whispering made her throat hurt.

He walked slowly around to the other side of the bed, where he filled a cup. His eyes only leaving her when he poured the water. She couldn't lift her arms or steady her shaky hands enough to hold the cup, so he carefully placed his hand under her neck and the bottom of her skull, avoiding the lump on her head, and lifted her so she could drink.

"Just small sips. Go slow," he murmured.

She eased down the soothing liquid. The coolness of the water felt good against her sore mouth and throat. It felt as though she'd been screaming. Nothing made sense. Water dribbled down her chin, she couldn't seem to hold her lips to the cup.

When she nodded to indicate enough, Drake lowered her head and put the cup back on the bedside table. Sitting on the bed carefully so that he didn't cause her any more pain, he patted her lips and chin dry with a tissue. Her hands started shaking uncontrollably and she felt sick in the stomach. She closed her eyes and tried to calm herself.

Drake's warm, strong fingers took her hand and held it. Opening her eyes at his touch, she could not read anything in his eyes. He seemed to be made of stone with no emotions, but his hands were warm and gave her comfort. A feeling she was safe. Her eyelids were growing heavy, she was tiring quickly. "What happened?" she rasped.

"It's okay, you sleep now, and I will tell you all about it when you wake."

"You won't leave me, will you?" She was already drifting back to sleep when he mumbled a reply.

"No, I won't leave you."

Drake sat on Kathryn's bed with his hands wrapped around her cold one, until Gail came in to do her observations. Kathryn was sleeping, but a little restless. She was in pain, and he hated seeing her suffer. They couldn't give her anything more, she was as comfortable as possible Gail told him as she walked to the side of the bed and took Kathryn's other hand to take her pulse.

"Has she woken yet?" Gail asked, watching her watch, which was pinned upside down on her shirt, counting.

Drake looked from her, back to Kathryn. "She did, and asked for some water and about what had happened. I told her I would tell her everything when she next woke. She went back to sleep."

Putting Kathryn's hand back to the bed, Gail walked to the end of the bed to write notes into the chart. "So, she recognised you then?"

"Yes." He was watching Kathryn, couldn't seem to move his eyes from her.

"How about you go and get yourself a coffee and something to eat. Give me about twenty minutes while I check on her other wounds."

Drake hesitated. "I promised I wouldn't leave her." He had not let go of her hand.

Gail's firm hand on his shoulder gave him no room to disobey. "She will be all right. I will stay till you get back. Off you go."

He left, with a last look at Kathryn laying in the bed and meandered his way back to the hospital cafeteria.

Half an hour later, Drake was waiting outside Kathryn's room. Her door was closed, but he could hear voices inside. One of the nurses had stopped him from entering; the doctor was checking on Kathryn. Gail had woken her so the doctor could inspect her head and ribs.

The medical ward had a low hum of voices floating around. Visitors were in many of the rooms talking to their friends or family members as the nurses made their rounds and answered the never-ending buzzers. Each time one went off, it lit up the board just above Drake's head. Room seven, room fourteen, then room twenty-four.

The nurses would look up to the board as they walked in and out of rooms, or while they entered data in to the computers at the nurse's station, if it was their assigned room they would go and a moment later the light would go out. The person was seen to, and their needs met. It was a never-ending cycle that seemed to flow with ease but was in constant motion of busyness and routine. It reminded him of the ducks he had seen with Kathryn yesterday. Openly calm on top, paddling like crazy under the surface.

With his hands in his pockets Drake quietly watched the goings on. No one took any notice of him, except the nurses or the two male wardsmen that were constantly on the ward. They would smile as they walked past, and he would nod back. They all seemed friendly enough, but he didn't like the feeling that he was being watched by them, he wanted to get in and make sure Kathryn was okay. The doctor was taking a very long time, and it was starting to worry him. As he walked another circle past her door it opened.

"You can go in now. She is awake and waiting for you," said a young doctor. He was slightly taller than Drake with a slim build and sandy coloured hair with oversized glasses.

"Is she alright?" Drake looked past the doctor into the room where Gail was packing up some medical equipment.

"She will heal. We changed her bandage and cleaned up some of her wounds. She's tired and should sleep peacefully tonight. I hear that you saved her." The doctor held out his hand to shake Drake's.

He shook it out of respect for the doctor but inside felt like a fraud. If all these people knew his past, they would not be trying to shake his hand.

"She is lucky you were there." He looked at his watch. "I'll call on her again in the morning."

Drake watched him walk off to the nurse's station and swap folders, then head down the hall to enter another room. It was late for doing rounds, but he guessed it was all part of the job.

Gail walked out and smiled at him. "She's awake and wanting to see you. I'll be back in a moment with something for her to eat."

Taking a deep breath, Drake walked over the threshold and into the room. Kathryn was sitting up in bed, self-consciously brushing at her hair and smoothing the blankets. She tried to smile, but her bruising and cuts made it look more like a lop-sided toothless grin.

He smiled back and pulled a chocolate bar out of his pocket. "I thought you might like something more for dessert then the stuff they have here." He placed it beside her bed on the table so she could reach it when she wanted. Sitting in the seat beside the bed, he noticed the tears in her eyes and her shaking hands. Taking her hand, he smiled again for reassurance. Not sure for who the most, himself or for her.

Inside, he was crumbling at her pain and despair. Reaching up, he gently wiped her tear away as it silently slid down her cheek. He couldn't leave her like this.

"I'm here. I'm not going anywhere," he murmured, vowing he would keep his internal struggle with the monster under control. He had to. For her.

Later that night, after he had helped her sip her soup, Drake lifted Kathryn and carried her into the bathroom, her head leaning on his shoulder. After making sure she was capable of seeing to her own needs, he gave her privacy, and when she was done, he carried her back to bed and tucked her in.

He tried to be gentle, but her ribs had given her pain. She was tired and her hands still shook occasionally, so he held one as she drifted off to sleep. He would stay and only go back to the motel room when he knew she was settled and fully asleep for the night.

Gail came in with another nurse. It was time for another shift change. Seeing him still there, holding hands with Kathryn, they left and came back pushing a recliner on wheels. The other nurse had a pillow and a blanket for him. He tried to protest but they wouldn't listen. Kathryn had been through a terrible experience and they were willing to break the rules for him, so that he could stay close to her to ensure she felt safe.

After they'd left, he tried to stretch out and find a comfortable position on the couch so he could continue to watch Kathryn sleep, making sure he was there if she had a nightmare or needed him for anything. Her brown hair lay across her pillow in silky strains. He reached out and touched it. It felt like the soft rose petal beside his bed at the motel.

Pulling the blanket up and over his lower torso, he put his arm behind his head and looked at the ceiling. He could hear the nurses moving around and the monitors in other rooms beeping away. Thankfully, Kathryn's had been removed earlier. Slowly his gaze drifted back to her, watching her; sleep slowly took over his mind and body.

Chapter 10

The dawn was yet to awaken the new day. Kathryn slowly looked around her room. She was sore and her eyes still hurt, but she was warm and vaguely aware of where she was. She was still awakening as the nurse left her after checking her obs.

A snoring sound drew her attention back from the door, where the nurse just passed through, to the side of her bed. She found Drake sleeping in a recliner beside her — a blanket pulled up over his shoulder and his arm tucked under the pillow, laying on his side. He was facing her.

With the bit of light that shone into the room she lingered her gaze over his handsome face. The growth of thick, dark stubble over his jaw and long eyelashes that shadowed his eyes gave him the appearance he was dark all over — but not to her. She had watched him sleep before when he had stayed at her house, the person she remembered then was nothing compared to the man who slept beside her bed now.

That he had slept right beside her all night touched her heart. All she wanted to do was reach out and touch the lock of hair that had fallen across his brow. She told herself it was to make sure he was really there, and that she was not in some beautiful dream.

He made a louder snore and rolled over onto his back, the blanket slipping down to his waist. His strong arm muscles were pulled tight in the rolled-up shirtsleeves. Those muscles had carried her last night when she couldn't get the strength in her legs and didn't want to embarrass herself by using a bed pan. He had known and lifted her with such ease and then carried her back and put her to bed. He was all muscle and strength. Powerful with a pure heart. He was Drake, and he was here with her.

A bird at the window sang its morning song to tell the world that finally a new day had begun, and it was time to celebrate. The bird's happy sounds were soon joined by another bird. Together, they sang until the first rays of the sun hit the window behind the thick, darkened curtains. The only announcement of the sun's rays were the beams that crept through the gaps between the window and the curtain.

Moving slowly so as not to wake Drake, Kathryn tried to sit up. Her ribs and head hurt but didn't throb like they did yesterday. She swung her legs over the side of the bed and the room spun. She'd moved too quickly. Holding the side of the bed and putting her foot on the ground, she closed her eyes to stop the world from spinning.

"Whoa, whoa, whoa. Where do you think you're going?" Drake was suddenly kneeling in front of her, his hands covering hers on the bed rail. She didn't even hear him until he was there in front of her.

Looking into his eyes she tried to smile, but her head throbbed and the room had not quite stopped spinning. He touched her cheek tenderly. The barely-there touch was a whisper against her skin, but it felt warm and tingled. She closed her eyes and leaned into his hand.

"Come on, let's get you back into bed," he said as he stood.

"I have to go to the little girl's room," she stated, lifting her head from his hand.

Smiling down at her, Drake chuckled at her choice of words. "Right then, let's get you to the little girl's bathroom."

She shook her head slowly, of course he had to laugh at her right now. She had unthinkingly used her grandmother's words. Once before, she'd used them without thinking in front of him and he had laughed so hard at her that she'd punched him in the arm. The thought of doing that now was a good one, if only she could do it without causing herself pain.

Wrapping his arm around her waist carefully, he helped her to the bathroom. She couldn't make it back to the bed when she was finished though, all her strength was gone in that one small act. Drake carried her back to the bed and pulled the covers up and over her. She was still wearing the hospital gown and smelt like an old dirty disinfectant cloth. Screwing up her nose at herself she leaned back against the pillows.

Kathryn watched Drake while he fussed around with the blankets and pillows. His masculine scent wafted around her when he stretched over her to fluff her pillows. As he worked above and over her, she noted his strong facial features, and how truly beautiful he was. Even more so, this morning.

His eyes were like emerald crystals in the early mornings it seemed. Her skin was growing warm at his nearness and her hands itched to smooth over his chest and shoulders. Kathryn allowed her eyes to roam his upper body and back up to his face and eyes. He was watching her.

His eyes scanned slowly over her face, seemingly taking in every line, indent, and imperfection on her skin, halting at her eyes that she was sure were even darker this morning with the bruises. She saw the intake of breath that seemed to catch and tighten as he breathed.

Gradually his intense gaze moved down to her mouth and the cut on the corner of her lip. It was healing fast but the swelling and split was still painful. Another tight breath from him and an emotional look that she couldn't quite figure out, flashed across his beautiful face giving her the sense of protection from him, before his knuckles, grazed down the side of her face in a touch that left her heart racing. From the side of her cheek to her bottom lip, where his thumb moved across her tender flesh, she sucked in a little extra breath to try and calm herself. Tilting his head ever so slightly, Drake neared her, the heat of their breaths mixing as the emerald burned into her soul.

Bang! The breakfast trolly collided with something and a tray fell to the floor outside her room. Startled apart, Drake stood taller and smiled at her shyly. He squeezed her hand and then went to help the person outside with the trolly.

Kathryn's heart was pounding. She wasn't sure if it was from the trolly or Drake being so close. In that moment, she'd wanted nothing more than to feel his lips on hers. To feel his tenderness and soft caress against her. To feel safe in knowing that he wanted it as much as she did.

Brushing at the blankets and her hair self-consciously, she noted again that she still wore the smelly hospital gown and was in desperate need of a shower.

Drake returned with her breakfast tray. Placing it on the table in front of her, he folded up his blanket while she nibbled carefully at the food, trying not to re-split her lip.

Lucy was back as her nurse this morning and seemed surprised to see Drake had stayed the night. "Gail never lets anyone break the rules. She must have a soft spot for you!" She teased Drake while she checked on Kathryn's wounds.

Kathryn giggled when Drake blushed. He hated drawing attention to himself. He always had. But she like to see him feel a little uncomfortable.

"The doctor will be around later this morning. How is the head feeling? Any dizziness?" Lucy asked. "Do you think you are up for a shower this morning?" Lucy searched around the room. "Do you have any clothes?" She looked between Kathryn and Drake.

"Oh, yes please. A shower would be good, but I don't have any clothes."

"I'll go and collect some for her this morning," Drake supplied to Lucy and smiled at them both. "I'll be back soon." After squeezing Kathryn's hand and promising he would be back as soon as possible, he left.

A quick shower and a change of clothes back at his motel room, Drake found himself at the café. He had hoped to see Annabelle, but she was not working today. After filling his stomach, Drake found a boutique dress shop and then a corner convenience store. Spying the shop next door, he went in there too, hoping that Kathryn still loved what they sold and that his choices were correct.

He hadn't intended to be as long as he was but found he couldn't stop himself from purchasing everything he thought she needed or may want. It was close to lunchtime when he returned to the hospital and found Kathryn asleep. The curtains had been pulled opened and her hair was damp from her shower. Placing his gifts beside his chair, he leaned in and touched her cheek. Cool to touch, her skin was silk. She had beautiful milky skin with no hint of freckles.

He remembered that she'd always looked after her skin, applying moisturiser and sunscreen daily. She had been astonished to learn that he'd never worn sunscreen and did not think that real men wore moisturiser. She had rubbed cream into his face just to prove that men did.

Smiling at the memory, he caressed her cheek again. Nothing had marked her beautiful skin — until Rob. Rage started to burn and he turned away, hoping her skin would not scar. Swallowing down his emotions, he tried to breathe. He walked to the window, but his thoughts and emotions kept rolling. She was sleeping soundly, so maybe a walk could help.

Drake was halfway down the hall when two police officers walked through the timber entrance doors of the ward, now locked back open for the day. Seeing him they directly walked his way.

"Drake Harrison?" the female officer asked.

His heart stopped. "Yes?" he answered tentatively.

"I'm constable Jacki Smith from the city police station. We met the other night." She raised an eyebrow at him.

Ah, looking more closely, he recognised the female officer from the night he had found Kathryn. A sick feeling roiled in his stomach. He remembered a similar conversation years before. Suddenly, he was back there in that moment. His heart tightly thumped and his stomach churned.

"How is Miss White?" enquired Constable Smith.

Blinking, Drake tried to focus and bring himself back to this moment. "She is sleeping. I was just going to stretch my legs." Drake became aware of another man standing just behind the officers. As tall as Drake, the man was heavily built. He was not in a uniform though. Drake looked between them all. Something was going on.

"May we talk privately with you before we speak with Miss White?" Jacki raised her eyebrows again and motioned back towards the nurse's station in the middle of the ward. It was not a question but a thinly veiled order.

"It won't take long, and I am sure Miss White would like you to be there with her when we speak to her. We would like to speak with you first though please. *If* you wouldn't mind."

Drake's protective instinct kicked in and he found himself studying the ununiformed man next to him as they all walked back towards the nurse's station. Something was definitely up.

At the nurse's station, Jacki asked to use Ruth's office. It was a small room with glass windows the full way around for a view of the entire ward. The nurses at the station politely moved away to check on patients. Ruth remained just outside the door, making herself appear busy.

Constable Jacki motioned for Drake to enter, then stood near the door behind him while her partner stood to the other side of Drake as he took a seat at the desk. The plain clothed man walked around the desk and sat down in Ruth's chair. After he had settled himself, he watched Drake for a moment before pulling out his note pad and flipping through the pages.

Drake's anxiety doubled. He couldn't read the man in front of him. What was going on?

"I am Detective Scott Cooper, from the city police station. I work with the drug trafficking department. I believe you saved Miss Kathryn White from a brutal domestic assault two nights ago. Is that correct?"

"Um, yes. That's correct." Drake was confused, and deep in his gut, it was shrieking warnings.

"Did you also have a confrontation with a Mr Robert Edgile?" The detective peered up at Drake.

"It was self-defence for me, and to protect Kathryn." He felt like he'd just said the wrong thing. Scott looked at his notes, then at Drake, then back at his notes. "He was really laying into her, and I had to defend

Kathryn, and myself once he started on me. I had to defend us both so I could get her to safety."

Drake turned to Constable Smith, who was leaning against the door, preventing anyone from disturbing them — or allowing him out. The thought that he might be in trouble caused panic through him in waves. His nerves were on end.

"How long have you known Miss White? You are friends, correct?"

"I knew her a few years ago. Yes, we are friends."

"When did you *re-connect* with Miss White?" The Detective was writing everything Drake said down in his notepad and was watching him intently.

"About three days ago."

Stopping writing, the Detective eyed Drake with a confused look. "Three days ago? How did you re-connect again?"

"I walked into the café where Kathryn worked to get something to eat, and she was there."

"Did you know that was where she worked?"

"No. It was by coincidence, that's all. We talked, and chatted again later that night at the pub she also works at. We went for a picnic at the park the following day."

"Did you know of the relationship between Mr Edgile and Miss White?"

"No."

"How did you find her in the alley, then?"

"I was walking back to my motel room after eating dinner at the pub."

"And *you* just happened by at the right time?" The detective raised his eyebrow at Drake. He was testing Drake's story.

"Yes." Drake rubbed his hands on his jeans to remove the sweat on them, Scott watched him do it.

"We know about your past, Mr Harrison."

Drake looked him directly in the eye and took a slow deep breath, a coolness coming over him. He knew what was going to happen. He sat back in his chair, which creaked under his weight, and folded his arms.

"Mr Edgile has gone missing. Miss White's and Mr Edgile's apartment has been broken into and ransacked. Do you know anything about this?"

Drake's heart leaped into his throat. Surely, they didn't think he had anything to do with Rob's disappearance or the break in? "I don't even know where Kathryn's apartment is, and I haven't seen Rob since the bastard took aim at us and shot her." Barely holding onto his temper, Drake swung around to face constable Smith. "You were there. You saw it. All I did was rough him up enough to get Kathryn out of there." He waited for her to verify his story, but she just looked at her comrade with an unreadable expression.

"Can anyone vouch for your whereabouts over the last 12 hours up till 6am this morning?" Scott pressed.

Drake turned his gaze to the detective and took a calming breath, his mind racing with relief. Thank God for nurse Gail and her bossiness. "I was here all night with Kathryn. She was upset and her nurse, Gail, told me I was to stay. The nurse that was on night shift and Lucy who is on today can also *vouch* for me being here until about 8am. I left then to buy Kathryn some personal things. I have only just arrived back now."

Scott looked above Drake's head and gave a barely noticeable lift of his head to Jacki. She opened the door and left. Turning his gaze on Drake he smiled, but it wasn't genuine. "Now we have that sorted, I need to speak with both you and Miss White." He stood and walked to the door, holding it open for Drake.

Drake led the way around the nurse's desk and passed Constable Jacki, who was quietly speaking with Ruth. They both gave him a little smile. At Kathryn's door, he knocked gently so that she would wake on their entrance. To his surprise, she was awake and smiled back at him when he entered.

His return smile faltered. His nerves were too frayed, and he knew the moment Scott and the other police officer followed him into the room. Her smile fading, Kathryn tried to sit up but winced, pain showing on her face. She looked from him to Scott, to the other police officer and then to the two other women as they entered and closed the door behind them. The room suddenly felt crowded.

Kathryn had a deep sinking feeling in her stomach as she looked at the man who followed Drake into her room. She noticed Drake had paled in the face compared to his normal bronzed tone.

Her thoughts raced. She had not yet asked about what had happened to her, all she could remember was that Rob had come home and found her packing, and then waking up to find Drake at the curtains in this hospital room. She knew she had been bashed. She didn't want to face it yet, and the feeling she was about to be forced to, set her heart thumping and her hands shaking.

Drake walked straight to her side, pulled up his chair and sat on it, his hand taking hers for support. He was shaking too, but she could see him trying to hide it. He remained looking at her hand wrapped in his. She looked back around at the group of strangers now standing in her room, who were watching them both.

Clearing his throat, the heavy-set man spoke first, "Miss White, I'm Detective Scott Cooper from the city police station, and I work in the drug trafficking department. Am I able to speak with you about Mr Robert Edgile and the events that happened two nights ago?"

Kathryn couldn't speak around the lump in her throat, so she nodded and gripped Drake's hand tighter. He squeezed her hand back.

"Is it acceptable for Mr Harrison to be in the room with you?" She nodded again. "If you wish at any point for him to leave, please let me know." She nodded, then looked to Drake, who tried to smile in reassurance while still staring at her hand. He would not look at her.

"What is your relationship with Mr Edgile?" Scott asked as he read from his note pad.

"We are, were, flat mates."

"Was there ever anything more to it than that, Miss White?" Scott raised his head to observe her response. "Did it start out as a relationship, or turn into one while you were living together as flat mates?'

He was watching her so intently she felt colour staining her cheeks. She didn't want to answer, it was embarrassing. She had always prided herself on her self-control and treating her body like a temple and now she had to tell them of her slip up. Drake seemed suddenly interested in a spot on his boots as he shifted back in his seat.

"One night I got drunk, and we slept together. That was all. We knew it was a mistake. We were never in a romantic or sexual relationship. Just flat mates."

"How did you become *just* flat mates with Mr Edgile?"

Frowning, she didn't like how he was talking to her. "We knew each other in high school, as classmates. Never anything else. I needed somewhere else to live when my old flat mate's boyfriend moved in. Rob offered a room, and I accepted."

"Do you know of Mr Edgile's friends or associates? Did you know where he worked?"

"No." Kathryn was getting frustrated and confused by the questions. Her head was hurting, and if she tightened her grip on Drake's hand any more, he would lose all sensation.

"Like I said. We were just flat mates. Only passing if we were home together, which was rare due to my working at the café and pub nearly seven days a week. Rob worked different hours and different jobs, from what I can understand."

Scott was busy writing notes and took a moment to ask another question. She took that time to look at Drake. Her head was throbbing, and the room had started to rotate. She tried to lie back but her ribs stabbed with pain, and her breath caught in a gasp. Drake instantly stood, helping her to carefully lie back. As soon as he sat down, she gripped his hand again. Hers was shaking and he held it with both his hands to calm her.

"Are you okay to continue?" Scott asked, concern in his voice.

Kathryn nodded, realising that everyone in the room was watching her and Drake's every move. Ignoring the panic the realisation brought, she refocused on the man at the end of her bed.

"Only a few more questions left to answer at this time." He glanced back at his notes. "Did you ever feel in danger for yourself with Mr Edgile?"

"Yes. I was saving up to leave and find my own place."

"Why did you feel in danger, Miss White?"

"Because he had started to take drugs and it was affecting his behaviour towards me."

"Was he ever violent towards you before the night of the attack?"

Taking an unsteady breath, she looked at Drake and then to everyone else in the room. Swallowing the painful lump in her throat she answered "Yes, the night before that. He was waiting for me outside the pub I work at. We walked home together, and it got a little scary."

The way Drake lifted his head and looked directly at her, she knew he'd realised it was the night Annabelle had come racing up and stolen her away from him.

Scott flipped back through his notes and looked up at Drake and then to her. "Was that the night you were talking with Mr Harrison at the pub? The night before you went on your picnic?"

She looked down at the blanket on her bed and picked off a piece of fluff. Embarrassment and humiliation heated her skin just a fraction as she remembered what had occurred that night back at her apartment with Rob and how he had pulled himself off in the kitchen while watching her. She should have run then and now cursed herself for not doing so. "Yes."

"Did you tell Mr Harrison what had happened the night before when you went on your picnic together?"

Kathryn looked up. She was not stupid and knew where the detective was going with this line of questions. Calming herself before she answered she breathed deeply. "No. I was planning on leaving the apartment that night and going to a friend's place. He didn't need to know."

"Were you going to Mr Harrison's and Mr Edgile found out? Is that what happened, Miss White?'

Drake was becoming agitated. He pulled his hand from hers and stretched out his legs, sitting back in his seat and crossing his beefy arms across his wide chest. She could see him trying to keep his temper under control as his jaw pulsated each time he gritted his teeth. He also understood they were trying to blame him for Rob's disappearance.

Kathryn took a slow deep breath and looked Scott directly in the eyes. "No. I was not going to Drake's. I'd organised to stay a few nights with my friend Annabelle until I could find an apartment for myself. Rob was taking drugs and stealing my money. He was becoming violent and controlling. I will not stand for that. I had my plan, and I was following through with that." She bunched the blanket in her hands.

"I had shared a picnic lunch with Drake that day because it was my birthday. After we'd said our goodbyes, I left to pack my few things from the apartment so I could take them to the pub, then go home with Annabelle. I thought that Rob wouldn't be home and that I would be safe." Kathryn took an uneven breath in. "I thought wrong."

A sob caught in her throat and Drake moved to sit beside her on the bed, pulling her into his arms. Ruth came to her other side and poured her a glass of water and checked her drip. A sign of support for her patient.

"I'm sorry to have upset you, Miss White. But we must ask these questions. I hope you can understand," Scott said placatingly.

Kathryn nodded and wiped her tears on the back of her hand, remaining huddled within the strength of Drake's arms.

"Miss White, I am Constable Jacki Smith. I was with you and Mr Harrison the night he found you. Can you remember what happened?" Constable Smith sat gently on the bed and touched Kathryn's leg through the blanket for extra reassurance.

Feeling more secure with Drake's arms around her, Kathryn sniffed and answered, "I remember packing and hearing Rob come through the front door, that's it. Running, maybe being carried. Everything is a blur, and nothing makes sense. I'm sorry." She started to cry, and Drake held her tighter.

"Do you know where Mr Edgile could be? We have been around to your apartment, and it has been broken into and ransacked. Do you have any idea where he might be hiding, Miss White?" Constable Jacki pressed.

Shocked, Kathryn calmed her crying and looked at the detective and the two police officers. She didn't know what to say. Didn't know anything. She shook her head and then cried into Drake's shirt. Her life was a living hell.

"If you think of anything more, then please contact us." Scott handed Drake a card with his details on it and after a nod to the others in the room, walked out, the officers following in his wake.

Ruth fussed with the bed and the room for a minute longer before leaving, closing the door behind her. Once the door was closed, Kathryn couldn't hold it in any longer and she sobbed into Drake's chest, her whole body quivering with emotions. He held her tight and tried to soothe her.

Wiggling himself gently down the bed, taking her with him, Drake pulled her head onto his broad chest. She felt safe and protected just like when her grandmother had held her as a child.

She remained that way, allowing her tears to fall, soaking into his shirt until sleep came for her again.

Chapter 11

The next morning Kathryn woke before dawn again, her awareness stirring at the sound of the tiny finches on the window ledge, singing their happy morning song. The day before she had watched them come and go to the ledge. They were a cute couple. He was always puffing out his chest in front of her as she hopped around him, then she would fly off and he would chase her.

The first show of love. Nature had it down to a perfect dance within the animal kingdom. Maybe, in the human kingdom, one day for her it would be the same — these had been the thoughts filling her mind yesterday while Drake had been away.

Before she knew Rob was missing and that the police suspected Drake of being part of it. That she had planned the whole thing of Rob's disappearance. The thoughts saddened and scared her. She hoped Rob would stay away from her so she could move on with her life, but something was amiss. The police were interested in more than they let on and knew more than what they were saying.

It was as if they needed to cross off the most logical possibilities first, that being she and Drake had planned it all, before moving onto the truth, which was that Rob had got high and then bashed her nearly to death. Drake had somehow, by divine intervention, been the one who saved her. Then she had been shot, and in his cowardness, Rob was hiding out and most likely getting high again.

The soft sound of snoring pulled her attention away from the birds at the window and her thoughts, to the other side of her bed. Drake lay stretched out on the recliner again. The blanket had fallen to his waist, revealing his bare chest.

The sight of his sculptured body and tanned skin made her mouth go dry. Not a small man, he had a large chest with muscles that led from his shoulders down to his stomach and beyond. Hair covered his chest and fed down over his stomach, disappearing under the blanket.

Her gaze travelled up to his face, which had more stubble on it. Yesterday, he'd held her while she cried and never let her go until she had fallen asleep. In the last few days, he'd become her saviour and protector. Something she had prided herself on never needing. She had learned to do things on her own and protect herself — that was before Rob — but now Drake was here, she felt safe and wanted him to be with her forever.

Forever.

Where did that thought come from? She blinked. Drake had his own life to get back to and, except for two close kisses, had done nothing but offer friendship. Was that all she was to him? A friend? From the first time she had laid eyes on him all those years ago, her heart had wanted more and had always fluttered and beat rapidly whenever she saw him. With each shared touch she had craved and wanted more of him. When he had said goodbye ten years earlier, never contacting her again, her heart had broken. The thought that all Drake saw her as was a friend was too much to take. Especially now. Swallowing the lump that formed in her throat, Kathryn closed her eyes against the pain from her aching heart.

She'd always fantasied about him taking her with him one day and living happily ever after, like in one of the romance stories she loved to read. Like the ones he'd brought for her yesterday.

She opened her eyes and looked at the three books stacked on top of one another, with a chocolate bar on top of them, now positioned on her bedside table. After she had woken late yesterday afternoon, Drake had shown her all the beautiful things he had brought.

She now had three new dresses, two sets of pyjamas, a pair of boots and slippers, plus toiletries: he'd even remembered moisturizer, lacy underwear and bras, that he blushed about when he handed them to her, plus the three new romantic books, all part of a series.

He had gone to one of the most expensive boutiques near the café and purchased it all. When she asked about how he knew her correct size, he'd blushed, saying the young serving girl had looked to be about her size, so he'd based his choices on that.

His blush had deepened to a near tomato red when he explained how mortified he'd been when the girl suggested she model the underwear for him to make sure it was the right sizing for Kathryn.

Kathryn had laughed so hard at him, and the look that came over his face when he told her about it all, her ribs had hurt and made her cry tears of both pain and laughter. The thought made her smile again now.

She'd never bought herself lacy underwear, preferring the comfortable cotton ones. He could not have known, she realised. Most men thought woman walked around in sexy lingerie all day, just waiting to rip their clothes off and be sexy like in magazines and porn movies. Cotton all the way for her, but she wouldn't tell him that. Not now.

All the other things he had bought her were beautiful and very much her. She passed that boutique daily on her way to work, and always stopped to look at the divine things in the window display, wishing she had the money to buy them. Her café dream by the river would always stop her walking in and drive her on her way to work.

The sun had started to send its rays across the earth and hit the window. It was going to be another bright and sunny day. Light was filling the room as it found its way around the heavy curtains.

Drake moved his leg, drawing her attention. She watched him sleeping, her stomach giving her the now familiar warm feeling she got every time she was near him. Her eyes lazily going over his sleeping body again.

"You shouldn't look at men that way, Kathryn. It will get you into trouble," Drake drawled with a teasing smile, watching her with the most intent green eyes she had ever seen.

She'd been caught allowing her eyes to travel the length and breadth of him. Her cheeks heated as she smiled shyly back. "I was just checking out the scenery, that's all." She turned away, shocked that that had just come out of her mouth.

Drake smiled to himself as he sat up and watched her get embarrassed at her words. It was the most brazen thing she had ever said to him, and he allowed it to feed his ego. He knew the work he did daily on his farm gave him the body many men spent hours in the gym achieving.

She wasn't the first woman to look at him like that. She was the first woman however, who made him feel her eyes touch him everywhere she looked. He wanted her hands on his body instead of her eyes.

That was not a good thought. He cursed to himself.

Standing up, pulling his shirt on, Drake turned to fold his blanket, anything to get his thoughts back to where they should be. His stomach growled loudly, complaining at his limited intake of food over the last few days. The hospital café did nothing for his appetite, and he never wanted to be away from Kathryn for too long.

If he hadn't arrived back yesterday when he had, she would have had to face that detective by herself. His temper started to rise. She would have been scared and upset. He would not let that happen.

In another time, he had allowed the police to place blame where they shouldn't have, and as a consequence he'd never trusted any of them again. No. They would not do that to Kathryn, he would make sure he was with her, and she was safe.

Outside the door, the breakfast trolly rattled to a stop. Drake moved to the windows and opened the curtains, letting light fill the room and clear away his heavy thoughts.

"Good morning." A woman who looked to be in her late sixties entered the room carrying Kathryn's breakfast tray. "Oh good, you're awake, my love. And looking much better then yesterday, I must say." The woman gave Kathryn a warm smile as she placed the tray on her table and brought it round to her bed so that she could easily eat.

When Kathryn moved to sit upright, she let out a groan of pain. Drake rushed to help her and the woman smiled up at him, her eyes full of admiration and something else.

"Oh, you're a good boy," she said. "We all knew you'd be here, especially knowing what you did for your girl and how you've cared for her these last days. You're a good'un, you are." The woman beamed at Kathryn and, nodding to herself, walked out of the room, only to return with another tray.

"Here, my boy, we made you a tray up as well, but don't go telling Ruth, she might not like us old girls spoiling ya and giving you a free feed." She lowered her voice and leaned in to get closer to Drake. He had to lean across the bed so he could hear what she was whispering. "Us girls are mighty proud that good men are still out there caring for their women. I might even sneak back later with a nice coffee and cake for ya. Better than the stuff they call food at the cafeteria." She winked at him and patted Kathryn's hand before she left.

"Thank you!" Drake called as she passed through the door, and she waved over her shoulder.

Feeling her staring at him, Drake looked down into her dark chocolate eyes that were dancing, his arm around her waist, supporting her. Her warmth was penetrating pleasantly through her silk PJ top, slivering its way up his veins.

"You could charm the ears off a cat, you know that," she said with a coy smile.

Giving her his most charming smile, and look of innocence "It appears so, but I have no idea how it happens."

"It's that country boy charm you ooze. It gets the girls every time," she said matter-of-factly with a teasing voice.

Raising both eyebrows, he turned his full focus on her, his arm still holding her as he bent closer to her and whispered. "Does it now? It appears to be only the old girls. Where is the fun in that?"

Kathryn rolled her eyes and shook her head, sitting up a little straighter and nearer to her breakfast. "Men. Really? Trust me, if you paid attention, you would notice it's not just the old girls."

"Is that right. What do you think?"

Smiling inwards, he could see he had caught her off guard. She didn't know what to say. He waited, almost sensing the thoughts flitting around in her mind.

"That you don't need me fuelling your ego?" She said dryly and lifted the cover from her food. She groaned at the sight of a Weetbix, tub of yogurt, a cup of juice and a cold cup of tea. "I hope you got something better."

Drake walked around the bed to his tray and lifted the lid. "Nope. I got Cornflakes, though. Do you want to swap?"

"Yes please, if you don't mind."

Drake swapped the trays. He hated Weetbix but knew she loved Cornflakes.

"You know what I would love to eat right now," Kathryn mumbled as she crunched her way through the Cornflakes.

Drake looked up from his soggy breakfast. "What would that be?"

"A plate filled with hot pancakes, loaded with fresh berries, flooded with warm maple syrup, with a dollop of cream on top, served with ice cream on the side. And a steaming caramel hot chocolate with marshmallows to wash it all down with. Mm mm."

Looking down at his breakfast Drake replied, "It sounds like a heart starter, sugar rush to start the day, but you know what, if I concentrate hard enough, I think I can taste it when I eat this." Smiling, he took a large bite of his soggy breakfast. "Mm mm, I can taste it... maybe not." He grimaced at her over the rim of his cup as he took a big swig of the cold tea.

Laughing softly, Kathryn sat back against the pillows with her breakfast bowl in one hand and her spoon in the other. "I remember the neighbours that used to live behind my grandmother's house. When they had an oversupply of strawberries, they'd give us some. Usually, Grandma would make jam with them, but a few times she made pancakes with maple syrup and strawberries. We would sit on the front steps and eat them slowly, savouring every bite." Kathryn licked her lips, looking like she was savouring the taste all over again.

Drake watched her tongue glide across her top lip and slide back into her mouth, his eyes taking in every movement and locking it into his memory. A crushing need to touch her lips with his own flooded him. As she continued speaking dreamily, reminiscing, he imagined himself tasting and nibbling her luscious bottom lip, hearing her moan as he sucked every part of her mouth and down her neck. Her lips once again caressed the spoon, sucking the cool metal deep into her mouth, making him mentally groan with the torment she was unconsciously doing to him.

Shaking his thoughts from where they had dangerously travelled, Drake forced himself to focus back onto her words as best he could.

"At Christmas time we would go over for the day, and they'd fill us with food." Kathryn smiled widely at him, her face lost in her memory. "A champagne breakfast with bacon, ham, croissants, oh the list goes on, lunch was the traditional roast turkey and veggies, with lots of French delicacies, and dessert was pavlova, trifle, ice-cream and jelly." Laughing, she added, "We never needed to eat for a week after and they always sent us home with a box full of leftovers. It was great."

Drake just smiled, not adding to the conversation as he finished his breakfast. His mind wandered to his own childhood Christmases. He had never spoken of his childhood much. He always made sure conversation, when he did need to speak, was always about his grandfather, the horses and the farm.

"Is that where you learned to cook so well? From your neighbours and your grandmother?" he asked, wanting to change the subject before she asked about his Christmases, or his mind took off down a road he didn't want to go down.

"Oh yeah. They were a lovely old couple. She was French and he was a typical Australian. They met during the war. She nursed him back to health after he was injured and then they married and came to live here. They never had children, but had lots of other family members, who made Christmas a very large affair. I had her and my grandmother's recipe books, along with some other things hidden behind a piece of old tin, in the laundry shed at the back of my apartment." Kathryn looked out the window. The happiness that was across her face just a moment ago died and was replaced with sadness. "I won't be seeing that again, I guess."

Drake watched the sadness of her dreams slipping away wash over her face and felt the stabbing pain of knowing that no matter what or how hard you want something, sometimes it was ripped away from you.

A few hours later, Drake and Kathryn sat playing cards. Lucy was on duty again and had brought in some roses from her garden for all her patients that day. The scent of the beautiful flowers wafted throughout the room. Delighted, when Lucy gave them to her Kathryn touched each rose delicately to her nose and studied the colours and soft petals. A simple joy had somewhat returned to her today.

They were on their fifth round of Go-Fish, and she had beaten Drake soundly every time so far. He was not a good looser and when she took his last card from his hand yet again, he suggested Snap. These were the only two games they both knew how to play.

He shuffled the cards and dealt them out. "I must tell you that I'm very good at Snap, so be prepared to lose."

"Like you were an excellent player at Go-Fish," she teased.

He squinted at her as he placed his first card down so she could place hers on top, then his on hers, she was watching the cards as intently as he was. He flipped his card over, and she snapped her hand on top of his before he had the chance to remove it from the stack.

"Ouch. How did you see that so quick?"

She had snapped on a pair of Queens. Laughing, she watched as he pretended pain in his hand. "You flip your cards towards me before you place them down on the deck." He looked so shocked she started to laugh.

"You're cheating!' he gasped, then stood and pushed the table away from her with the cards now scattered across the fake timber top.

She laughed even harder while he tried to glare at her, hands on his hips, but his eyes full of humour. Next thing, he leaned in and grabbed her hips, pulling her down the bed. He tickled her waist and she screamed with laughter as she tried to wriggle away. Her ribs hurt even though he was being gentle with her, and she tried to push his hands away. Twisting, she moved her head from side to side, her hair flying around her.

Her neck made a loud popping sound and a tight pain locked her neck. Kathryn stopped instantly and Drake's hands froze where they were on her hips. She gaped at him in terror. Should she move or not? Drake didn't move. Not an inch.

Someone had to move.

Slowly, she moved her neck and head, and relief washed all through her. It was just a bone cracking back into place and felt better now but her neck muscles were stiff. She remembered she'd experienced the same thing when she was a teenager and had been playing a game in sports class. The teacher had explained that it sometimes happened within the body. She breathed a sigh of relief.

Drake still had not moved, his hands were still on her hips. His eyes were wide and fearful. "Are you okay?" he finally breathed out.

"Yes, but my neck muscles are locked up."

Instantly, he was up and moving to the door. "I will get the doctor."

"Drake!" She halted him before he could exit. "I'll just rub it. It's only the muscles." Sitting back up on the bed, she lifted her hands and began to massage the taut muscles, closing her eyes in concentration, and enjoying the small relief.

She heard Drake walk back from the door. Her breath caught and her heart raced when he slipped in behind her, so her bottom was pressed up high against his inner thighs as he wrapped them around hers, straddling the bed.

Taking her hands, he slowly removed them from their massaging and placed them on her thighs. His warmth and protectiveness surrounded her, sending heat spiralling into her lower stomach.

Tentatively, his fingers brushed her neck as he gathered her hair and placed it over her shoulder. Her shoulders now nearly bare, he began to massage her neck with surprisingly good pressure and ability.

His hands, his heat behind her, the delicious relief he was giving her, made her eyes close and she involuntarily leaned back against his chest, a barely noticeable sound escaping her lips. His movements and gentle touch sent shivers all over her body.

Drake pressed his body closer to hers. His chest at her back allowed her to lean into him so he could support her as she relaxed. His body was reacting to her closeness, but instead of trying to pull away and not feel it, he stayed and kept moving his hands across her silky skin.

She was hurt and he knew his hands were helping her. Kathryn moved her head and her hair fell across his shoulder and down his upper arm as she settled her head comfortably against him. The smell of vanilla surrounded him, and his body pulsated more. Her eyes were closed as she relished in his touch. Her full lips were parted as another moan came from deep in her throat.

Drake shifted his head so he could watch her enjoyment. The small frowns and smiles that animated her face as he worked his hands, captivated him.

His hands worked their way ever so slowly from her neck to her shoulders, pushing the thin dress straps to the edge and letting them fall. Her shoulders were now completely bare to his eyes and touch. She had the most beautiful cream skin he had ever seen, and it felt like warm silk to touch. His hands wandered from her shoulders to the tops of her arms and back again. She was fully relaxed against him, her weight only adding to his awareness of her.

Slowing his hands at the edge of her shoulders, he let his fingertips slide slowly over her upper arms and down along her forearms. His heart beat wildly in his chest.

Kathryn dared not move, other than to subtly angle her body and head to face him. They had been at this point twice now and he had pulled away each time. She had to fight every instinct to not move, but to wait and see what he did. She didn't want to scare him, but so desperately wanted him to kiss her. Her mouth was dry, and it felt like her heart was beating so loudly he could surely hear it. Slowly, she ran her tongue over her dry lips. Drake's eyes darted to the movement. She did it again and he leaned in, curling around her, their breath mingling as he whispered her name and pressed his lips to hers.

Her heart leaped with joy and excitement as Drake's lips moved across hers. She didn't react too much at first, not wanting to scare him, but when he started to pull away, she followed his retreat and kissed him back. Slowly, nothing too passionate, instinctively knowing she had to let him set the pace.

He pressed his mouth back to hers and slipped his tongue inside tasting and dancing with hers then nibbling carefully on her bottom lip, the sensation travelling down her body, feeling as if his mouth and tongue were loving her entire being, not just her lips. Kathryn raised her hand and touched his face, tenderly pulling Drake towards her so he couldn't pull away. Not before she was ready.

She had waited and wanted this for so long, she was not going to let him leave so soon.

His veins were pulsating with heat and his heart was beating so loudly he couldn't hear anything but the rushing in his ears, and he didn't care. He only wanted more, and when he felt Kathryn's hand tenderly holding him to her, pulling him closer, he obliged and kissed her deeper.

His hand trailing from her arm to her stomach, he pulled her flush up against his body, the heat from her bottom now firmly pressed against him so intimately, aroused his male senses fully awake. He couldn't think, only react. His hand slid from her stomach, back up her arm to her cheek and along her jaw, missing her bandage, then into her hair as he angled her head to taste more of her. Her taste, her touch, her smell, they all became part of him.

The world around them disappeared to nothing as he continued to taste and explore her mouth. Her hand on his face, held the ground he was standing on sturdy and strong as the rest fell away. Her pull against him, too much, he wanted more of her. To have her breathing for him as the very last of his air was pulled from his lungs just to keep kissing her.

The need to breathe forced them apart. Breathing laboured and heart racing, Kathryn was staring into his eyes, wide and dark. He watched her carefully, his hands remaining where they were, not letting her go. Gently, Kathryn moved her hand across his face and rubbed her thumb across his lips, as if to reassure him. He kissed her thumb, then her forehead.

His hands shaking, he helped her sit back up and righted her dress straps. His body protested when he forced himself to move away from hers.

The coolness rushing over him was a bittersweet relief. He needed a moment to compose himself before he could apologise for his actions. He didn't want her to think there could be anything between them. Not when he was leaving once she was healed and safe, and he didn't want to hurt her like he knew he would. They were friends and that was it: that was all it ever could be.

He could not weaken around her again.

Chapter 12

Kathryn reached for Drake while he was regaining his balance from climbing off the bed. He took her hand and pressed it to his lips with a tight smile. Her heart still raced, and her body protested where his hands had left her. Her eyes smouldering, she smiled up at him.

"Ooh. It's good to see that a young man can still hold hands and make a girl smile." The lady holding Kathryn's lunch tray smiled as she entered the room and sat the tray on the table beside the bed.

Drake instantly pulled his hand from Kathryn's and ran it through his hair as he turned away.

"Here you go, my girl. You eat up now and rebuild your strength." The woman looked at Drake's back. "We've brought you something too, my dear." She smiled when he spun and regarded her with all his country boy charm. "Both of you need to eat up. I'll be back later with the tea and biscuits." She bustled out of the room.

Kathryn looked at the tray. She had a large salad and some ice-cream and jelly, and Drake had a large salad roll wrapped in clear film. It looked good. With a sigh, she picked up a fork to tackle the salad.

She had just finished scooping up the last dreg of ice-cream when Lucy walked in with the doctor, announcing that they would remove the bandage and replace it with a smaller cover over the stitches on her head.

Drake had taken his salad roll and stood near the window looking out at the city while they had both eaten in silence. Their minds, she was sure, were both on that kiss but neither wanted to talk about it, it seemed.

"It's looking good." The doctor drew her attention from her thoughts as he removed the bandage from her head. "You're healing well and should be able to go home in a few days."

Pleased, Kathryn looked at Drake, now leaning against the wall just a few steps away from her bed, but he avoided her eyes, studying the ceiling instead.

She felt something within him had shifted towards her. Just a fraction, but enough to make her heart give a kick. A kick from a naughty child. Her eyes followed his back as he wordlessly left the room to allow Lucy and the doctor to check her ribs and other cuts and bruises.

While they lifted her dress to check the bruises on her ribs, they asked questions. She answered when needed, but her thoughts were on Drake. That kiss had shaken the earth under her feet. For years, she'd wondered what his lips would taste like on hers and how it would feel to be in his arms while he stole her breath away. It was more then she had ever dreamed. He was a damn fine kisser, and his hands had such strength and tenderness all at once.

Since the kiss, however, he'd done his best to avoid eye contact with her. She could see him watching her, could feel it, but when she turned to him, he would look away, concentrate on his lunch or the ceiling.

Kathryn needed him to talk and say what was on his mind. He was a quiet man, he never did say much, least of all about his feelings. Her heart pounded: he'd be gone in a few days. She knew he was only here to see her get better. Well, when he came back into the room, she would ask him straight out what his true feelings were about her and that kiss. And if he wouldn't say, then she was going to have to make him open up somehow.

Drake paced just outside Kathryn's room, his mind racing. He should never have kissed her. Never led her to believe that he could give her anything more than friendship. Those moments with her in his arms, wanting more, were too dangerous for them both. He wanted more, much more with her, but he couldn't. He was who he was, and nothing would change that. He could never let her get close.

Hot anger swelled within his body as he walked back and forth in the hall. The heat was rising and his stomach was rolling; his temper was getting the best of him. Stopping, he ran his hand through his hair again and leaned against the solid wall at his back. His eyes closed, trying to shut out his turmoil.

"Mr Harrison."

The stern but friendly voice jolted Drake's his eyes open and he stood to attention immediately, hating that the police could make him do that still after all these years.

"Can we have a moment of your time please?"

Drake nodded, expecting them to lead the way to Ruth's office again. They didn't. Instead, the two of them stepped closer around him, locking him against the wall. His anger from before turned to cold fear.

"We have some information about Mr Edgile and his activities." When Drake did not say anything, only looked between them, Scott continued. "We believe that Mr Edgile has been murdered." He waited, watching Drake's expression.

The only clue Drake gave Scott that he had heard him was the smallest lift of his eyebrows and a more intense look.

"Execution-style, to the back of the head."

Drake felt sick to his stomach and panic started to flow through him. His hands shook and he could feel stickiness on his palms. He resisted the urge to rub them or wipe them on his jeans. The memory of the smell was with him as he fought to breathe and stay calm.

"Where did you find him?" he managed to ask in his normal voice, looking between the constable and the detective.

Constable Smith answered. "In the fire-ravaged shell of his and Miss White's apartment. It was set on fire last night at about 11pm. His body was discovered soon after."

Struggling to hold his composure, Drake wiped a hand over his face and took another deep calming breath as he looked up at the ceiling. This was not good. Kathryn had lost everything now. How would she take the news? Not only of the apartment being burned but Rob being found murdered. He wasn't sure she was going to cope.

Although she'd said she didn't care about Rob, she was such a kind and caring person that it would affect her on some level. This news could forever affect her to her core. Drake shifted his weight from foot to foot. "Do you have any idea who would have done this?" He knew they knew. They always knew before they asked questions.

They looked between each other and then back at him. "We believe so, yes."

The hairs on the back of Drake's neck stood up. He was missing something.

The doctor and Lucy walked out of the room and came to a stop just out of view of the room and Kathryn. "Right," said the doctor, nodding at them all. "This way. It will be more private, and we can discuss things without fear of witnesses or being heard." He walked past them and down the corridor.

Lucy smiled and waited for Drake to take a step forward and then fell in next to him. Scott and Jacki followed behind them. Drake felt nauseous as he followed the doctor down the corridor, past the elevators to a small but bright room tucked away to the side. It was an abandoned office, with a few chairs and an old wooden desk in the centre.

The doctor walked to one of the chairs behind the desk, as did Scott. Lucy sat next to Drake on the opposite side of the desk as Constable Smith closed the door and took up a guarding stance.

Drake looked around. Every eye seemed to be focused on him. His heart was beating fast and there was a ringing in his ears.

Scott spoke first. "For the good doc and nurse here, I'll explain why we need privacy and for you both to be here." The detective looked at Lucy and then the doctor before returning his gaze to Drake again.

Drake still had no idea what was going on.

"Miss White's former flat mate, the person who attacked her, was found murdered when the fire department was called to a fire at their apartment last night. Nothing could be saved, unfortunately. However, we believe we know who killed Mr Edgile."

Lucy let out a gasp of shock and stared at the doctor, her eyes wide.

"It appears Mr Edgile was part of, or associated with, a gang of bikies who are the target of a major investigation by my department due to their illegal drug smuggling and dealings." Scott looked directly at Drake as he leaned his arms onto the table.

"One of our undercover officers within the gang has been in touch and confirmed that the order was given to remove Mr Edgile. It appears he had stolen and used some of the drugs he was meant to be selling and re-locating. It is also believed he owed a great deal of money to the club and that he had evidence against them stored in his apartment."

Drake's heart was beating fast, and his temper started to boil. Kathryn had been living in that apartment. The thought of her being there and the bikie gang finding her and doing God knows what to her, had his hands clenching and unclenching in rage. He was struggling to keep himself composed as he listened to Scott. She could have been killed because of Rob's connection to this gang.

He had to stay calm and thinking clearly for her sake.

"But if he has been taken care of, surely Kathryn is now safe and of no concern to them?" Drake said cooly with a dry undertone. He was confused about why this meeting had to be private. The tension in his shoulders started to burn as he tried to understand what the hell was going on. Something was missing.

Scott cleared his throat and looked at Jacki, then back to Drake. "We believe Miss White is still in danger. By her association with Mr Edgile and the fact that she was living with him."

White-hot rage took over Drake. He abruptly stood, his chair falling over as he did. He ran his hand over his face and through his hair in anger and frustration, swearing under his breath. It was a poor way to regain some control over his emotions, but it happened before he could rein it in. The puzzle pieces started to come to together and the more they did, the more he lost control.

Hell, he had only come to this mad place to ensure that one part of his life had ended and to ensure that the monster was in fact dead and buried. Now he found himself and Kathryn in the middle of a bikie and drug investigation, all because he had randomly gone for breakfast in a café and reconnected with her.

He stalked to the window and glared out over the city. It was a beautiful day. The sun was shining, and he could feel the summer warmth radiating through the window onto his face. At that moment, all he wanted was to go home. Back to his farm and be with Sophie. Back with the smell of hay and dust. Back where he could control his emotions and keep to himself. Back where he was content and knew what he was doing daily without worry. Closing his eyes and heaving in a strained breath, knowing his temper would not hold.

"How? How can she be in danger? She has told you she knows nothing about what that asshole did. All she knew was that he was taking drugs. That's all!" Drake roared. It was only when Lucy flinched that he realised his mistake in losing control. Cursing under his breath at himself as he paced the small, enclosed area like a caged beast, he struggled to restrain his temper as he sat back down as calmly as he could and apologised.

"I'm sorry, Lucy. I never meant to upset you or scare you."

She nodded and tried to smile but she was shaking and moved to the end of her seat, away from him as much as possible without falling from wooden chair.

"Mr Harrison." Jacki said from behind him. "We understand and appreciate your concern regarding Miss White. This is why we have come up with a plan to see Miss White safe."

"For how long?" he shot back. The room was silent behind him as he reeled his emotions back under control yet again, just enough to think as straight as he could. Turning to look at Scott, he saw the answer.

His heart sank.

Drake had known men like those who would now be hunting Kathryn. They would not give up, would never give up until they found her and got what they wanted. They would see to it that she would disappear forever once they got their hands on her. He couldn't allow that to happen.

"We believe they still want their money, plus to ensure that whatever information Miss White knows, she will remain silent."

"But she doesn't know anything." He said through gritted teeth "That's the problem. She can't give them anything if she doesn't know anything." Drake was growing hot again. This was crazy. No one was listening to him. Could they not understand?

"They will want the money back that Mr Edgile owes them. If they believe Miss White knew anything, or has the funds, they'll search for her and take it from her any way they see fit." Scott leaned on the table again and held Drake in position with his eyes. "We believe Miss White, Mr Harrison. We will do all we can to keep her safe, but she is in a lot of danger. Do you understand?"

Hell, yes, he understood — he knew better than anyone else in that room what monsters were like. That they would never give up if they even remotely thought that there was a whiff of their prey being found. "Yes. I understand. But you never answered my question. How long can you keep her safe?" he growled through clenched teeth, pinning Scott with his own stare.

"Not us Mr Harrison. You."

Drake's heart stopped. Were these people insane? He couldn't keep her safe. Shit. She was in more danger from the monster he was than the monsters that now looked for her.

This could not be happening. This was a nightmare. One he needed to wake up from, and now. Running his hands over his face, Drake braced his elbows on his thighs, intertwined his fingers and hung his head. They didn't know what they were asking. A hysterical laugh bubbled to the surface and came out sounding eerily chilling to his ears. This was ludicrous.

Raising his head, he glared at Scott. "How the bloody hell do you think that I can keep her safe? Don't tell me that in all your wisdom you believe someone like *me* can keep her bloody safe and away from these monsters." His narrowed gaze locked onto Scott. "How the hell can *I* do that?" he growled.

"We have eyewitnesses that saw Miss White had been shot in the head, that she was seriously hurt and rushed away in the ambulance. They do not mention anything more." Scott shifted in his seat as he read from his notebook. "We have witnesses who have provided us with proof that it was Mr Edgile who assaulted Miss White and that it was he who shot at her and then got away from the police officer who gave chase."

Drake looked at him, not sure where all that information was leading.

"Miss White needs to disappear for good, Mr Harrison. No one knows she is here. The staff have all been protective of her given the domestic violence situation. It's part of the protocol here at the hospital. This ward is specifically for domestic violence patients and there is always undercover security here. Other patients are here only when other wards are full. To the outside world, Miss White has disappeared. For the time being," he added with emphasis.

Drake sat back in his chair, which protested under his weight, and knotted his fingers in his hair. He had the sinking feeling he knew where this was going now. Taking a deep breath, he let it out slowly and dropped his arms, folding them across his chest as he asked, "So, what is your plan then?"

"That you take Miss White with you, back to your property. Her features are nothing special. She won't stand out. Just another brown-eyed, brown-haired girl. She won't be noticed."

Drake's world came to a complete stop. Staring at Scott with his mouth gaping. That was not what he thought they would say. Apart from the insult Scott had just given Kathryn he couldn't believe what he was hearing.

"No, no, no, no, no," he said slowly as he dropped his hands and leaned back onto his thighs. "No. I can't. You don't understand. I can't take her back with me. She can't be living with me." He darted his glance between the doctor and Scott. This was maddening.

Lucy spoke, her voice quiet. "Your partner or wife. She will understand. She will be proud you saved Kathryn, and it's only temporary. Just until the police can make sure everything is safe for Kathryn. That's all." She reached out and touched his hand.

Pulling his hand away, he stood and started to pace next to the window. "That's not the issue."

"Then what is the issue, Mr Harrison?" Constable Smith asked.

He stopped and looked at her. "She won't be safe with me. Don't you understand? I can't keep her safe. You have to know that." He moved towards the door; the room was caving in on him and he couldn't breathe. He needed to get out.

The constable looked at Scott and when he nodded to her, she opened the door for Drake. The coolness in the corridor helped him to breathe. He could hear movement from behind him; someone had followed him out of the room. They followed him to a seat at the opposite end of the corridor, near the elevators.

"Drake." The young constable squatted down in front of him as he sat on the chair near the window, trying to get his emotions and head right as he held his head in his hands and rocked back and forth. "I know this is a lot to take in, but you have to know I put this plan to Scott because of you."

He looked up, his eyes burning with his emotions. "Why?"

"Because you saved Kathryn. You took a beating yourself and stopped her from being hurt more. You fought back against Rob. You held her till the ambulance guys arrived and even then, you held her to you. They had to work to make you let her go and told me that it was only you who could calm her when she became conscious again." Jackie touched his hand. "The emergency staff all said the same thing, and the nurses here said that you've barely left her side. That you've cared for her and brought her clothing and personal items. That you are the reason she has recovered so quickly."

She was looking at him like he was more than he really was. He stood and left her where she squatted. He knew manners stated he should have helped her up, but he couldn't at this moment. "I can't keep her safe." He turned, willing her to see that he was telling her the truth. Willed for her to see it clearly.

The constable stood "All you have to do is hear out our plan and then make your choice. Can you grant us that?"

Frustrated and resigned that he had no other option, Drake nodded and walked with her back into the room.

Half an hour later they all emerged from the room. Drake was not happy with the outcome, but it was now up to Kathryn and her choice. He would do as they asked if she agreed to it. He couldn't see another way out. He stopped Scott just before they reached Kathryn's door. "If she agrees, I need you to do something for me?" He proceeded to explain, Scott finally agreed.

Kathryn was brushing her hair, which was much easier to do with the bandage off. She'd even rinsed the parts of it, missed yesterday, to remove some of the dried blood. Her head didn't feel as sore and heavy now the restriction was gone.

The stitches would apparently need another week before they could come out, but Lucy had commented how beautifully the doctor had stitched her up. There would only be a little scar and her hair would grow over and cover that in time.

Her lip and other cuts were nearly healed too. They said the bruising would take another week to be completely gone, but were fading fast with the cream Gail had given her. It was going to be good to get out of here and home again.

The thought registered. She had no home to go to. She didn't have anywhere to go. Nowhere, and to no one. Rob would go to Annabelle's, the café and the pub searching for her. She had nowhere to go that was safe, nor did she now have any job to go to. No job meant no money. She would be homeless when she was able to leave. Panic bubbled. What was she going to do?

Drake walked into the room with a tight smile on his face, although he wasn't actually looking at her. The reason followed behind him. The detective, the policewoman, her doctor and Lucy, all followed him. Panic surged through her.

"Miss White," the detective nodded "We have some information about Mr Edgile and we need to speak to you now, if that's okay?"

Kathryn looked to Drake. He was standing near the wall with his arms crossed across his chest, his recliner between them, but it felt like an ocean. He didn't meet her eyes. She focused back on the detective. Lucy closed the door.

"We will get straight to the point. Mr Edgile was found this morning in your fire-ravaged apartment. He had been killed with a bullet straight to the head."

Kathryn gasped, and her hand flew to her mouth.

Drake was at her side in an instant. He put his arm around her and glared at the detective. "You need to be more sensitive, Scott. That was cruel and disgusting. Have some manners," he snapped.

"My apologies, Miss White." Scott didn't look sorry. He was watching her intently to see her reaction to the news. "We believe the bikie gang Mr Edgile had been working for is after the money he owes them and, further, that he was in possession of information about them that they didn't want to get out. Do you know of any such information, Miss White?"

Kathryn gripped Drake's hand, leaning against him, shaking. She felt shock pouring over her like cold water. "No. I thought he was just buying drugs and using, not working for anyone, especially not a bikie gang," she trailed off into a whisper.

Lucy moved to her other side and pulled the blanket up over her legs to keep her warm. She then took Kathryn's other hand for extra support.

"They may have found what they were looking for when they ransacked the apartment the other night." Drake peered at Kathryn. "Was there any money in the apartment that you were aware of?"

"No. None. Rob had taken all that I had hidden in the apartment to pay for his habit. Or so I thought." Fear and sorrow rose. Her money, any that was left, was gone too.

"Our department is building a massive case against this bikie gang and their drug trafficking. We have been information that Mr Edgile was doing the wrong thing by them and that the order had been given for him to be 'taken care of'." Scott stopped to allow the depth of what he was saying to her to sink in. "Through your association with Mr Edgile, and the fact you lived with him, they may think you also know information about them or that you have the money to repay what is owed."

The reality hit Kathryn like a slap in the face — the truth of what had happened, and everything Rob had been involved in, how that extended to her — hit hard. Panic started to set in, and she struggled to breathe. She gripped onto Drake's body and held tight. He tried to soothe her by rubbing her back and shoulder, reassuring her that she just had to listen more, and everything will be okay.

"But I don't. I don't know anything, and I have no money to give them. Can't you just tell them that? I have nothing and know nothing!" She knew she was becoming hysterical. Lucy tried to calm her, but she buried into Drake's side more.

"Can you give us a moment?" he asked, trying to unwrap her arms from around him. Once the others had left, he knelt on the floor and lifted her chin with his fingers to make her look at him. "Kathryn. Stop, look at me," he said quietly but firmly.

She gazed at him, despair flooding her. She tried to speak but only a moan of sheer hysteria and pain came out. Immediately, he stood and gathered her to him, holding her tight while she cried into his shirt.

After a while, his words rumbled against her head. "Kathryn, look at me. Do you trust me?"

She didn't look up but nodded.

"You need to listen to what they have to say and if you agree, this can all be over, and you will be safe." He waited for her to look at him. "You're going to be okay," he said, brushing the tears from her cheeks with his thumb.

Kathryn was more composed a few minutes later when the others re-entered the room. She didn't let them speak first, she did. "What is the plan?"

Everyone's eyebrows raised at her direct question.

Clearing his throat Scott replied. "No one knows you're here, or your condition," he looked over his notes. "We will put out a media release that you died from your injuries and that Mr Edgile died in a suspected accidental suicide. We'll make sure it gets across all media outlets and on the news. Hopefully, this will alert the gang that there's nothing to come after from you. However," he cleared his voice again and stared at her, "to make this work you must disappear forever, Miss White." He was stern and serious. "You can't contact anyone from your previous life. Remember, you died."

He continued to stare at her, but she couldn't release the breath she was holding. Her whole life was gone.

"Do you understand?" he prompted.

"Yes," she whispered and let go of Drake's hand, folding hers in her lap and looking down at them. Her life was over. She would spend the rest of her days running and hiding from people who wanted her dead. She would never have her dreams; she would never be able to have a family or friends. She would never be able to see Drake again. It was over. Tears blurred her vision. "What happens to me then?" she whispered.

"We'll give you a new name and identity, you can start your new life well away from here. Safe in the knowledge that everyone will think you are dead and you can live your life as you wish."

"But never having any contact with anyone ever again?"

"No. Not with those from your previous life. You are dead."

"I don't have a choice, do I?" Kathryn raised her head and looked at the detective. Her eyes had lost all the vibrancy that oozed from her naturally. Her voice sounded deathly calm.

"Not if you want to live, Miss White, no," he quietly answered.

The weight of her choice hung throughout the room. No one said a word.

"How long before I have to leave?"

"As fast as Mr Harrison can get himself sorted and packed and the nurses and doctor here can get you prepared. We want you out of the city immediately."

"What?" Kathryn turned to Drake, her heart pounding. "Do you have to leave as well?" She began to cry. She had ruined his life as well. "I'm so sorry, Drake. I'm so sorry."

"Kathryn." Drake said to her, his tone firm but quiet as he saw her add the pieces together but incorrectly. "Scott thinks it's a good idea that you come and stay with me until all your new documents are completed and we know for sure that the gang thinks you're dead. They don't know anything about me, or who I am or where I live. I'm not in danger. I live hours away in a sleepy town, remember? No one knows I'm here. Anyone who does, thinks I left after our picnic because no one has seen me since. Except you."

She gaped at him. What? She was going with Drake? To the country?

"Only if you want to, that is. No one will force you. It's your choice."

Slowly, she studied her hands in her lap. This was all too much. Her life had somehow just ended. She was dead. To everyone. She'd never be able to live in the city or have her café or be free to do what she wanted. She would be forever looking over her shoulder in case someone found her. How could she live like that until she died? Her head began to hurt. Her eyes filled with tears; she couldn't see anyone standing in the room anymore. Anybody but Drake. Looking up, she whispered, "Are you sure about this?"

"If it keeps you safe from these monsters, then yes." He replied with a warmth that reached out and touched her heart.

Trying to calm herself down, Kathryn took an unsteady breath. "Yes. Okay, I agree. I will die and go with Drake."

Chapter 13

Sunset was already approaching. Drake left the hospital when Scott did so he could get his things packed and pay his motel bill. He took longer than she thought he would be, but during his absence, on the advice of Jacki, the nurses dyed Kathryn's hair a darker brown and gave her some baggy dark clothes, a black cap and sunglasses.

On his return, Drake was dressed in his dark clothes, a similar cap and sunglasses. She almost laughed when he had to look at her a second time when he walked into the room. She was sitting in the corner waiting for him and he didn't recognise her.

He had parked his Ute at the maternity entrance and when they walked out of the hospital, she leaned on him for support. Her ribs ached and caught as she moved. Lucy was at her side, along with one of the wards 'special' Wardy's, a blanket to cover her and a note which had her pain medication wrapped in and that said good luck. When Drake drove out of the laneway and into the traffic, she hid under the blanket in the passenger seat, letting Drake take her away from her old life. Her dead life.

They hadn't spoken as the darkness of the evening descended. Her heart had been beating rapidly since Drake had entered her room with the police behind him; it only began to slow now with the cocoon of the night around her. Kathryn kept her eyes focused on the road in front of her. A tension hung in the air between them. She couldn't bring herself to look at him or speak.

The further the Ute took her from the city, the more the reality of her situation hit her. Her dreams were gone, and she was totally reliant on a man. A man who seemed not very happy at being forced into this situation. She had never been solely reliant on a man before — something that her grandmother would not have approved of — but she needed Drake and his protection. His security. Just until she healed fully and could work out the next step in her new life. Until then she would just have to put her worries aside.

Unfortunately, Drake had been forced into this situation too, just by walking into a café and getting breakfast. He hadn't really said anything to her since he'd returned to collect her. He was hard to read sometimes and watching him now, she noticed the tension in his jaw and throughout his body.

He kept flicking his eyes behind them, watching as every car passed them on the highway. Ensuring that the cars kept moving on their own journey. His grip on the steering wheel was white knuckled as each vehicle passed, and his jaw only slackened a touch once they did.

The hours slowly passed as the Ute ate every kilometre of the black road. The traffic thinned, only large trucks carrying goods to wherever they were needed were on the road at this time of night. Homes in the distance with internal lights flickering were becoming sparce. Each town seemed to take longer and longer to get to than the last. It was becoming never ending in the deathly quietness of the Ute cab and the blackness of the journey.

Drake still hadn't spoken more than a few words to her since she had made the decision to leave with him. No one had said anything. Everything had happened so quickly, but now there was nothing. Just the darkness cocooning them as they blindly followed the white lines into the night.

After stopping to refuel and get some takeaway to eat because he didn't want her getting out and caught on the security cameras, Drake continued out of a little town, pulling off into a secluded truck stop a few kilometres further on in the middle of nowhere. Two large semi-trailers were pulled up, their drivers asleep in their bunks. Drake reversed in behind the shower and toilet block and some bushy shrubs, concealing his Ute from passers-by.

Opening her door, Kathryn stiffly got out. Her legs had little feeling after sitting for nearly five hours straight. She kicked them out trying to get her circulation moving again. Her ribs pulled and her head ached, but she was safe and with Drake, and thankfully it appeared they hadn't been followed. She felt the Ute move behind her as Drake pulled the tailgate down then searched for something on his back seat.

Kathryn gazed around at her surroundings. In front of her, beyond the bushes, was the highway, down a few steps was the toilet block and showers, behind her were trees shrouded in darkness. She drew her blanket tighter around her. Her hands shook slightly. She had always prided herself on her confidence, but since her attack she had noticed that her hands shook ever so slightly at the strangest of times. Taking a deep breath, she mentally steeled herself — she was made of sterner stuff.

She walked to the back of the Ute to find Drake was laying out a blanket. It was dusty and smelt of horses, but it would be soft to sit on. He removed two burgers, some hot chips and a bottle of water each for them from a plastic bag that sat on the back near the freshly-laid blanket. Stepping in front of her, he tenderly placed his hands on her waist and helped her up onto the tailgate. Her ribs hurt with the movement, but she didn't show it. She would not let him see that he had hurt her.

"Do you think anyone followed us?" She hadn't allowed her thoughts to go there, but in the semi-darkness of the truck stop she couldn't help it. She was scared and needed his reassurance that it was all okay, that she was safe.

Drake looked at her from where he was perched on the tailgate. "I don't think so. No one knew where you were."

Nodding, she looked out to the highway as another large truck thundered past.

"You will be okay, Kathryn."

Not looking at him, she only nodded. She did know. She was always safe with him — it was when she had to leave him forever that she was fearful of. If the police plan did not work, then she would always be unsafe and on the run. The Ute suddenly rocked with Drake's weight. He stood up on the tray, moved to the front of it and pulled out a large heavy canvas that was rolled up.

Kathryn watched as he untied the straps and unrolled it. "A bed!" she exclaimed.

Smiling, Drake corrected her. "Swag, actually."

"Oh, right," she said with her first attempt at a genuine smile since that morning. Their food now finished, she felt his eyes watching her as she walked to the bin and deposited their rubbish. She saw him scanning the area around them. An undercurrent of nerves surrounded them both as she surveyed the area again and moved back to the safety of the ute.

Unrolling the swag, Drake removed one of the blankets and his pillow for her. Jumping down, he opened the door and placed them along the back seat of the Ute.

"You can sleep here." He whispered and scanned the area again "The night will get colder, and you need the warmth. Lock the doors if you want. I'll be on the tray at the back." He stepped back from the door. "I need to sleep. We're at least another four hours from home."

Carefully protecting her ribs, Kathryn nodded and steadily climbed into the back seat. He closed the door behind her, avoiding her eyes. Moments later, she felt the Ute move with his weight as he climbed in the back and crawled under the canvas cover of the swag. Wriggling carefully, she tried to get comfortable, and stared at the Ute's interior roof.

Home.

He'd called it home. He had a home to go to, he had a life to go back to — and she didn't. She had nowhere and no one but him, and she could never stay with Drake permanently; he was making that perfectly clear by his actions. She had become a burden to him. She never wanted that, she never wanted to be a burden to anyone. She yearned to be wanted and loved, to achieve her dreams, her café by the river and her own apartment. A family and friends. A man who loved her. Now, she'd never have those things.

Instead, she would be forever looking over her shoulder wondering if someone had recognised her or was following her. She would never be able to place those she loved in danger. She was going to be alone forever once she healed and said goodbye to Drake.

Somehow, she had to learn to be okay with that. She was a strong, independent and resourceful woman. She could get through this. She was stronger than her emotions had been these last few days, but that didn't stop the tears as they fell onto Drake's pillow beneath her head.

Drake couldn't sleep. His mind was filled with too many thoughts. Lying there in his swag he heard every truck that thundered by and now he listened to one of the semis coming to life parked just down from them. He had no idea what the time was, but guessing by the distance the moon had travelled across the sky while he had been lying there, he reckoned it was only a few hours before dawn.

The sound of the truck driver's door slamming shut made him sit up. He wasn't going to get any sleep tonight and, as if to confirm it, the truck roared and slowly moved forward. It was fully loaded and by the time it was pulling out onto the highway, Drake had counted about four gear changes. The diesel fumes wafted across the truck stop and over him.

Looking out, he could see the truck moving and then noticed the second truck moving away too. Both trucks pulled out and headed west, all lit up. Once they gained speed, they would be just a blur of lights on the road as they thundered by.

"Are they always that noisy?"

Drake just about leaped out of his skin. He had been so engrossed in watching the trucks leave that he had not heard his own Ute's door close. Kathryn stood beside the tray, his blanket wrapped around her.

"Yep." His heart thumping against his rib cage, he ran a hand over his face and his stubbly beard. "Did they wake you?"

She moved to the end of the tailgate and sat. "No. I can't sleep." She was watching the highway. From a distance they could hear another semi rolling along the road. It was about to pass the truck stop. She waited and watched it pass in a blur of lights.

"Come up here with me." Drake held up the canvas as an invitation for her to climb in beside him. "I won't bite," he added when she hesitated.

Smiling, she climbed up and under the blankets. "Aren't you worried I will?"

"I might like it," he teased back as she laid her head against his shoulder, his arm closing around her. Without thought he pressed a kiss to the top of her head. Vanilla swirled around him, his heart giving a kick at the aroma. Her warmth surrounded him as she snuggled against his body and he felt some of his tension melt away.

The fading night was clear and now very quiet as Drake looked up at the stars. He still wasn't sure how he had got to be in this position. He, the protector. Ha.

He knew he couldn't call himself that, he was as dangerous to Kathryn as the men who could be looking for her were. He only hoped that Scott's plan would work, and once they knew for sure it had and she had her new identity, Kathryn would leave. He would make her leave, for her own safety. That one thought had made him agree to take her with him in the first place — that eventually she would leave and be safe from him.

Peering up at the stars, he wondered if they were looking down on him. If they would understand his decisions. If they knew he had been to see them. Had they heard his apology for failing them? Thinking about them now, he inadvertently tightened his arm around Kathryn.

The stars shining down on him, the night wrapped around the two of them, the thoughts of those he'd already failed made him realise he would never have left Kathryn in the city to fight the monsters chasing her. He would never do that, but once she was secure, he had to let her go. For her own good.

Her hand moved over his chest to lay across his heart, her warmth seeping through his shirt. He covered her hand with his, and she raised her head back to look into his eyes. Nothing moved. The world disappeared. It was only them.

His lips claimed hers slowly as his hand slid up her arm to cradle her jaw. She opened her mouth and allowed him to taste more of her; to claim her mouth as his. Heat spilled around them, flowed through him and made his heart beat faster. He rolled his body to face her as her hand tangled in his hair and pulled him deeper into the kiss. Her tongue darted into his mouth and he suckled it, making her moan tenderly and press her body against his. Her curves fitted against his body perfectly, he followed her tongue back inside her mouth and tasted her again and again. She pressed her body against his more firmly, until he was straining against his jeans. She wiggled her body against him.

Drake froze and stopped kissing her. His muscles locked as he rested his forehead on hers and tried to smile.

"At least you didn't bite me," he said softly as he slid his thumb over her bottom lip. Another truck roared past, and the world intruded. Drake rolled over onto his back and placed his forearm over his eyes. "We had better sleep. Dawn will be here soon, and we need to keep moving."

Kathryn lay there listening to his breathing slow and become even as he slipped into sleep, while her mind remained confused. Every time they touched, he pulled away, yet he was the one always drawing her into it.

She wanted it, more now than ever, she wanted it and him. If she was going to have to say goodbye once she healed, then she'd take every touch and kiss she could, so that on the nights when she was scared and lonely, she could remember every detail of him. She wanted to be with Drake, to feel his touch and lips against her skin. If he wanted her like she could feel he did, then what was it about her that made him pull away?

She was still awake when the dawn of a new day came to life, her head still resting on his chest as she listened to the birds awaken and sing their morning song. She was a strong woman. She was safe and would rebuild herself a new life — without Drake — but until then she would savour every moment she had left with him, and when the time came, she would walk away with her memories.

Chapter 14

It was mid-morning when the town Drake called home, River Flats came into view. The river was wide and flowing steadily as he drove over the bridge and into the town. The main street had trees growing through the centre and gardens lined the sidewalks. It was a complete contrast to what Kathryn was used to seeing in the city.

Drake followed a busy street that turned off, stretching away from the main road through the town, to run parallel to the river that meandered along the outskirts of the little town. People were walking in and out of shops, others were talking in the middle of the sidewalk, greeting others as they passed by on their way to another shop. A little café that was very busy and had people sitting at tables outside, caught Kathryn's attention.

There was a liveliness to the town and a sense of friendliness. People were genuinely smiling and greeting each other with a warmth she had never witnessed before. Growing up in the city, Kathryn was accustomed to the cold acquaintance that was part of city living. Watching people as they moved and interacted with each other in this small town gave her a warm feeling. A sense that she had somehow missed out on something big in the city. With the sense of comradery and security in knowing each other came a sense of safety.

Drake pulled up across the road from the grocery shop. In front of her was a large sandstone building with the Australian coat of arms on display above the door. The gardens around it were well kept, and beside it was a beautiful park filled with flowers and native trees and a children's play area. A town centre oasis.

Drake left, saying he would only be gone a few minutes to get some groceries and she was to sit in the Ute and avoid being seen. Given she still had bruises and cuts on her face, she did not wish to draw the attention of others.

A few minutes after Drake had left, a mother and child arrived at the park. The little black-haired boy was so excited about the slide and finding out how many different ways he could go down, his laughter and excitement echoed around the play area. His laughter and delight escalated when his mother played a game of missing him each time as he slid past her, filling the play area and surrounds with his pure joy.

Watching the simplistic scene playing out in front of her through the windscreen, Kathryn had a lump in her throat and fought the sting of tears trying to break through. She would now never be able to experience for herself, what she was watching in front of her.

A knock on her window made her jump out of her skin.

The older man looking in at her smiled as she wound the window down just enough to speak to him, her eyes darting around anxiously searching for Drake. "Can I help you?"

"Hello, Miss White. I just saw Drake in the supermarket, and he said you were here waiting for him." He reached his hand through the small gap she had allowed, to shake her hand. His toughened, stubby fingers wriggling wildly as he did.

"I'm Senior Constable Richard Ferguson, one of the officers in charge around here. Well, there are only four of us and I'm the boss, you could say." Pride showed on the casually dressed police officer's face as she shook his fingers in greeting.

The driver's side door of the Ute opened, giving Kathryn another fright, as Drake hopped in, placing his bags of goodies in the back behind Kathryn's seat.

"See you found her, Richard," he said dryly to the older man.

Pulling his hand back through the tight gap in the window "I sure did. I was just about to tell her that she'll be safe here, and once we know for sure that things have worked out in the city, I'll be in touch." Richard smiled at her and winked. "'til then you have this man here watching over you." He squinted playfully. "You just let me know if he doesn't and I will sort him out for you, miss." Richard looked up as car drove past them. "Right then, I'll let you folks go." Standing straight, he thumped the roof of the Ute. "Off you go."

"Yes, sir!" Drake gave a tight smile as he started the Ute and began to pull out of his parking spot.

"I didn't think Scott would tell anyone. I thought I was meant to just arrive here with you?" Kathryn's hands started to shake again. Placing them under her thighs to hide them, she watched as the main street disappeared behind them, replaced by farm machinery places and rural supply distributors, a fuel station and other farm shops, which then disappeared behind them into paddocks filled with wheat and other crops, cattle and horses and homes in the distance.

"Scott only let old Richard know just in case. He's been here for thirty years and knows everyone and their secrets, but he will never say anything. I promise you, you're safe here with me." Leaning over, he squeezed her shoulder gently, the touch sending warmth through her and helping to settle her nerves.

It was a short forty-five-minute drive to the farm Drake called home. The track was dirt and lined with tall gum trees. On either side were paddocks with tall grasses and horses feeding. Cattle on the distant hills looked like white rocks in amongst the grass moving like waves across the rising ground. The sun's rays capturing the crest of the grassy waves as the wind moved them along.

The beauty of it was mesmerising and Kathryn sat up to take as much of it in as possible. The house and sheds came into view as the Ute crested a small rise. The house was an old cottage and as they got closer, Kathryn could see an old climbing rose had snaked its way up and over the veranda posts and along the railings. An old picket fence surrounded the house, a few of the pickets had fallen to the ground or were leaning sideways. The sheds were made of timber, and looked to be solid and cared for. It was truly a picturesque quant looking farm he got to call home.

Drake stopped the Ute near the house yard by the front gate and helped her to slowly walk to the house. Going up the steps pained her ribs and he took her elbow as she eased her stiff and sore body up them and into his house. Holding open the screen door, he allowed Kathryn to cross the threshold.

The room was modest but cosy. An old leather couch with a blanket over it faced the window. In the corner was a tv, and old photos filled the walls. A cowhide lay on the floor with a small coffee table in the middle of the room. At the back of the room was a tiny kitchen with an old wooden bench which gave the space separation from the lounge room.

The cupboards were a mint green, and the walls had a tainted yellowing to them. Over in the corner was a square table with four chairs surrounding it that looked to be from the 60's era. This little timber box was small, cosy and her home for a few weeks. Kathryn took a slow breath.

Drake closed the door behind her and pushed past her. "Your room is this way." He led the way down a very short hallway to the right of the main living room.

On one side was the bathroom and laundry, and on the other were two small bedrooms. The first one had baby blue walls and old duckling stickers peeling off the walls. The second room, which Drake was now standing in, had white walls and looked to have been repainted in the last twenty years. A large bed dominated the room, along with a timber cupboard and a window that nearly took up the entire wall overlooking the driveway and the sheds. Kathryn looked around the room, her eyes coming to settle on Drake standing next to the bed. He was watching her.

Clearing his throat, he placed her meagre belongings on the bed. "I will leave you to settle in. There are sheets and things in the cupboard in the laundry if you can manage, otherwise I'll help you later." He walked out of the room and out of the house, leaving her standing in his home — alone.

This was bad, very bad. He had to get himself under control. All he wanted to do in there was take her in his arms and kiss her until the despair in her eyes disappeared forever. She looked so small and scared standing in that room — a room that held so many of his own memories. He would have to keep his distance while she was here. He wouldn't let himself slip. He couldn't. For both their sakes.

He had just reached the half fallen-down gate into the yard when he heard Sophie coming. She wasn't quiet and before he had a chance to kneel, the dog was leaping into his arms and licking him all over his face. "Sophie!" He laughed as he struggled to hold her wriggling body.

She felt heavier. Reggie had been feeding her well while he had been away. Sophie was so excited that he nearly dropped her. He put her on the ground and squatting, he scratched her behind her ears and kissed the top of her head, telling her constantly how much he had missed her and that she was such a good girl. Whimpering with excitement, she flopped over onto her back so that he could scratch her belly. Belly rubs were her favourite.

"I don't get that welcome, Sophie. You only sat on the veranda sulking the whole time I was caretaking. That was till this morning, mind you, when she decided to go for a walk, looking for you, I'm guessing. Found her near the road."

The man Drake had come to love like a second grandfather and now called his closet mate was leaning on one of the fence panels. An old beaten-up hat covered his eyes, but the smile that showed the lines of years of hard work in the sun and his age was clearly visible.

"Morning, Reggie." Drake stood and shook his hand. Not happy about her attention being given to someone else, Sophie sat up and barked at him, then flopped back down, telling him that she wanted more. Laughing again, he rubbed her belly with his boot. It was good to be home.

"You have never left the house yard, girl, unless on the Ute or with me. Where were you going all by yourself?" As if knowing she'd done the wrong thing, Sophie rolled over and sat up with a big sneeze, then leaned on Drake's leg, contented now he was home.

"You were gone longer than I thought you would be, me boy." Reggie had been Drake's grandfather's best mate and neighbour since they were both in nappies and running amuck. Reggie had been there through everything with them both, and when his grandfather had passed, they became closer. They needed each other to fill the void that his grandfather had left. Reggie had even taken over the protective fatherly nature that his grandfather had always provided him with.

"Yeah," Drake said on an exhalation. "Something came up that needed my attention."

"Did you get it all sorted then?" Reggie had a gruffness to his voice that spoke with an authoritativeness laced with concern.

"In a way, yes." He didn't want to tell Reggie about Kathryn just yet. He didn't know how he could answer all the questions that would need answering. He wouldn't lie to Reggie, couldn't, but he had to keep Kathryn safe and the fewer people who knew the truth the better.

"By yes, you mean you brought that *something* home with you?" Reggie was looking behind Drake with a small knowing grin. He must have spotted Kathryn in the house.

Sophie suddenly leaped up and ran towards the house, whimpering with excitement as she went, a friendly bark at the stranger emerging from within the house. Drake watched Kathryn retreat a few steps against the now closed screen door at her back, as Sophie hurriedly approach her. She looked from Drake to the dog and then back again.

Sophie wouldn't bite, but she didn't like strangers, especially not in her house. Drake and his grandfather had found her in the middle of the road the day before his death as they were coming back from Reggie's. The dog had been covered in dust and her nose was cut up and bleeding, like she'd fallen from a vehicle and landed on it. She had buried her face, shaking, in Drake's arms the whole way home.

Since that day, the dog had been his constant companion. Sophie would not go any further than her invisible line of the house and sheds, and if she got desperate enough in the heat of summer, the creek. But only if Drake was walking there.

If it wasn't for her, he would not have recovered from his grandfather's passing or the loneliness that sometimes became too much in the darkness of the night. She had arrived at just the perfect time; when he needed her.

Sophie was walking up the steps slowly to Kathryn, her tail between her legs and she was low to the ground, as if she sensed Kathryn's fear and was trying hard to show her that she just wanted to smell her. That she wasn't going to hurt her. Sophie's stomach was nearly touching the boards when she finally reached Kathryn's feet and then, to everyone's surprise, she flopped over onto her back to ask for a belly rub, revealing her full vulnerability to Kathryn.

"Oh. You beautiful girl." Kathryn kneeled and let Sophie smell her hand, and when Sophie wriggled closer, Kathryn rubbed her belly. She was rewarded with lots of licks and kisses to her legs.

"She must really like you, Missy. The only person she ever let's rub her tummy is Drake here. She must sense you're something special." The elderly man Drake had been talking to at the fence when she'd walked out of the house to ask Drake if he would like some lunch, was now standing at the bottom of the steps.

His foot was resting on the first step, his arm leaning on the railing, but when Kathryn looked up from patting Sophie the man stood straight and studied her harder. His eyes averted at first but quickly came back before looking away again. He had noticed her bruises and swelling, the discolouration still visible as well as the large Band-Aid covering the stitches from the gun shot.

"Reggie this is Kathryn. Kathryn this is Reggie. Reggie lives next door and has been looking after Sophie and the horses while I've been away." Drake stepped up the few steps, avoiding Reggie's eyes, to stand in front of her, holding out his hand to help her up. Although she tried to hide the pain of her ribs, he saw it. "You should be resting," he whispered in her ear when she stood.

"I'm fine." She placed a hand on his chest to steady herself and the contact sent tingles up her arm.

"Pleased to meet you, missy." Reggie climbed the rest of the stairs and held out his hand to shake hers around Drake.

His hand was large and rough, but he loosened his grip to allow for her smaller, softer one. "If I had known Drake had company, I would've cleaned myself up a bit." He grinned at her and removed his hat, dusting it against his jeans and smoothing his few strands of white hair in an old comb-over style.

"It was a last-minute decision," Drake said roughly, still looking down at her. "Kathryn needs to rest. It's been a long drive." Reaching behind her, he pulled open the screen door. Sophie shot up and raced inside, onto the couch, in her spot.

"Hopefully I will see you around," Kathryn said quietly as she stepped back through the doorway.

"It would be my pleasure," Reggie called as she went. Putting his hat back on, he walked down the steps.

Drake closed the door and followed him. They walked in silence to the Ute.

"You want to tell me something, me boy?" Reggie said sternly.

"It's not what you're thinking."

"Don't accuse me of thinking nothin'."

Drake didn't know what to say. He was tired and sore from the drive. The last thing he wanted was to be questioned so soon about Kathryn. Rubbing a hand over his face and stubble he leaned on the tailgate. He had to tell Reggie the truth. "She is May's granddaughter."

"I can see that."

Nothing escaped Reggie. He had the eyes of an eagle and the memory of an elephant. Reggie, Drake's grandparents and May, Kathryn's grandmother, had all been friends before May up and married and moved to the city. She had remained close friends with Drake's grandparents, especially his grandmother, but when May and her husband had come to visit, Reggie had always stayed away. So his grandfather had said. Drake had always wondered if Reggie had wanted more than friendship with May, but he would never ask.

"We caught up while I was in the city and now, she is here. Okay?"

"I can see that." Reggie replied, a little drier than normal, but with weight behind the statement.

"What do you want me to say? She is staying here for a few weeks then she is leaving. End of story."

"I think you're spinning me a load of bull. Something that is not you, young man. What about those bruises?"

"It's not what you think, Reggie. Just leave the bloody thing alone." He'd never got upset with Reggie. Looking up into the sky, Drake took a deep breath to calm down.

"It looks like there's a lot more to her being here then you're willing to tell me. I'm just looking out for you, you know that. Nothin' more."

"I know that and appreciate it." Knowing that Reggie deserved more than his bad temper and frustration, Drake opened the door to remove the food he brought earlier in town. "She got herself into a situation and I'm just helping her out. That's all."

"Okay then. That's all." Reggie walked towards the large shed which operated as the stables. "By the way. Nothing to report and everything is fed for the day."

"Thanks!" Drake called back to him.

"You had better see Vicki soon, too. She has been worried about you." After a moment, Reggie added as he continued to walk to the stable, "Think she would like to meet Kathryn."

Drake knew that Vicki would want to see him but taking Kathryn was not a good idea. She was here to heal and then leave privately without the whole world knowing she was ever there. That was all.

Later that afternoon Kathryn sat on the front steps of the house, watching the last of the sun's rays dip behind the trees. Sophie had not left the house since being allowed inside but decided to venture out and keep Kathryn company as the day slipped into night.

The dog sat with her head in Kathryn's lap and a paw on her leg. Sophie was completely black apart from four white socks and a white patch on the back at her neck, and she had the brownest of brown eyes. She was a gentle and sweet girl, who loved her belly being rubbed, but was content to have her ears massaged now as they sat together. When Kathryn woke from her nap earlier that afternoon, Sophie had been asleep next to her bed.

She hadn't seen Drake since they had shared a quiet lunch after Reggie left. He'd said he needed to check on things, but it was getting late now, and he was not back. She figured he must be on horseback as his Ute remained where he'd parked it when they arrived.

Around her, the crickets began to chirp. She felt safe here in the seclusion of the surroundings. Nothing but nature. No traffic, no one yelling or blasting their horns, just a peacefulness and quietness of nature. Her tummy growled, loud enough that Sophie sat up and looked at her with her head turned to the side. With a giggle and kiss to the top of Sophie's head, Kathryn stood and went back inside.

Drake was still not back after she'd made herself a toasted sandwich and cleaned up. Sophie sat at the door to the bathroom while she showered and when she crawled into her bed later, Sophie found her spot on the mat right next to her bed. She didn't know if she should be worried about Drake or not, but her body was so tired she fell asleep as soon as her head hit the pillow.

Drake did not leave the stables all afternoon. He mucked them out and worked two of the new horses that had arrived just before he had left. If he was honest with himself, he was hiding from Kathryn.

He told himself it was best for her that he kept his distance. She would heal faster and there would be less chance of him hurting her. From within the darkness of the stables, he watched her while she sat on the front steps with Sophie. He remained enclosed in his dark spot and watched her move through his house, eating alone and then crawling into bed. He watched her light go out, and still he hid in his dark corner. Eventually, about an hour later, he gave into his hunger and his fatigue and snuck into his own home.

Sophie was asleep next to Kathryn's bed and didn't stir when he entered. He stood and watched Kathryn's steady breathing in the moonlight. She had opened all the curtains in the house and most of the windows. The heat of the day was now replaced with a cool breeze flowing through the home. A sweet fragrance of a flowering tree caught on the wind, floated around the room.

Touching a piece of her hair that had fallen all over the pillow, the silky strand sliding through his fingers, his heart gave a kick. She was beautiful.

Reminding himself he needed to keep his distance, he crept out of the room, leaving Sophie to keep watch over her.

The shower burned against his skin as his soaped his body clean. He had eaten and cleaned up without disturbing Kathryn. Now as he bathed, he hoped the noise wouldn't wake her. He had always heard his grandfather bathing. It was hard not to when the only bathroom in the house was right next to his room. He'd tried to turn on the water quietly, but the old pipes banged and whined. It wasn't until after he turned the water off and was drying himself that he heard the scream and then a muffled sound.

Heart leaping, he pulled on a pair of shorts and raced out of the room. Kathryn was frantically thrashing around in her bed. She was having a nightmare. Her hair was entangled around her face and neck, and she was trying to escape the confines of the sheet that had tangled her arms and legs tightly. She started to cry and scream. Drake tried to grab her arms and soothe her, but she screamed louder and fought harder.

He knew it was not good to wake a person in such a nightmare, but he didn't know what else to do. She managed to get her arm free and lashed out. He avoided it, but only just. He grabbed her arm and pushed it down onto the bed, his leg locking her to the mattress. The adrenaline and her fight in her dream had her hips lifting him and nearly unseating him on to his butt on the floor.

He managed to weigh her down and calm her with his voice like he had at the hospital. After a few hushed words of reassurance, Kathryn calmed and drifted into a more settled sleep. Drake removed himself from her body and cradled her in his arms, her body pulled flush against his, the only thing separating his body from hers was the twisted sheet and his thin shorts.

Bringing his own breath back under control, Drake watched Kathryn as she slept, her head on his shoulder and her arm draped across his chest. He could smell the scent of her hair and the heat of her body against his. His body responded, though he did not move. He would not let his emotions take over him. He couldn't risk it.

Being here with her like this was torture enough, if he touched her, the slightest move, he didn't know if he would be able to stop. It had been easier in the hospital to stop himself. The fear of anyone walking in and the knowledge that he would be leaving her there was enough, but now she was here, in his house, and there was no one to stop him, bar himself. He didn't know if he had the restraint to stop if he started. He had to stay in control and away from her.

Dislodging her from his body, he sat on the edge of the bed.

A soft hand touched his bare back. "Drake. You're back."

Her sleepy, raspy voice sent a thrill through him. "Yes, I am. Go back to sleep".

"Will you stay with me?" When he didn't answer she added a sleepy, "Please."

He couldn't say no, so he lifted the sheet and pulled up the blanket and lay beside her, his arm draping over her slender body and when she rolled over to her side, he pulled her to him, her back against his chest. Her hair was around him and he inwardly sighed. She was asleep and unaware of his growing arousal pressing into her. He willed himself to not think but to sleep.

It was hours before that happened, but eventually his body agreed, and he fell into dreams of holding her and pressing himself deep within her warmth.

Chapter 15

The first rays of a new day were just starting to awaken the earth when Kathryn woke the next morning. Her body and head did not hurt, for the first time since that awful night. Rolling over, she cuddled the pillow beside her. A distinctive male scent filled her senses and made her come alert and sit up.

Drake had been in her room. More than that, he had been in her bed and had slept there. Closing her eyes, she tried to remember what had happened. She was tired and had gone to bed when he had not returned. Her nightmare. He'd come to her. Then she remembered asking him to stay.

Looking over the side of the bed, Kathryn found Sophie asleep on the mat. The dog had fast become her friend and never left her side it seemed, even at night. Falling back on her pillow, Kathryn listened to the birds singing and a new sound. Horses nickering. Somewhere close by horses were moving and whinnying, talking to each other — or someone. Drake must already be out in the stables.

Flying the blankets back, Kathryn gave herself a new mission for the day. To complete it she was going to have to get up and get dressed. Finding her boots, she walked out of the house, heading toward the stables, a coffee in her hands and Sophie beside her.

She had only just reached the bottom step of the veranda when she saw Drake walking back across the yard from the stables. He was in a pair of old jeans and a work shirt. His cowboy hat on his head, even though the sun had yet to fully rise from its bed. He looked as she had often dreamed. Her vision had come to life and was walking right towards her. A thrill of excitement raced over her and settled low in her stomach.

He smiled as he approached. "I didn't think I would see you up so early."

Stepping off the last step and walking to him she smiled up at him as they met in the middle of the yard. "I love getting up at this time, there is something so special about starting the day as the sun rises. It's my favourite time of day."

He leaned down and for a moment she thought he was going to kiss her, but he leaned past her to give Sophie, who was sitting patiently at her side, a pat. She felt giddy at the thought of his lips touching hers again and then embarrassed as he lovingly stroked the dog's ears and kissed Sophie good morning instead of her.

"Is this your normal time to rise? Before dawn?" Kathryn enquired, handing him the coffee she had made for him as he stood back up.

"Not usually this early, but I need to catch up on some work so for a while it will be. Breakfast?" He moved around her and started toward the house. Kathryn followed.

Over the next few days, they developed their own little routine. Drake was usually gone when Kathryn woke but would return so they could eat breakfast or lunch together, but not dinner. He would always be late.

She tried waiting for him the second night, but she'd gone to sleep on the couch. Finding herself later tucked in her own bed, alone. So, she would eat with Sophie and then crawl into her bed. Most nights, Kathryn hoped that Drake would come and lie with her to help keep the nightmares away, but he seemed to be keeping his distance. Maybe to allow her to heal and give her space. Maybe he really did have so much work to catch up on.

Over those few days, she found a large veggie patch in desperate need of some love and attention and three rows of fruit trees at the back of the house yard. Realising that was where the boxes of fruit had come from when Drake had come to visit her in the city years before, made her smile.

Deciding to focus her energy and thoughts into cleaning up the veggie patch, she was delighted to see some self-seeding happening with some corn and tomatoes. With some daily tender love and care, the little plants should flourish.

Sophie was forever by her side, seemingly to Drake's surprise. The dog had not left her since her arrival and he had told her it was the first time Sophie had not followed him to the stables. He had stated, in mock sulkiness, that he missed Sophie's company, making Kathryn giggle.

When she suggested he could take them both with him when he went to go somewhere, he turned serious and said no. So, Sophie was her constant companion instead of Drake. Kathryn talked to the dog a lot and at night, when it was just the two of them on the front steps, she'd stroke Sophie's ears and had taken to singing to her. Sophie would paw at her if she stopped. The dog seemed to like her singing voice.

Kathryn had been at Drake's farm for nearly a week. Tonight, the temperature was hotter than normal and there seemed to be no breeze. Kathryn was lying in bed, trying to stay as cool as possible, the sheets were sticking to her skin and making her feel uncomfortable as she tried to read one of the books Drake had bought for her while she was in the hospital.

Hearing the squeak softly echo through the house, she stopped reading and listened as the back door opened and closed quietly. Sophie, who had been asleep, sat up and pricked her ears. A low growl coming from the dog made Kathryn's heart beat faster. Silently creeping out of her bed, Kathryn moved to stand behind her door, hairbrush in her hand.

She had no idea where Drake was. Her hands were shaking, mouth dry and her heart beating so loudly in her ears she barely heard the soft laugh of Drake as he peered around the door to look at Sophie who took that moment to solidly bark at him. Scaring Kathryn and making her jump at the loud noise.

"Since when do you bark at me for coming into *my* house?" he asked half sternly at the furry animal.

Wagging her tail, Sophie walked to him to say hello and Kathryn let out a sigh of relief.

Looking up to her, he added "Lucky I came in slowly. Between her growling and you ready with the hairbrush I don't think I would have walked out unharmed." He smiled at her in a teasing way.

"Maybe if you didn't sneak in, we wouldn't have been scared out of our wits."

"I'm sorry. I thought you may have been asleep." Noticing that she was shaking, he stepped over Sophie and taking the brush from her hands and placing it onto the timber dresser, cuddled her to his body.

He was warm and smelled of sweat and horses but that didn't matter. She'd grown accustomed to his smell, and it filled her with security and something uniquely erotic.

He thought her weak, Kathryn chided herself as she let him hold her. She was not weak, she knew this, but be dammed if she was jumping at the slightest noise, especially at night. She was made of sterner stuff. At least, that's what her grandmother would have told her. She needed to calm down and trust she was safe. But she didn't want to be strong right at this moment, she wanted to be held and cuddled. To feel protected and safe in the security of his arms. She was allowed that, and as Drake was there doing that for her, she would allow it. Soon, she would be by herself and never feel this secure again so she would hold on tight to what she had this very second.

Drake stepped back and looked down into Kathryn's chocolate eyes. She had the most beautiful eyes, framed with long eyelashes. His gaze moved from her eyes to her full lips. She was drawing him to her, stripping away any chance of will power. Watching as her tongue darted out to wet her lips, his hand moved up to cup her chin, he tilted her head back ever so slightly, then leaned in to touch his lips to hers. Just a brush. A taste. A gentle hot brand of skin to skin.

He pulled back just enough to see her eyes close slowly. Her bruises were nearly gone, except for the one around her eye, which had a lingering yellowing tinge to it. Her stitches would be able to come out in another two days and she hadn't mentioned her ribs hurting, even though he suspected they still might be tender. She was healing fast, which meant that once the news came through from Scott, she would be leaving.

The thought sent a pain to his heart and looking at her now, eyes closed, he couldn't help himself. He wanted to touch her. Leaning in, Drake pressed his lips to hers again. She responded and opened her mouth for him, slipping her tongue into his as she tasted all of him. He let her tongue tangle with his, and when she slipped her hands into his hair and pulled him deeper into the kiss, a groan escaped from deep in his chest.

She was everything he had always wanted but could never have, now she was standing in front of him in a pair of skimpy silk pyjamas that outlined her curves and breasts perfectly. Her heat surrounding him, her hair smelling of vanilla, a smell that had become her and only her. He let himself go as much as he dared and breathed her in.

Standing on tiptoes, she pulled him to her more, the force of the movement overbalancing them, and he fell forward, catching himself from landing on her, his arm caught her body stopping her from hitting the wall to hard. Breathing heavily, he broke the kiss, but she was not letting him go. Her hands were still entangled in his hair.

He was looking into her eyes, when she pulled him in again. He didn't fight, he couldn't. She had started to heat his body to burn like a furnace. His heart was beating fast and the ache in his jeans was starting to hurt. He could barely think. Any control he had was fast fading.

All he wanted was to taste, touch and to breathe her into his body. To get lost in her touch. His hands moved over her; one found its way down her back and over her bottom, to her thigh. He lifted her leg and wrapped it around his hip, holding her there and pressing her harder into the wall at her back.

She pulled away from the kiss with a gasp and he froze thinking he had hurt her, but she shook her head and pulled him back into the kiss as her hips pressed into him. His other hand trailed slowly down her neck to the lacy frill of her pyjama top. Her breath faltered a fraction as his fingers traced the outline of the lace against her skin.

His hand slipped lower, fingers walking down over her breast and nipple, which erected at his touch, and kept going to where her shirt ended, and her tiny shorts started.

Drake pulled away just enough to look into her eyes. Her breathing was laboured, and her eyes were filled with passion and wanting. It burned at him.

She studied his face as he slowly moved his hand under her top and retraced his path back up, ever so slowly. Her silky skin formed goosebumps, and a shiver vibrated through her. He found the curve of her breast and with one finger traced its outline all the way from the outside to the inside where it gently touched the other one.

Her eyes became heavy lidded as his finger traced a slow line around the tender flesh, chewing her bottom lip as waves of shivers passed throughout her body — all created by the sensation of his finger caressing her skin.

She was intoxicating to watch, and he leaned in to kiss her, taking her bottom lip between his teeth and biting ever so gently hearing her gasp in pleasured pain. He suckled her lip and tongue until she melted against him, her hips pressing and grinding up against his to get some sort of release from the pressure building in her and between them.

Gliding his finger back, he gently cupped her breast and squeezed. She broke the kiss with a cry and pressed her breast against his hand harder, her head falling back against the wall exposing her throat for him.

Drake trailed a line of kisses down the slender softness of her neck to the delicate spot at her collar bone. Laving and suckling her sweet-tasting skin, he pressed her hips back against the wall and raised both his hands with hers to pin them to the wall together near her head, his knee now holding her grinding hips pinned between the plasterboard at her back and his erection.

His lips moved down further to find her nipple through her thin top. He took it deep within his hot mouth and sucked. The sensation had her trying to move but he had her locked. All Kathryn could do was push her breast further into his mouth and moan out her cries of need for him.

The pleasure and heat that he was giving her body was driving them both crazy. He could feel how much she needed to touch him and feel all of him against her body, could feel how badly she wanted him to take her to a place and give her the release she so desperately needed.

"Drake… Drake. Please," she breathlessly whispered, but he shook his head and moved to her other breast. It was throbbing and heavy with need as much as the first one. He took it and drew it into his mouth as Kathryn's breath faulted and fractured. He was sucking her that hard, it made her grind her hips against him.

He released her hands and they grabbed his hair; holding him to her breast as little cries escaped her lips causing him to feast harder. He was straining and pulsating against his jeans and she lifted her other leg to wrap around his hips as he raised his head to kiss her lips again. His hands moved to her bottom and kneaded it as he kissed her with a fevered hunger.

Some part of his brain was screaming at him to stop, that this was not right, but he ignored it as he turned and carried her, still pressed against him, lips locked, to the bed. He hit the edge of it and tumbled down, catching himself above her.

Her hair fell all around her, like a halo, and he was caught by her beauty and for what seemed like a lifetime, all he did was stare at her. Burning her into his memory.

Her breathing was ragged and her tension was building with his weight now pressing on her. His jeans were hard against her most sensitive spot, and she ground herself against him willing for release.

His eyes locked on hers, neither saying anything. Only their breathing filled the room.

Like a moth to the flame, Drake couldn't fight it. Lowering his head, he kissed her slowly and passionately, the flames leaping higher as they both burned.

Kathryn moved her hands and started to unbutton his work shirt. Shaking his head, he pulled away. "No."

"But-" He stopped her words as he kissed her harder and deeper, his tongue dancing with hers in another round of heated passionate need.

Pulling away, Drake moved to lie stretched out beside her, his head resting on his hand as the other one, pressed a finger to her lips, halting her protests, before gliding down and finding her breast and squeezing.

A throaty sound escaping her lips made him smile and continue. She was moving her hips and wiggling with pleasure as she chewed her bottom lip with her eyes closed. When his hand moved lower and circled her belly button, she lifted her hips off the bed and grabbed for him, trying to pull him into a kiss. He gave her a quick one then pulled back just enough so he could watch her eyes flutter open, full of need and desire before she closed them again. He moved his fingers lower still, slipping them under her silk pyjama shorts and then stopped. He would not go any further unless, she was sure.

Sensing his gaze and his frozen movements, Kathryn opened her eyes, the darkest glazed chocolate he'd ever seen, looked into his. Stealing his breath as he watched her chewing her bottom lip, she lifted her hips and closed her eyes.

That was all he needed.

Gently, wonderingly, he slid his hand slowly lower, and lower, until his fingertips came into contact with her curls. She had no underwear on. He grunted in surprise, as he continued moving ever so slowly down further, until he found her wet hot mess and cupped it as she raised her hips to meet his hand.

Opening her eyes, Kathryn pulled him down so that she could press her breasts into his chest. Frustrated and desperate for his lips to be on hers, she reached up and forcibly pulled him to her, kissing him hard as he gave a soft laugh at her demands for him.

Drunk on her kiss, Drake didn't move his hand, until Kathryn reached down and pressed his finger into her wet heated body.

She was scalding and silky wet to touch. His finger slipping into her, felt like warm silk. Her gasps were filling his lungs as she kissed him, taking everything he had, and still, needing more.

Slowly he moved his finger within her. She was so tight and so wet. Her passionate movements were pulling away his restraint so fast he was worried he might embarrass himself, very soon. She was far more passionate than he had imagined in his dreams. Her body moved and pressed to him with a rhythm and sway that left him yearning for more. To join with her and feel the passion she exuded with such beauty and wanting need. To have her take him and ride him hard until she exploded, leaving her wet and wanting body all over him in elated bliss.

Groaning with his image of her, he found her spot and drawing back from her kiss, he watched her as she became fully lost in the pleasure he was giving her. She was tightening around his finger over and over and her hips were grinding against his hand, her moans filling the room and her breathing was fast and heavy.

He could feel her nearing the peak, so he fastened the speed of his finger deep within her sweet body and held her tight as he watched her plummet over the crest, her body wreathing and twisting, she grabbed him and pulled him to her hard. Her fingers dug into his hair as she shook with the waves of release, crying out his name breathlessly, she held him tight to her with all she had.

Drake stayed where he was as Kathryn floated back down to earth. He removed his finger from deep inside her but left his hand sitting on her lower belly, feeling it rise and fall with each breath she took. Her hands had dropped from around his neck at the same time she let a satisfied sigh escape her beautiful lips. His own pain was still very much in need of attention, something he would deal with later in private, for now he was satisfied to watch and hold her.

His heart beat an unsteady rhythm as his mind tried to wander to places it shouldn't. He was not going to listen to it now and slammed all those thoughts down. He would deal with them later. Keeping a relaxed but controlled restrain on them, he let them wander wherever they wanted to go about her. He was here with her now and he would deal with the other consequences later.

Kathryn woke to the sound of distant thunder and wind blowing her curtain around. Drake was not in the room but had covered her with her blanket and turned out the light. Rolling to her side, her body ached, especially her ribs. Sophie was not in the room either. Steadily she pushed back onto her back, a heat rose and tainted her face as she remembered what had happened between them.

He had touched her and made her come without removing a layer of clothing. She had never been touched so intimately. Her first sexual experience was horrible and only lasted about five minutes, not enough time to even get wet. The boy had basically entered and exploded. Yes, it was both their first time, and they were young, but still ... and her second experience with Rob was a drunken mistake. One that had changed her life in a way that she would never have even thought of.

Yet that event had brought her here, with Drake, and now he had shown her what intimacy could actually feel like. What a real orgasm with a man could feel like. It was amazing. If only she had experienced something like this on her first time she may never have settled for a drunken moment with Rob. But then she would never have reconnected with Drake.

A bolt of lightning drew her attention away from her thoughts. She got up and closed her window and curtains. It wasn't that she disliked storms, she liked to watch them, but from the safety of behind closed windows. Another clash of thunder, this one was louder and made her go looking for Drake. She knew what to expect in the city when a storm came, but here in the country, she didn't know. Would it be rougher because of no buildings, would it be louder and the rain heavier?

Opening her bedroom door, she was surprised to find him sitting on the floor in the laundry opposite her room, next to a thick blanket on the floor and a sheet covering it. His shirt was half opened and showed a small line of hair across his chest. His long legs, stretched out and crossed at his ankles, filled his jeans to perfection. A thrill of excitement and the memory of how he had touched her gave her goosebumps from her head to her toes. Crossing her arms across her chest to quell her body's reaction to him, he looked up at her, a faint smile on his lips.

"What are you doing?" she asked as she stepped into the tiled room. It was a very small room with a hot water system, a large linen cupboard and an old washing machine that rattled and groaned when it washed clothes.

"Sophie doesn't like storms." Drake gave her a crooked smile. Heat spiralled up her body.

"I usually make her a bed here and cover her over with a sheet. She settles once the rain comes but hates the build-up of the storm. She senses them long before I can ever hear the rumble."

Sophie lay under the sheet panting and whimpering, only the tip of her nose visible from under the sheet. Drake was stroking the shaking dog through the thin fabric. Her fear was something Kathryn could relate to. Reaching up and over Drake's head, that was resting back on the cupboard door, Kathryn looked down at him and smiled into his eyes as she straddled his hips, standing on her tiptoes and took a towel from the top shelf. Her skin was warm as she felt the intensity of his gaze. Stepping over him and finding a place on the floor, she sat down next to Drake and Sophie.

He looked away; his jaw tight. "You don't have to sit here," he said moving his legs as if his jeans were pinching him. "Sophie will be okay, and you need your rest."

Frowning at him, Kathryn leaned in and kissed Sophie's head through the sheet. "She has not left my side since I arrived, so I won't leave hers when she needs me. Hey girl."

A flash of lightning skittered across the sky just outside the window, quickly followed by a loud clash of thunder that rattled the house. Kathryn jumped and looked at Drake. He didn't seem to be worried or fazed by it, he just continued to stroke Sophie's head, his own leaning back on the cupboard door, his eyes closed.

Kathryn watched his chest deeply rising and falling steadily. In ... out ... in ... out. He was such a contrast. He was all muscle and strength, yet he could be tender and soft and caring. He seemed to fight that side of himself, when he realised it was there, but it was also natural to him.

She allowed her eyes to travel the length of him, taking in all his curves and rises. The way his clothes fit his body. Some men's clothes wore them, but Drake wore his clothes. They fit him and, in a way, made him appear larger, stronger and more of a man than she could have ever thought a man could be.

She had spent many nights thinking and dreaming of him, of his touch, of his kisses and of the feel of his naked body pressed up against hers. She had been given another chance to experience all her desires with him and knowing her time would end here no matter what Scott said, she wanted to have all she had thought and dreamed. She wanted it now.

The first sounds of rain, drummed on the tin roof. A few drops at first, then it rushed down. The sound was deafening. Drake sat up and, with a last pat to Sophie's head, stood and held out his hand to help Kathryn up.

She saw his hand shook slightly. Not sure why, she gave a last cuddle to Sophie and allowed him to help her up. They stood so close to each other that her shirt touched his. She raised her gaze from his chest, up to his eyes. Those emerald eyes that she could never look away from and that always seemed to be looking directly into her soul, were staring back at her. He seemed to be at a loss as much as she was.

Taking her hand, he walked out of the laundry and shut the door. "Sophie will be ok here 'til morning." He looked towards her room, at her bed. Suddenly, he stepped back away from her, dropping his hand away from hers, "Goodnight, Kathryn." He turned and stalked his way to the other end of the house, opened his bedroom door and slammed it shut with his foot.

Not sure what just happened, Kathryn walked to her bed and sat down. She listened to the rain pound the roof and the lightning and thunder rage around the house. It was as if the emotions of Drake were raging and fighting within him, just like the storm outside her window. He was running hot and cold with her. When he was cold, he was ice, but when he was hot, he could burn her to ashes. He was such a contradiction. He wanted her sexually. She knew that. Could feel it pulsate through him, but then he would shut it down and turn to ice.

Another bolt of lightning streaked across the sky, its fingers spreading out to light up in a spectacular show of beauty and danger, before it disappeared never to be seen in that formation again, Kathryn decided enough was enough.

She was a strong, independent woman. She had been brought up to work for what she wanted and taught that if she worked hard enough, she could get it. The question was: did she want Drake? She would never be able to have him for life, but she could have him now if she wanted? Couldn't she?

The power flicked off, sending the house into complete darkness as she walked a direct line to Drake's door. Her confidence high and her mission set, she would not stop until she got what she came here to get.

Not bothering to knock, Kathryn turned the nob on the door and walked in. The room was completely dark except for the flickering of lightning outside. In the middle of the room was a large bed, larger than hers. A chair sat in the corner, next to a large window that was open. The curtains were blowing and twisting in the wind from the storm raging outside. Walking to the bed she couldn't make out anyone lying in it. She turned in a circle and when another flash of lightning lit the room, she found him. Standing near his cupboard.

Naked.

Kathryn's mouth went dry. Her eyes widened. Who was in more shock she couldn't tell, but neither moved. Her heart was racing. He was naked and she didn't look away. He was pure muscle from his shoulders down to his rippled torso. Her eyes continued down, over his hips and to his manhood, now coming alive. Past his toned thighs and down his calves. She took her time, allowing herself to take him all in. He was truly beautiful. Her excitement grew as she took another thorough look at his body when lightning flickered and lit up the sky again, finally coming to meet his eyes.

He had allowed her to take in her fill of him. He stood there watching her as she took every inch of his body into memory and he did not move. Finally, when her eyes came to his, he asked, "What are you doing in here, Kathryn?" His voice was a hushed whisper over the storm. His emotions raw.

"I came for you," she said more confidently than she suddenly felt, walking up to him, her hand finding his chest. His heart beat wildly under her touch. She smiled at him as her thumb rubbed over his nipple, bringing it to attention.

"We *can't*, Kathryn." he growled sounding almost painful with restraint "You need to leave and go back to your room." He took a step back, but she stopped him with her other hand on his face.

Her palm caressed his warm, roughened skin, as her fingers intertwined into the hair near his ear. It was then, she felt the wetness on his cheek and felt his body shaking. He was not shaking with lust but with something else and he had tears sliding down his face. She stepped away, letting her hands drop from him. "Drake? Are you alright? Why are you crying and shaking?"

His temper rose, and he pushed past her to the end of the bed where his jeans lay discarded.

She watched him pulling them on again, seeing the corded muscles in his back work to yank on his jeans. He was jerky and unsteady in his movements. Agitated.

Lightening lit up the sky when he turned to face her, all his emotions were focused on her, and he growled, "Just leave me alone, Kathryn, and go back to your room. I'm not strong enough to fight it."

"Fight what, Drake? Me?"

"No dammit. Not you." Frustrated, he ran a hand through his hair and started to pace the room. She didn't understand, how could she? He stopped in front of her, careful not to touch her and taking deep breaths to keep everything under control, he begged, "Please go back to your room."

He was pleading with her and the rawness she saw in his eyes as another streak of lightning blazed across the sky, tightened her chest. She reached for him, her fingers on his arm. "No."

His eyes closed and his head dropped as if in pain. Her heart was beating so fast but she was going to stay her path no matter what. She had made it this far and though things had not gone as she had played them out on her way through the house, she was in fact now here, and he had not removed her as yet from the room. A mini accomplishment. Maybe.

"What do you want from me?"

His sorrowful plea snaked its way into her soul. There was something about it that made her want to cuddle him to her chest until his fear went away, but another part of her knew that if she didn't say it now, it would never happen. She would lose her nerve, or he would never grant it to her.

"I want you. All of you, now. Right here, tonight," she said clearly, watching as he raised his head to the ceiling, letting out a slow breath through clenched teeth, his eyes closed tightly like he was in serious pain.

"And that's it, because I can't give you anything more, Kathryn." His eyes opened, and he looked down at her, pleading with her to understand the truth of it.

Nodding, she shyly looked up into his face. "Yes. I understand what you're saying." She gripped his open jeans in both hands, pulling him to her. "But please give me this." Standing on tiptoes she pressed a kiss to his lips — and they were both lost to the taste and need of each other.

Drake pulled her to his body, and she could feel her erect nipples pressing into his bare chest through her silk pyjama top. Hungrily he feasted on her, his need turned primal and heated her to scolding and still he demanded more from her. His hand slid up her spine to cup the back of her head, he fisted her hair roughly and pulled her head back near painfully as his lips pressed harder to hers. It felt like he was devouring her entire being. His other hand rose slowly up her back and gripped her shirt, preparing to rip it off.

Through the noise of the pelting rain, wind and thunder, came the sound of someone pounding on the front door.

Drake froze and lifted his head, listening. Kathryn waited, her heart pounding hard. Surely, no-one would be out in this weather. But there it was again, pounding, and someone calling for Drake. He looked down at her, thoughts flickering across his face as he stepped her back into the darkest part of the room. His body shielding hers in the dark corner, his heat surrounding her as his body pressed against her.

She nearly leaped into his arms when the person who had been knocking on the door suddenly bashed on his bedroom window.

"Drake. God dammit. Get out of bed. I need your help." *Reggie.* Thank God. A second passed before he bashed again, this time harder, then moved back to the front door.

Kathryn's knees felt weak with relief. Drake cursed under his breath through the darkness as he did up his jeans. Another flash of lightning and thunder lit and crashed through the sky as he stepped back away from her, avoiding her eyes before he opened the bedroom door and suddenly the lights flicked back on in the house, lighting up the lounge room.

Kathryn stayed hidden in Drake's room listening to the muffled voices, her heart still beating hard against her chest.

Drake returned and pulled his work shirt back over his head. "One of Reggie's horses got spooked and has run through a fence and cut its leg. I need to go and have a look. He is too upset to do it himself. I may be a while." He quickly finished dressing and as he left, kissed her on the forehead.

She reached for him, grabbing his shirt to hold him. He stepped back through the door and twisting a fist full of her hair in his hand, tilted her head back and kissed her. The sensation went all the way to her toes and curled them.

Pulling away he smiled tightly. "I won't be long. Remember, you are safe here." With that he left with Reggie in the pouring rain.

Chapter 16

Surprisingly, Kathryn slept in for the first time since she was a little girl. It was nearly nine o'clock. The day was already warm, and the air smelled sweet. After Drake had left last night with Reggie, she had gone to sit with Sophie while the storm had continued to rumble around the house, the intensity passing quickly, leaving only the beautiful sound of rain on a tin roof. A sound that was completely new to Kathryn. Its gentle, soothing rhythm had eventually lulled her and Sophie it seemed, into a calm and relaxed state of mind, so she had gone to bed and straight to sleep with her loyal friend on the mat next to her like normal.

Rising, and seeing Sophie sitting happily on the veranda, she peeked into Drake's room. The bed had been slept in, but he was already gone. By the looks of the kitchen, he had not eaten tea last night or breakfast this morning.

His actions last night were so confusing, and the shock of finding him when she had stormed his room with tears in his eyes and shaking made no sense. He was running constantly hot and cold with his emotions. Giving her mixed signals.

Looking out the window at the sound of horses whining, Kathryn decided to put last night out of her mind for the time being and just enjoy the moments she had left here with him.

The day was too beautiful to waste. Feeling inspired, Kathryn set about cooking up a hot breakfast for them both. Collecting freshly laid eggs from the chicken coop and thanking the girls, her fear of them now gone, Kathryn made a beautiful omelette with fried tomatoes and homemade hash browns. She was just serving it up when Drake came in through the back door. He looked tired.

"That smells good," he said as he walked over to make himself a coffee. He avoided touching her, opting instead to stand on the other side of the counter as he prepared his brew and then wearily sat at the table.

Kathryn placed his hot breakfast down in front of him and took a seat opposite to eat her own. Pushing her worried thoughts about last night to the side, and his demands for her to leave him alone, she settled in her seat, her focus on filling her ravenous stomach.

"I thought I would take you to get your stitches out today. Old Gerald at the nursing home was the town doctor until he retired a few years back. He wouldn't ask any questions."

Swallowing a mouth full of food, she nodded.

"Vicki, a friend of mine lives there too. Reggie told her you were staying with me, and she wants to meet you. Is that okay? You don't have to if you don't want to," he added when she gave him an unsure look.

"No that's fine. I would like to. I just thought you said you didn't want too many people to know that I was here, that's all."

"I think if we word our story right, no one will ask too many questions." He took another bite of his breakfast, watching her.

"And what is the story you think we should say?" They discussed it further over their breakfast.

An hour later, Kathryn was sitting in Drake's Ute, wearing one of the pretty summer dresses he had bought for her and her boots, going to meet someone who she suspected he respected very much.

The retirement home was a network of buildings joined together by covered-in walkways. The gardens were beautiful and there were lots of birds singing in the trees. Kathryn's nerves increased as she followed Drake through the first set of double doors leading to the main office reception desk.

A short, stout woman, with greying hair and glasses smiled and greeted them when Drake signed his name in the entry book. "She's been waiting for you to come and visit, and she's not been very patient, I can tell you." The woman looked over at Kathryn and her smile grew bigger. "Mind you, when she sees what you have brought back from the city, I think she will be very pleased."

The woman had a soft spot for Drake, it was clear to see. Completing his signature, he looked up and gave her one of his charming country boy smiles. Kathryn sighed, suspecting he knew he could nearly get away with anything when he used it. Like a little boy who had been caught with his hand in the lolly jar only to get told he could have the whole thing.

"We will see, Mrs. B," he said. Taking Kathryn's hand, he led her through the second set of doors when Mrs. B opened them by security lock. Kathryn loved that he kept hold of her as they walked down the corridor hand in hand. It was bright and airy to one side with windows open to the breeze, letting in the sights and sounds of the gardens outside.

On the other side were rooms. Each one had a bed, private bathroom and very small kitchenet. Some of the occupants were in bed watching tv, others were reading or knitting or doing a crossword. Some were sitting in big armchairs just outside their door talking to their neighbour. The place had a good vibe, Kathryn felt.

As Drake passed the rooms, he greeted the residents, most by name, and commented on the day or the rain of last night. They all seemed to know him and were eager for him to stop and talk, however he kept moving, telling them Vicki was waiting and they all knew to never keep her waiting. Nodding their agreement, they peered with interest at Kathryn, smiling broadly at her. She heard them whispering after they'd passed by.

By the time they reached another set of double doors, Kathryn's nerves were sending butterflies flying in her stomach. Pushing the green button to open the double doors, Drake walked into a room that functioned as a dining room. Lots of solid round tables and plastic chairs filled the space. An industrial stainless-steel kitchen was at the back and a tv worthy of a sports room at the local pub was on one wall.

On the other side of the room were old leather lounge chairs and timber coffee tables for a more private chat if needed. On the wall behind her, Kathryn was amazed at the wall-to-wall bookshelves filled with books from roof to floor, finishing just near the double doors they had just walked through.

The room was vacant except for two elderly ladies sitting and reading quietly in the corner. Both looked up when Kathryn and Drake entered the room and began to whisper behind their books.

"She must be in the garden." Drake placed a hand on the middle of her back, steering her towards yet another set of double doors, just beyond the kitchen.

The sunlight was bright and made her squint as they stepped out. The burbling of a fountain filled the space, and a pale cement path led the way, meandering in a gentle way, like a river through the country into the garden oasis. At its end was an open area of green grass and outside tables.

There were people sitting in the sun, some were digging in the garden and others were sipping tea in the shaded areas. Nurses were chatting and helping where needed. The whole scene was beautiful. Nothing like she had witnessed in the city.

She had worked briefly at a nursing home in the inner city — a brick place where people came to die. The patients did nothing but watch tv and eat. No one seemed to visit them or care. There wasn't much of a garden, so they never went outside, and never really talked to each other. It was a grey life and one she had no desire to experience. But here was a life full of colour. Everyone looked happy and healthy, and they were active. There was laughter and talking to each other and they shared meals together. A loud cheer came from behind the shaded picnic area, and everyone turned to the noise.

"There must be a game on. They get pretty competitive here, so watch out," Drake leaned in to murmur in her ear. With the slightest of pressure on her back, they walked up to one of the nurses.

A young girl, around her own age, Kathryn guessed, with midnight black hair and the prettiest cobalt eyes she had ever seen. The nurse straightened and smoothed her hair as they approached, she smiled prettily at Drake but eyed Kathryn with a covered-shock look. Looking Kathryn up and down, the nurse stared at Drake's arm resting on her lower back before she turned her eyes to Drake and fluttered her eyelashes at him. Completely ignoring Kathryn's presence.

Kathryn was not stupid — the girl was clearly keen on Drake and did not like that his attention was taken up by her. He apparently didn't notice the nurse batting her eyelids at him. This girl was stunning, but there was something about her that made Kathryn uneasy.

"Is Vicki out here, Brigid?" Drake asked, looking over the girl's head towards another group of ladies.

"Yes, over in the corner talking with Gerald." Brigid touched Drake's arm gently leaning in to him and pointed to the corner. "How was your trip?"

Drake smiled blindly and un-answering at Brigid before taking Kathryn's hand and making a direct line towards the back tables.

Vicki was a tall woman with a slender build. Her hair was tied up in a bun high on her head and earrings dangled from her ears. Her face was nearly wrinkle-free and glowed with health and happiness. She stood when she saw them approaching and, to Kathryn's surprise, Drake walked straight into her open arms and gave her a big hug and squeeze, lifting her off the ground, making her laugh with the shock and delight of his actions. She smacked him on the back and told him to put her down. He did, and as she pulled back to look at him, he kissed her cheek. The man sitting with Vicki rose to his feet and reached out his hand to shake Drake's in a welcome.

Drake took it and greeted the man with a wide smile, then stepped back. "Vicki, Gerald. This is Kathryn." He put his hand on her back, moving his thumb in circles, soothing the nerves that were plaguing her.

Kathryn stepped forward to say hello.

Vicki grabbed both her hands and squeezed, looking her up and down before leaning in and giving her a kiss on both cheeks. "It's lovely to meet you, my dear. Please sit and tell us all about yourself."

Drake held out a seat beside Vicki for Kathryn and took up the one beside Gerald for himself.

"There's not much to tell, really," Kathryn said as she looked to Drake to help with the story they had planned to tell.

"Oh, my dear, there would be lots. Tell us how you two met." Vicki was onto them and could see straight through them both.

"We met years ago, and then recently caught up in the city. Just before Drake was due to leave, my house burnt down and I lost everything. So, I thought I would come for a visit with him for a while before I moved on to my next adventure."

"Is that how you got your cut?" Gerald asked. He was a tall man, about Drake's height and size, with a large grey beard that was nearly to his chest and a bald head.

Kathryn tenderly touched the spot where the bullet had grazed her head, annoyed to feel her hand shaking slightly. "Yes. It was all very scary, but I'm safe now." She looked at Drake and smiled shyly. She didn't like lying, but it was best for everyone's safety. He squeezed her hand and the conversation moved on to the sights of the city and their trip home, the storm last night and Reggie's injured horse.

It turned out she and Vicki had much to talk about and got along well. They talked food and recipes and Sophie while Drake and Gerald spoke about the weather and farming. He looked so relaxed, being here with what were obviously two of his favourite people.

She could see Vicki was watching Drake from the corner of her eye, noting the way he sat with his arm casually draped around her chair, one ankle resting on his knee. The woman was watching closely, probably taking in a lot more than what she was hearing.

Kathryn couldn't decide whether to be uneasy or pleased that Drake had someone so alert and aware looking out for him. The lunchtime bell rang — their visit had gone quickly. Everyone stood.

"You will come back and see me again before you leave, Kathryn dear, won't you?" Vicki said as she squeezed her hands goodbye.

"Of course," Kathryn replied and stood close to Drake as his hand once again rested gently on her lower back.

"Gerald, I was wondering if you could help us out?" Drake asked. "Kathryn needs the stitches taken out and while I am happy to remove them from a horse, I'm not too keen on doing it for her. To save us waiting at the hospital or trying to get an appointment with all the information they need just for a two second job, would you be able to remove them for her?"

Drake had worded it so well that even she would not have suspected that there was another reason for not wanting to have to give her personal details away.

"It would be my pleasure, my dear. If you would come with me my bag is in my room." Gerald gave her a warm reassuring smile and, tucking her hand in his elbow, his warm hand covering hers, led the way to his room.

Drake stayed behind, at Vicki's request. No doubt she was going to ask him a lot of questions. Vicki would no doubt have been intimidating in her younger years, she still was now, but Kathryn really liked her and found that while stern, she was also kind and understanding. Her heart was big, and she had a lot of love for Drake. It was written all over her face.

Kathryn sat in the chair Gerald indicated, he was extremely gentle and professional as he assessed her stitches. He bathed her wound and checked that it was indeed ready to have the stitches removed, constantly remarking at what a beautiful job the doctor had done in sewing it up. That once the hair grew over the scar, you would never know it was there. It had healed beautifully.

Kathryn felt only the slightest of tugs on her skin when he started at the stitches and that was it. Band-Aid applied, she helped him to clean up and pack away his things, saying her goodbye when another gentleman walked into his room to talk.

With a smile for them both and reassurance she could get herself back to Drake and Vicki, Kathryn retraced her steps back down the hall. The men's wing of the retirement village had their own nurse's station, just like the women did.

As she passed the station the pretty nurse from before, Brigid, stopped her. "You know, you don't have what you think you have with him. He's not what you think, he can't commit to anyone," the girl said in a nasty tone while her eyes raked Kathryn up and down with distaste. "Drake has secrets and a past no one knows about, but it's rumoured to be violent. He'll make you think he wants you, but in the end, he'll reject you. Just like all the others." Brigid stalked off towards to the station. Turning back with a sneer she added, "You've been warned."

Kathryn stared at Brigid's back, shocked at her rudeness. She was definitely in love with Drake and wanted to scare her off! Giving a shudder at the girl and her words, she continued her way along the hall.

All she knew was that Drake was the least violent person she had ever known, and whatever his past was, it was his and his alone. If he ever shared it with her, that was his choice. She knew the man he was today.

Drake and Vicki were deep in a serious conversation when she returned to them. Drake was leaning forward, his forearms on his knees, looking at the floor, shaking his head as he listened to what Vicki was saying. On sensing her approach, they both stopped their conversation and he stood and tried to smile normally, but it was strained. "All good then?" he asked.

"Yep. He did a beautiful job. Is everything okay? Am I interrupting something?" Kathryn looked between them both.

"No, my dear, not at all! I was telling Drake that we should go shopping and buy you some more clothes. You'll need some more after losing everything in that horrible fire."

"Oh, that's very kind of you but I have enough."

"Pish posh, my dear" Vicki scolded. "A women can never have too many clothes and accessories. Good lord, did you hear that, Drake?" She seemed shocked at Kathryn's statement. "Drake will bring you by in the next few days and I will teach you how to shop. There may not be much here in town, but we'll find you something more. Now, if you will excuse me, I am hungry and if I don't arrive soon all the good food will be gone."

Vicki hugged Drake and whispered sternly, "Remember what I said, my boy." She tapped his face gently, before hugging Kathryn. "Lovely to meet you, my dear girl, and I am so excited about our shopping spree. It will be so much fun." Waving over her shoulder, she marched towards the dining room.

On the way home, Drake was quiet. Whatever Vicki and he had been discussing, it had not been about clothes shopping and had unsettled him. When they arrived back at the farm, he got changed and went straight to the stables, saddled one of the grey horses he had been working earlier in the week and rode out through the gate. She was once again left with Sophie.

After spending the afternoon tending to the veggie patch and reading, Kathryn grew restless. Putting on her boots, she decided to explore the stables and surrounds. With Sophie beside her, she headed to the stables first.

The shed was spacious, with a high roof, and smelled of hay and horses. One side of the shed had square hay bales piled high nearly to the roof, on the other, four stalls, all empty. In the very end stall were bags of grain and a cupboard filled with medicines and creams.

On hearing horses nickering beyond the tall, solid double metal doors at the end, she continued her exploration. Outside, there was a large round yard and two smaller circular pens that were filled with sand. An extensive cement pad with a hose attached to a tall moveable pipe, was near the shed and tanks. Two brown horses with black manes were lying down in one of the sand pens.

Following around to her right, Kathryn found another shed. It smelled of leather and had lots of saddles, ropes and many other things she had no idea about. Everything was organised and had its own special spot. This was his world. It was organised and controlled; nothing was out of place.

As she explored, her thoughts wandered to the words Brigid had said about his past. She could not think of Drake as being violent now, but had he been? She had known him years earlier and the man she knew then was the same one she still saw today. She knew that Drake's grandfather had been his world. He'd loved him dearly. Besides, the horses here all seemed to welcome and trust him. They wouldn't do that if he was ever violent or rough with them. Hadn't he said something about them being rescue animals?

Today, she saw that he was loved by everyone at the retirement village. If he was a violent person, or had been, surely he would not be so welcomed there? Yet, apart from Reggie, no one else had come to visit him. The phone never rang, and he hadn't spoken about friends or what he does for fun. It had only ever been Vicki, Reggie, the farm and horses that he spoke of.

He seemed to have no friendships with people of his own age, nor did he seem to care. If these were the only people he had in his life, then what was he doing in the city? Why did he travel that far, every few months all those years ago and then abruptly stop, only to come down a few weeks ago? There were so many questions she now had about him.

Maybe she really didn't know the person she was now living with. Maybe she had only chosen to see what she had wanted to see in him and not the Drake he was.

A coldness prickled her neck and moved down her spine. Had she done it again? Had she moved in with another person she barely knew, thinking it was right? Had she put herself in danger again? Maybe Brigid was right. Maybe she didn't know what she had got herself into. Her hands began to shake.

The sun was setting when she reached the house, after wandering around the horse yards and paddocks mindlessly in thought for hours. Showering quickly and making herself a sandwich, Kathryn went to her room before Drake returned. She didn't want to see him. She needed time to think about the revelations she had made that afternoon. She also needed to know the person who she was now living with and his past. Before she did that, she needed to form an escape plan — just in case.

Kathryn was in bed sleeping when Drake finally arrived home later that night. He had not meant to be as long as he had been. He had ridden over to Reggie's to check on the injured horse, on one of the horses in training that he had been sure was nearly ready to go — but it had shied on his return and, much to his disgust and self-embarrassment, it had bucked him off onto his ass.

The horse had then bolted off towards home, which meant he had to walk the rest of the way home on foot. Given the rain the previous night, he had to walk nearly all the way back towards the main road before he could cut across the creek in the dark and then make his way back to the house and stables.

He was cold and soaked to his bones, thanks to a misjudged deep hole in the creek crossing. His boots were sodden, and his temper was boiling. He had found the horse waiting for him near the saddle shed, grazing happily on a patch of green grass, totally unaware of the grief it had caused by shying at a fence post.

Dammit. He'd hoped to talk with Kathryn tonight, but the day's activities had worn her out. She appeared to be healed, but her fatigue must have caught up with her. After showering, he had to check on her. He didn't know why but he needed to touch her, to know she was safe in his house.

Pushing the door to her bedroom open just enough to allow a sliver of light into the room, he stepped through the door and over a sleeping Sophie to the bed. Kathryn was lying on her side, facing the window, her hair fanned out across her pillow. Her shoulders were bare and uncovered. She was cool to touch. Pulling the blanket over her, he surprised himself by pressing a kiss to her temple. Just a light one so as not to disturb her. She smelled of vanilla.

It was her.

His body reacted, something he was growing accustomed to. Touching her soothed him somehow, but also scared him. He didn't want to desire her this much and knew he was fighting a losing battle, a battle he couldn't afford to lose. She needed to leave soon, and he needed to make her go.

Stepping back over Sophie and slipping out through the door, he was surprised to find his dog, who had not left Kathryn's side since she had arrived, following him out and into the lounge room, taking her usual spot on the lounge chair. Maybe she sensed that Kathryn didn't need her as much anymore, which meant that Kathryn would be leaving soon. Not wanting to think about it, Drake went to bed.

The following afternoon Kathryn was watering the veggie patch. The day had turned out to be hot with hardly any breeze. The mist from the hose cooled her legs and eased the intenseness of the heat. Sophie too, had wanted to be hosed off and cooled down, so Kathryn had soaked the dog and washed her all over to help her quell the heat. To thank Kathryn, Sophie had shaken water and hair all over her, then decided a game of tag was required.

Once Kathryn figured out the game she wanted to play, Sophie loved it, racing around the yard and veggie patch, weaving in between the fruit trees and then coming close to Kathryn, but not close enough to get 'tagged'.

The dog's antics had Kathryn giggling and laughing. She hadn't laughed for so long. Her ribs pained her a little, but she didn't care — she was laughing, and it felt good. Picking up the hose again, Kathryn decided to try and 'tag' Sophie with the water instead of catching her. The dog barked and raced around again, even more excited.

Drake could hear Sophie barking from inside the stables. He had just finished repairing one of the leather straps on his bridle that had a tear in it from last night's incident. She never barked liked that. Turning his head to listen more, curiosity got the better of him. Following the path around the side, to the back of the house, he stopped at the corner and leaned on the timber weatherboards of his home and watched what appeared to be the game at play.

Kathryn was barefoot and nearly soaked through. Her hair fell down her back, dripping water at its ends and her dress was wet from the game she was playing with Sophie — his dog who never played anything but fetch the ball and that was only when *she* wanted to. Which was normally when he was sitting on the back steps with her at the end of the day, having a cold beer.

This game of water tag was new. Sophie raced around with an exuberant amount of energy and would come close to Kathryn but dodge the water from the hose and tear off again, barking with excitement.

She was teasing Kathryn, making her laugh and the sound filled the air. It was a sweet melody. He had never heard her laugh like that; it was a true happiness. Watching from his place leaning casually, his ankle crossed over the other, his arms lazily across his chest, the corner of his mouth lifted slightly as he spied Kathryn move backwards, step by step, closer to the house.

Each pass by, Sophie had to run further away from the veggie patch, meaning that Kathryn was getting closer to wetting her. A game of tactics and calculations between both girls were at play. Intense, Sophie halted for a second, her look at Kathryn, teasing her to make a move. Kathyn stopped and stared back at Sophie.

A standoff.

Sophie made her run again, racing directly for Kathryn but instead of turning and racing back to the right she veered to Kathryn's left and raced behind him, under the house and back out from under the steps. Back to the safety behind the veggie patch and fruit trees. Kathryn blindly followed the dog with the hose.

The water hit him as it followed Sophie's path. "Oh!" He gasped, the water cool and refreshing against his body.

Sophie forgotten; Kathryn stood with her hand covering her mouth. He must have looked funny as he stood next to the corner of the house wet, looking at her, his eyes wide with the shock of the cold water hitting his body instead of Sophie's. She burst out laughing at the sight.

"So, you think that's funny, do you?" He started to slowly stalk towards her.

She took a step back, hose still in hand, giggling. "You looked hot, like Sophie, so I thought a cool down with the hose would help." She couldn't keep the smile off her face as she stepped back again; matching each step he took forward.

"Is that so?" He raised his eyebrows with a wolf's smile.

Kathryn took a quick glance at the distance between her and the veggie patch, he saw her decision to run for it reflected in her eyes as she darted away. Drake was on her in two steps, his arm slipping around her waist as he lifted her off the ground. She let out a squeal of shock and delight, but she held tight to the hose as he tried to hold her with one arm and retrieve the hose from her with the other. Water was going everywhere. Sophie was jumping and barking around them in excitement and wanting to be part of the game.

Drake was soaked, water was hitting him in the face and drenching his clothes, his hat slipped from his head, landing in the mud as he fought Kathryn for control of the hose. The laughter bubbling up and out of him felt strange but good and he couldn't stop, it just kept flowing out of him. Kathryn was laughing and squealing along with him as she managed to squirt the hose into his face again, stinging his eyes. His grip on her released enough that she slipped from his arm and ran.

She darted around the side of the house towards the front and had just stepped onto the side path when he wrapped his arms around her, her body slamming into his. His breath coming in gasps, he laughed and pinned her to him while she tried to wriggle free. She nearly managed the task, but then he spun her around and in one fluid motion lifted her up and flung her over his shoulder and marched back towards the hose on the ground where she had dropped it.

She was kicking and pummelling his back, wriggling and fighting to get free as she laughed; ordering him to put her down. He jostled her, making her lose some of her fight, before she started again. Sophie was jumping around his feet barking.

Using all the strength she had, Kathryn managed to push herself up and half turn, getting her arm around his neck, she twisted her body in one fluid motion. He nearly dropped her but regained his balance and forced her back to her position, hanging over his shoulder.

"I don't think so, my love. You're going to pay for getting me all wet. I will punish you." And to emphasize it, he smacked her on her butt.

"Oh, you're going to pay for that, Drake Harrison," Kathryn said with indignation as she stopped wriggling and forcibly sat up straight, the momentum forcing him to stop so he wouldn't fall forward. Taking that second, and the fact she was wet and slippery, she slipped a little down his body, wrapped her legs around his waist and kicked his knees forward with her heels, causing Drake to fall to his knees with shock on the ground, half dropping her, before she slipped from his grasp and sprinted away.

It was his luck that she was laughing so hard about felling him that she lost her speed. He grabbed her again and, this time holding her back to his chest, he walked backwards. Their chests heaving with their laughter and the exertion of their private game.

"That's a nice trick, but you're going to wish you hadn't done that," Drake teased her.

Her skin was warm through her wet dress and the air around them started to crackle and heat. His breath was on her ear and she gave a little shiver when he playfully nipped at her neck.

"Hope I'm not interrupting anything?"

Drake stopped and looked up; Kathryn froze. She felt him take a frustrated breath. "Have I ever told you, you have the worst bloody timing of anyone I know, Reggie?"

Drake said standing tall. Kathryn tried to move away but he kept her locked to him.

"Not that I can remember." Reggie smirked back. The old man was incorrigible, and he bloody knew it.

"Why aren't you at home with your feet in a bucket of ice water? It's hot enough for it."

"It's definitely hot enough here, I can see." Reggie winked; cheekiness written all over his face.

Kathryn wriggled again, trying to loosen Drake's grip, but he held her tighter and whispered in her ear, "I'm not finished with you yet."

"That horse of mine is running a fever. I wanted to get some penicillin, but the vet in town is gone for the day. Useless bugger he is, anyway. Wouldn't know a sheep's ass from his own."

Laughing at Reggie, Drake asked "Is the wound weeping more than last night?"

"Looks like it. He's off his food and won't drink." Reggie sounded worried.

"I can come and have a look if you like," He could sense Reggie's distress and concern for the horse.

"No, it's okay." Reggie didn't look at them, instead, he took off his hat and beat it against his leg. "I just need the penicillin."

"How about I come and inject him for you, so that the old bugger doesn't play up on you and I can see for myself? It would put my mind at ease."

Reggie's eyes lit up. "Oh, only if you're worried. I'm not, if the old bugger dies, he dies." But that was just a cover. Drake knew that the old horse was Reggie's pride and joy and that he was very worried about him, but his pride wouldn't let him reveal that.

"Meet me at the shed. I'll change and we'll go over together, how does that sound?"

"Well yeah, okay." Reggie smiled at Kathryn, still locked tight within Drake's arms.

She smiled back. "Would you like a cold glass of cordial? I made it myself. It's great for days like this. You could have one while Drake changes."

The old man nodded his thanks and headed towards the back door; relief written all over his face.

Drake released Kathryn and, after turning off the hose, she followed him into the house. Reggie drank two glasses of her cordial and then asked if she could make a bottle for him. After promising she would, she excused herself to go find some dry clothes.

Kathryn had been gone a while, and he was ready to go. Setting the needle and penicillin on the bench as Reggie finished his third glass of Kathryn's cordial, Drake walked down the short hallway to her bedroom door and knocked just before he peered around the door. "I promise I won't be long. I will needle the horse and come straight back."

She was still in her wet dress.

"That's okay." She chewed her lower lip, then turned around, pulling her hair to the side. "Could you please undo my buttons? They're too wet for me to manage."

Smiling, Drake wiped his hands on his jeans and stepped into the room. One by one he fumbled to undo the tiny fabric buttons, eventually getting them opened.

The skin on her back was creamy and he couldn't help but touch it, tracing his fingers slowly up her spine from the last button to her neck. Her skin goosebumped at his touch, and she leaned back slightly. His fingers trailing back down the soft curve of her neck to where the dress sat on her shoulders, he pressed a soft kiss to the spot, feeling her jump with the touch. He continued the line of kisses up her neck to the little indentation below her ear.

"I will see you later and I *will* have my revenge," he whispered, a laugh in his voice. Then he backed away, leaving her standing there.

Holding her breathe, Kathryn didn't move until she heard the front screen door close and their footsteps heavy on the steps as they left. Releasing the air in her lungs, a warm shiver ran through her body at Drake's words and the images her mind created.

Kathryn sat and read to occupy herself, next to Sophie on the lounge chair until the sun was starting to dip behind the trees. Her stomach rumbled and she realised she was ravenous after all the games and laughter that afternoon.

Now familiar with the kitchen and feeling relaxed, she felt inspired to cook. Tonight, she decided to make steak and salad with a potato bake. It was the first decent meal she had cooked since her world had fallen apart. She'd been craving the comfort of potato bake but had no energy to prepare it. The laughter and fun with Drake that afternoon had changed that, and had also given her the answer she had been looking for.

His past was his. She wouldn't ask about it, she would just enjoy the time she had left here with him. She knew she couldn't stay, no matter how much she wanted to, she couldn't. It would put Drake and all he loved at risk. It didn't matter what Brigid had said — she would be gone before it mattered.

If it was the truth that is.

Opening the oven, she placed the potato bake in. The salad was already done and in the fridge. She would cook the steaks when Drake arrived.

Thud!

The sound made her jump. Something or someone was on the veranda, near her room. Instantly, her hands began to shake. Holding her hand to her chest and as quietly as she could, she edged to the back door and closed it, sliding the dead bolt silently into place. Then with as much inner self-talk as she could, to give her strength and courage, she moved to the front door. Her footsteps making no sound, she was about to shut it when Sophie came racing up the stairs, her fur up and her teeth bared. Kathryn didn't even look to see what or who was out there. She slammed the door shut and dead bolted it. Her heart was racing, fear rising.

They had found her.

Before her mind caught up, her feet raced her to her bedroom where she pulled her door closed then running into each room, she slammed windows and closed the doors. The last room was Drake's. She slammed the windows and pulled the door closed. Looking around for something to hold against the door, she saw his chair. It was a heavy thing and she had to try and lift it, so it didn't scrap across the floor. She placed the back of it under the doorknob, then opening Drake's cupboard, she climbed in and pulled the clothes in front of her as best she could. It was now dark; Drake had promised he wouldn't be long. She just had to hope he was on his way back now.

Kathryn could hear Sophie barking and growling, attacking whoever it was with such aggression. Her heart beating in her ears, Kathryn was shaking violently. The roaring of her fears and memories flooded back. She was drowning in it all, tears flowing as she tried to not scream or make any noise.

Nightmare memories came rushing back. Rob's hands were on her throat, his foot to her ribs, and then she was running. Her feet hurt as she tried to get away, but he had her. Her head ached, and she let out a scream of fear, the sound bringing her back to the moment. Biting her fist to try and control herself she tried to listen for Sophie. But she couldn't hear anything. Time froze as with each agonising second that ticked by, her heart ached for Drake to come and save her but also pounded in fear for both their safety if he did.

Trying her best to slow her breathing, she listened harder to who may be out there or where they now were. She heard a grunt. Like someone being hit, but it didn't sound like that either. Listening even harder, she couldn't hear anything.

The front door rattled and banged. "Kathryn ... Kathryn! Open the door. It's me, Drake."

She nearly cried out in relief but stopped. What if it wasn't Drake and she ran straight into their trap? She was too scared to move. Couldn't think straight above the impatient bashing at the door. Then it stopped. Nothing moved outside or in. Her breathing was all she could hear in her safe place as memories began to swamp her again. The only thing keeping her half in the here and now were Drake's clothes surrounded her. She could smell him on them, and they soothed her a little.

The bedroom door jiggled. Then nothing.

Her stomach rolled over.

They were in the house. They had found her. She was going to die. They would take her away and kill her, bury her body in a place where no one would find her. She was dead.

The door smashed open. The chair slid across the room with such force it hit Drake's bed. Kathryn stopped breathing, her head swimming. The cupboard door flew opened and then slammed shut.

They had not seen her.

Then the cupboard door slowly opened again, and the clothes moved apart.

"Kathryn?" Drake whispered. "Kathryn, it's me Drake, look at me. You're okay, I've got you."

She didn't want to open her eyes. If she did, she would see that her mind was playing tricks. The roaring in her ears sounded as if she was being crushed by wave after wave in the ocean. She was drowning.

His hand touched her shaking one, making her jump. Her eyes flying open she was ready to fight for her life. "Oh!" She flew out of the cupboard and into his arms.

Drake was squatting on the floor and her force knocked him flat on his back. He locked her to him, his heart racing as wildly in his chest as hers was. He struggled to sit up as she cried hysterically in his arms, her arms wrapping around his neck and gripping him for dear life. She was shaking and sobbing and gasping for air all at once.

Rolling to his side and picking her up, Drake carried her the two steps to his bed, sitting with her on his lap, he held her tight, cradling her. She knew he was trying to calm her down, but she couldn't get her hysteria to settle.

Drake held her for all he was worth. How could he get through to her to explain that he had returned to find the house dark and Sophie barking and growling near her bedroom. His first thought was that someone was inside the house with Kathryn. He had raced up the stairs ready to do battle, when Sophie dragged a long and angry snake by its tail down the stairs at him. It's head just missed him as it swung around to get whatever had it.

He had found a large piece of wood and hit it a number of times to kill it, using such force it had made him grunt. He had tried to get inside the house once the snake was dead, but all the doors and windows were shut and locked from the inside. He had tried to let her know it was him by calling out but now as he held her, he figured out what had happened.

"I thought ... I thought ..." was all she kept repeating.

He needed to reach her somehow, to break her out of her fear and shock. Sitting her on the bed, Drake kneeled in front of her and took both her hands in his one.

"Kathryn. Look at me." She just cried more. "Kathryn, look at me," he said in a gentle voice as he raised her chin, forcing her to finally look at him. Her eyes swollen and red, tears stained her cheeks.

"You're okay, you're safe." He wiped her falling tears away with the pads of his thumbs. "It was a snake. Sophie hates them and will kill them on occasion. Usually not that big, but she was protecting you. No one was here. You are safe here, remember."

She just stared at him, tears still streaming down her cheeks. He was worried about her; she didn't seem to understand what he was saying. A state of shock maybe, but he had never seen anyone this bad with shock before.

"Would you like a glass of water?" He started to rise, but she reached out and pulled him to her.

"No. Just hold me and never let go."

Her words cut him deeply as he scooped her up and laid her on his bed, then stretched out beside her. Her arms locking around his neck to hold him as close to her as possible, she pressed her body to the length of his, in the dim light from the lounge room, now the only light on in the house. He pulled the blanket over her to help with her shaking and to stop her slipping into more shock.

Lying there, Drake held her tight until she finally drifted off to sleep against his heart.

Chapter 17

Later that night, after Drake had cleaned up the mess of his broken door, he ate quietly at the table. He had seated himself so that he could watch Kathryn sleep.

Her potato bake was amazing. She was a good chef and would easily find a job wherever she went. He knew the day was coming closer. She was healed. All they were waiting on was a message from Scott that everyone believed she was dead — then she was free to go find herself a new life. She had to. It was for the best. He couldn't be what she needed. Having once before failed to protect those he had loved, he couldn't possibly risk failing Kathryn.

He also knew what he was — a monster — whose control was starting to thin quickly, especially around her. Reining it back was becoming harder and harder. He would give it another week before he contacted Scott to find out what was going on — one more week, that was all.

Movement in his room had him refocusing. Kathryn had sat up and was looking at him, her dark eyes on his. Nothing moved and no one spoke. But her pull on him drew him up and moved his feet to her.

When he stood at the side of the bed, she reached up to him and, one knee on the bed, his arms around her, he fell with her back onto the bed. Side by side, they lay staring at each other, breathing each other's air.

Nothing in the world mattered. The world was only them and this moment. Kathryn placed her hand on his face, her thumb moved across his stubbled jaw, scratching her thumb. When her hand moved to his lips, eyes still locked with his, Drake kissed the palm of her hand and felt a thrill of excitement race through her.

Her eyes were a dark, liquid chocolate, so focussed on his with such intensity it sent his heart quaking. Twining her fingers in his thick hair, she pressed her body to his, and brushed her lips across his once, twice. He hesitated for half a heartbeat, she pulled him to her, opening his mouth and tasting him with her tongue. Rolling her tongue across his teeth, drugging him with desire for her.

He kissed her back. Slowly at first, until the ambers that had been sitting, waiting over the last weeks between them sparked and started to burn.

Drake couldn't pull his mouth from hers; she was earthy and salty and everything he had ever wanted. He needed more, more of the taste of her, more of her body pressed against his. Pushing up on his elbow, never breaking the kiss, he rolled her onto her back, his hand cupping her jaw so he could kiss her deeper.

Mixing heated passion with tenderness, their mouths continued dancing with suckles, licks and nips. Her body was heating, and fevered shivers were running through her, vibrating to him and creating his own body to respond with primal need. A growl thundered in his chest and escaped out of his mouth, pouring into her, as he hungrily feasted on her lips. Her body rose and pressed hard against his, her hand found his shirt and pulled it up his back to tell him that she wanted it off, and he broke the kiss. They were both beathing hard.

He kissed the top of her nose. "What do you want?" he asked. His voice sounded husky and gravelly.

Smiling seductively, Kathryn pulled at his shirt again. "This off, and now," she demanded. He liked the orders she gave and responded by giving her one of his crooked smiles, while sitting up just enough and pulled his shirt over his head, returning to his spot against her. Ready for his next order.

Kathryn's hands glided over his back and shoulders. Her nails digging into him; staggered his breathing as a shiver rippled over his body causing his eyes to close and his mouth to claim her needllingly. She moaned back with pleasure.

Drake left her mouth and trailed a line of kisses to her ear, where he sucked and gently bit on her soft lobe. The sensation gave her goosebumps and made her gasp, fuelling his line of pleasure and sin to brand down her throat to her collar bone and then between her breasts, as far as he could with her dress on. She pushed her chest up to feel more, as his hand pulled on the top of her dress in the same way she had let him know she wanted his shirt off.

She nodded and begged, "Please."

Gathering the dress in his hand, he pulled it up and over her head in one swift move, her hair falling around her when she fell back against his pillow. She was simply stunning. He had seen pretty girls, but nothing could compare to the perfection of Kathryn lying like she was now. Her lips swollen and wet from him, her silky soft hair fallen around her on his pillow and her creamy skin glowing and heated lying on his bed. Breathing seemed a challenge.

She was here and she was his in this moment. Desire knifed through him, and he wanted her with everything he had, even if it meant his life, he had to have her and now.

Pushing away every bit of screaming in his mind as to why he shouldn't be doing this, Drake kissed her again, somehow even more hungrily and passionate than before.

Kathryn was struggling to keep up with Drake's renewed need for her. His hands were in her hair keeping her still as his lips moved to her breasts. He ran his tongue along the lace of her bra and then playfully bit and pulled at the top of it, first one side then the other. Her nipples were becoming tender against the roughness of the lace. She tried to reach around her back to unclip the bra, but he wouldn't let her. Instead, finding her nipple, he began to suckle it through the lace. The sensation made her buck in sheer pleasure and moan from her throat loudly.

Her hands found his head and pulled him to her body for more. Pleasures she had dreamed of experiencing were streaking through her body and settling low like a coil that started to tighten. When she thought she could take no more, that he might suck her nipple completely through her bra, he changed sides and repeated the action.

Driving her near insane with pleasure, her nails dug into his skull. Causing him to groan and feast harder on her body. Pleasure and pain mixed together in extremes as tension of need built quickly, causing her to move and grind her body against his, trying to seek release. She pushed at his chest hard, making him roll onto his back. She followed and climbed onto him.

"My turn." She kissed him deeply while positioning herself over his bulging manhood, which was straining so hard against his jeans it felt like a rock between her thighs. Rubbing herself against it gave her some relief but was agony too.

He grabbed her hips and stopped her torturous sexual movements. "If you keep doing that, this night will end very fast."

Smiling at him with sin, Kathryn lowered her head and playfully bit each of his nipples, grinding them between her teeth until she heard him hiss. Proud of herself, she continued to tenderly bite, first his ribs and then his stomach, her body pressed to his, she glided her wet lace bra over his skin, giving him the same goosebumps he had given her.

Her nipples were tender, but the sensation kept the pleasure building low. Giving a last bite just below his belly button, she looked up to find him watching her, his green eyes filled with wanting and curiosity. His hand stroked her hair.

Sending him another smile, she concentrated on undoing his jeans. First the belt buckle and jeans button, then slowly the zipper. Their eyes locked together the whole time, her heart racing with excitement and wanting. He was letting her do anything she pleased and the power that brought, filled her with confidence.

Sliding down further, she slipped off the bed and grabbing the bottom leg of his jeans, she removed them and stared down the bed at him. She was in only her lace underwear, but the way he stared back at her, she felt totally naked and exposed in an erotic way.

Drake didn't move. His chest rising and falling more rapidly than before was the only sign he was as affected by her, as she was with him. She saw him swallow and take a deep, steadying breath. Just as she was thinking she would burn to ashes if he looked any harder at her body, he sat up and came to his knees on the bed, his hand stretched out to her. Taking it, she allowed him to pull her onto the bed and to fall back on top of him. He kissed her back into submission, slowly exploring her mouth as his hands roamed all over her silken skin.

With a sleek move, he rolled her over onto her back, his body still pressed to hers now nestled between her thighs, he continued his roaming. His hand found her calf and slowly he trailed his hand up and over her knee to her thigh and higher still. It skittered around to massage her bottom then hip, then higher still to her breast.

Her moans and sighs of pleasure fuelled Drake on. His mouth found her nipple again, and he fanned the flames to near combustion. Arching her back and grabbing at his head, her finger nails skimming through his thick hair, and when he finally reached around and freed her from her bra, she threw it across the room with a tortured release of frustration at the innate object and hungrily kissed him.

Finding the line of her underwear, he butterfly-touched his way along the lace line, then grabbed, squeezing her sensitive spot, he made her cry out on a gasp and lift her hips.

Sliding his body down and over hers, kissing first each nipple then her belly button and still down further he went. When he got to her underwear, he took it between his teeth and pulled them down. A nervous little giggle escaped through her kiss swollen lips as Kathryn raised her hips and allowed her lace nickers to slide down her legs, where Drake finished their descent from her body with his hand.

Gazing back up her body, with eyes the colour of heated emerald glass, a rush of embarrassment took over her and she covered herself with her hand. Feeling fully exposed and vulnerable having him look at her from that angle, she sat up and went to explain, she'd never had anyone's face down there before. But before she could get a word out, her cheeks felt like they were on fire, Drake rose up onto his hands and knees, meeting her halfway and kissed her, stealing her words from her mouth until she relaxed: he laid her back down. He was holding himself above her, their foreheads nearly touching.

"I won't do anything that you don't want me to or that will hurt you." He kissed the tip of her nose as she nodded. Her heart beating a little different with a rush of excitement and nerves and a feeling that he had just stripped away more than her underwear. His hands finding her outer thigh, he distracted her from her thoughts and watched her as she stared back at him. His rough, calloused hand circled and then slid up her inner thigh, the sensation making her moan as he found her curls.

Gripping, rubbing and sliding his hand over her, alternating between hard and soft, rough and tender, he kissed her until she was a moaning melting mess against his lips then he slid one finger inside. She was hot and slick.

They both moaned.

She tightened around his finger as he moved it inside of her. Her body relaxed and she opened her legs a little more for him. He inserted another finger into her. She was so tight that was all she could take as she gasped and arched back. Swallowing her cries with a soul stealing kiss, Drake continued to build the tension in her body.

She was rising to the peak too fast. She pulled back on a gasp and shook her head, confused at all he was doing, wanting more but not wanting to go over the peak just yet. The coolness that touched her lips as they parted from each other gave Kathryn just a second of reprieve, before Drake's tender voice drew her eyes open.

"Do you trust me, Kathryn?"

Not sure of the question in her passion-hazed mind, she frowned. Did she trust him? Her heart beating rapidly, her breathing heavy, she knew the answer. "With my life," she whispered. He was taken back by the words, she could see it on his face, but not for long.

Wriggling himself back down her body, he spread her legs wider apart. Her hands flew down to cover herself again. Drake gave a small chuckle and kissed them slowly as his hands removed each finger, one by one.

When he had lifted them enough, he licked her. She backed up the bed and away. Drake had barely enough time to grab her hips and lock her to his bed, he held her tight and this time dove straight in. His hot mouth licked and kissed and suckled her as she cried out in pleasure and ecstasy. Her mind filled with only the need for him to keep doing what he was doing and for him to never stop. Her hands, now free, slid into his hair and gripped, holding him to her, pleading and demanding for more. She raised her hips to his mouth and spread her legs wider so he could feast deeper into her dripping body.

"Drake please, come to me" she pleaded with him, but he didn't stop, just shook his head and continued to feast on her harder and harder, drawing her clit into his mouth, flicking and sucking it just like he had done to her nipples through her lace bra.

She was so close; he could taste it. He couldn't take much more himself. As it was, he was fighting his own restraint with as much grit and determination as he could. He had never hungered for any other woman like he hungered for Kathryn, and he didn't want this to end but knew he was not going to last long once he entered her. Pulling back, he removed the last of his clothes with shaky hands and ragged breath. He watched her floating on his bed, in the ecstasy he had just given her. Primal need pulsated through him. He climbed over her.

Kathryn kissed him, he could taste her again on his lips as she tasted herself on his mouth and it made her even more ravenous for him.

His manhood was at her entrance. He gently pushed into her and then slid out. She cried out in protest. He lifted his head just above hers. "Are you sure?" he asked hoarsely. Barely restrained, he was on the brink of explosion and complete desperation for her.

"Yes," she begged, "now."

He didn't need any more encouragement, he ploughed into the depth of her scalding wetness. She was so tight, he nearly lost himself immediately. He paused to allow her to adjust to his size and for him to gather the last of his restraint. She was chewing her bottom lip and holding her breath as her body tensed with his thickness and length.

"Just breathe, Kathryn. I won't hurt you. Do you trust me?" She nodded, and he kissed her deeply until she relaxed. Gradually, he withdrew from her body just a little and then drove back into her, burying himself completely inside of her. She took him all in with a throaty cry and when she relaxed again, he began to move. She wrapped her legs around his hips and forced himself further into her sweet body with each solid thrust of his hips.

It was heaven and they raced up the mountain to be together. He was close and pushed harder as she clawed at his arms and cried out his name. Her head thrashing from side to side, her breath gasping with small cries between her throaty cries of pleasure, filled his room and drove him on and into her until, on a last cry, she grabbed him and pulled him to her lips and cried her pleasure into his body as he groaned the same into hers. Their bodies rocking and lifting, holding and locking together with sheer pleasure and release.

Drake didn't move from his place on top of Kathryn's sated body. She had wrapped him to her and now her arms were lazily around his neck, her finger nails circling little pieces of hair as they both floated back to earth. He was shaking. He had just experienced something he couldn't describe. All he knew was that he was still off-balance and fighting to find solid ground as he floated back down. Knowing that when he finally did hit solid ground, nothing would ever be the same again.

Taking a deep breath and forcing himself to move off her, Drake rolled from the safety of her warm body and positioned himself so that her back was pressed up against his chest. His arm over her, he cradled one of her breasts. She slipped into sleep, her breathing smooth and rhythmic. Everything about her surrounded him as he, too, slipped into a deep sleep holding her to him.

Chapter 18

*"**D**rake! You know I will find you. If you don't come back now, I will take her from you. You know I will, and you can't save her. You're just like me, you know that. Come back here now so we can sort out this little problem we have... Drake!"*

Drake sat up, his heart beating wildly against his ribs. The bed was wet and for a moment he thought he had pissed himself. He kicked back the blanket and let the coolness of the night wash over his naked skin.

It was only a nightmare. He rested his arm across his eyes, his heart was still beating madly, and focused on his breathing. IN. OUT. IN. OUT.

That voice still had the power to shake him and take him back to that horrifying night. To a split-second time in his life when nothing would ever be the same again and he was powerless to save them both.

A warm body beside him stirred and rolled over, draping her arm across his chest before snuggling closely to his body for warmth. She made a small snuffling sound as she drifted back into a deeper slumber.

"You're just like me, you know that. You can't save her." With that voice ringing in his ears and memory, Drake dislodged himself from the beautiful woman sleeping next to him and got out of bed. It was not yet dawn, but the sun was about to rise. Another day was about to dawn and here he stood, butt naked as the day he was born, shaking and sweating with a deeply pitted pain low in his chest growing and taking hold. He padded silently to the bathroom to shower.

He could smell Kathryn's scent all over his body and that only made the pain worse. He had betrayed himself and her. Sleeping with her was a big mistake. He knew it, and yet he couldn't stop himself. He had needed her like air last night. Needed her for his life and breath. He needed her now with every fibre of his being.

Shaking his head, he turned on the cold water, wanting to be shocked into the real world and not the one he was allowing himself to imagine with Kathryn. The thought of waking with her naked beside him every day for the rest of his life had passed through his mind more times than he wanted to acknowledge.

Her kisses and touches through the day and the lovemaking all night long had started to take root in his thoughts. If that wasn't proof enough, his need for her was physically evident all day and night too. He wanted Kathryn. But he couldn't have her. Someone like him didn't deserve a person as beautiful as she was.

The lust he had just a moment ago turned into anger and hatred for who he really was. He couldn't be what she wanted, and what they had shared last night had been wrong. No matter how much they had both wanted it, it was not right. He was a monster and that was not going to change. She needed to leave and soon, very soon.

His emotions were raw, and his temper was starting to boil. He didn't know how much longer before the real him came to the surface and he lashed out at her. He was twice her size — she'd never stand a chance against him. She would end up where the other two lay in the city, and he would be left rotting where he had fought so hard never to be. It was safer that she left.

For a time yesterday he had wanted his life to be more, to be a different person. Maybe the person she thought she saw, but the reality was, he wasn't. He was who he was — and now he needed her to leave.

Kathryn groaned as she untangled the sheets from her body. Annabelle had told her many things about what she and Johnny got up to and Kathryn had fantasised about Drake doing them to her, but the reality was very different to anything she had dreamt up.

Drake had touched her and done things to her body that she could never have thought of. He had licked her in places that she'd read about and wanted to try, but when he did, she had nearly come all over his face. The thought had her blushing. How could she look at him this morning knowing where those lips had been last night?

Annabelle said that men loved doing this for their woman. Did Drake like doing it? Importantly, did he like doing it to her? Did she taste good? Hopefully she didn't smell bad. That thought made her eyes open wide. She would never be able to look at him again if he didn't like it or she had smelled horrible.

Oh, but the thought of his naked body against hers and the cries he had wrung from her lips started to warm her skin. He was skilled and gentle in his love making. He must have had many women. *No Kathryn, don't ever go there. He is with you and you're here with him. Nothing in the past matters,* she sternly told herself.

But she wasn't here with him, at least not forever. Maybe only a few more days now and she would have to leave. She would be forever on her own — would never be able to call herself his, to feel his arms around her, to feel the pulse of him buried deep inside her body. She would only have her memories of what it was like to have been held and made love to by Drake Harrison.

A nickering of a horse outside drew her attention from the sombre thoughts rolling in her head. Drake was not beside her. The wind carried his voice through the bedroom window above her head. Standing on the bed, the sheet tucked around her body like the Queen of the Nile, she watched through the window as he led a light-coloured horse in a circle with a long lead. He was talking to it in a reassuring and calming voice. It seemed a little nervous and kept looking around and even kicked out at him once, but he never wavered in his calming approach.

It was as if he wanted the horse to trust him, to see that he was no threat. That the animal, no matter how scared or nervous it was, would understand that Drake was in control, and it could fully trust him. It was safe with him.

Kathryn watched, mesmerised, as around and around he went with the horse. He would change direction every so often and the animal was visibly becoming more and more relaxed. Drake continued for another quarter of an hour before he stopped and called the horse to come to where he was standing in the middle of the ring.

It tossed its head around and snorted at him, refusing his order, but he was patient and eventually the horse gave in and step by step walked to the centre where he was waiting, to then be rewarded by a pat and rub over its long nose and ears. Drake continued holding his hand on its nose as his other hand moved over its neck and shoulders.

She could hear him talking to the large, solidly muscled animal constantly. It pawed at the ground with its black front foot and tried to shake his hand away from its nose, but he remained firm with it, soothing it until he was ready to finish the pat.

When he was finished, he picked up the lead and walked to the gate in the ring. To Kathryn's surprise, the horse followed Drake. It didn't seem to want to but was somehow drawn to do so. Hearing the gate close she was about to hop off the bed, when she saw Drake come back into the ring. He had nothing in his hands and with a quick step to the right, he moved.

The horse shied for a moment and looked at him. He moved again, this time not so quickly, and called to the horse. It came over to him and this time he moved away. It followed. Kathryn couldn't understand what was going on. Drake would run and then the horse would follow or turn and kick up its heels and trot around the yard, throwing its head around. He would move and call after it and the horse would stop and either repeat what it was doing or come to him. It looked like an odd game of tag and the horse seemed to love it. She even heard Drake laugh out loud when he nearly lost his footing and almost stumbled face-first into the sand in the ring, saved only by putting his hands out.

The sound stopped the horse and made Drake not move, but wait for the horse to respond. He was kneeling with one knee on the sand, the other poised in position to stand. He talked and called to the horse and eventually it came close enough to touch his hat. Drake reached up slowly and rubbed its chin then over its nose. The horse snorted and stepped back, allowing him up. He gave it a pat and a hug, his arms going around the horse's entire neck, the mane tickling Drake's face. The game was now over, having lasted for no more than a few minutes, but it was beautiful.

Kathryn couldn't take her eyes from him. Drake was sexy as hell, but he was so much more than that. He was kind and gentle, even though he was large and strong. His instincts of patience and understanding for the animal's nerves and fear was truly beautiful to watch. He was so self-assured in his ability to help the horse overcome its fear, that it gave him an aura of confidence that she had not seen.

He seemed to even understand what Kathryn wanted and needed without asking most of the time, and he knew the right time when she needed to be held and how to hold her. He had no idea that she was watching him and was his true self when he was with the horses — the man she always knew him to be.

A warm feeling flowed over and through her, giving her goosebumps. Stepping off the bed, Kathryn headed for a shower and some food. Wanting to be outside and in the sunshine had her hastening her steps. It was a new day, and it had a magical calling to her; she needed to touch it and breathe it all in.

Showering quickly, then gulping down a coffee and toast, she found that Drake had ridden out on a different horse. She'd missed telling him of her plans to go exploring. Disappointed, she called Sophie, but the dog refused to come. So, she was left alone to happily explore this place that made Drake so happy.

Setting out, Kathryn followed the path that Drake seemed to always take when he rode out on one of the horses. It was lined with fences and horses of all colours and sizes for the first bit then, after climbing over a metal gate, it stretched out before her into a large wide-open space of nothing but grass, which moved like a rolling wave in the wind, the rippling grass-heads flowing up and around the hill in front of her.

Seeing no clear path, Kathryn walked through the grass, her hand touching the softness and sharpness of it, the sensation tickling her palm. The complete silence of nothing but nature surrounding her filled her with such a sense of peace that she laughed out loud and gave a skip and twirl in the air. It was amazing to be out here. The sun on her skin, the heat of the day and the grass at her feet. She felt free and totally alive for the first time in her life.

The climb to the top of the nearby hill was steeper than she had first thought. Her ribs were tender from her exhaustion the night before and they pulled at her side now as she made her way up to the peak. After finding a rough track just near the top that made the last bit a little easier, she discovered a hidden tree oasis. Standing on a large rock she could see everything that surrounded the hill in a full circle. She could see Drake's farm shed and house. The horses looked like large rocks in the middle of each paddock.

She could see the road and entry to the farm. Still turning, she peered down at a large herd of cattle grazing and, behind her, in the very far distance, she discerned what looked like another house and sheds. Turning to fully complete her circle she noticed the creek lined with trees. It looked inviting, so she made a path directly for it.

The creek was lined with bottlebrushes and gum trees. The chatter of rainbow lorikeets and other birds eating the flowers from high above made Kathryn look up and watch.

In the city she used to sit and watch the birds in the park going about their day, eating and socialising with each other. As a form of entertainment, she would often make up the conversation they were having between them. Today though, the birds added to the excitement and fun of exploring this world she was now in.

The creek flowed over rocks and fallen branches, gushing and gurgling like a waterfall. The air was cooler here than out in the open with the grass. Finding a barely visible path, she continued along the water's edge. The water was clear, and tiny fish were swimming in and around the rocks. It was beautiful here.

The creek rounded a corner and the tranquil spot that opened before her was enticing. Bottlebrushes hung over the water, touching their leaves to the surface. Birds and bees were busy flittering about, the hum of their movements made her smile. The fragrance of the flowers drifted around her, and on finding a rock that looked easy to sit on, she sat and took her boots off, poking her toes into the cool water.

This was pure joy: just her and nature and the beauty of this world. Nothing in the city compared to this. There was always the grumble of the traffic intruding on the sounds of nature, the air always had a taint of acid to it and the birds were always busy compared to the ones here. Here they seemed to just do their thing and play.

A couple of afternoons ago, while sitting with Sophie on the front steps, she had watched a number of pink galahs playing on the power lines. They'd flown in and started nosily chattering to each other. Then one had flopped over and hung upside down for a time, still conversing with its friends, then flapping its wings, righted itself back on the line to the others' loud screeching and bobbing of their heads. Kathryn had smiled as she watched their game, they truly were the clowns of the bird world, and they didn't seem to care about it. They were simply enjoying life to the fullest.

The water was so cool and inviting against the building heat of the day. Looking around her to make sure no one was around, Kathryn slipped out of her clothes and into the water. The briskness chilled her skin, but the exoticness of swimming naked where anyone could find her filled her with excitement — and a wild hope that Drake would be the one who would find her and join in.

After a long time of swimming and floating on her back, she climbed out and got dressed. The sun was making its way towards the west, which meant it was mid-to late afternoon. She'd been gone nearly all day and the water and snacks in her pack were almost depleted. Retracing her steps back along her track, she found a spot where she could use the rocks as stepping stones to cross and, if she had remembered right, she should come out onto the road that led right back to Drake's house. It shouldn't take too long.

She couldn't wait to tell him all about her day and her find. He probably already knew about the creek oasis, but she would tell him anyway. With her clothes wet against her skin, the heat of the afternoon warming her and the exhilaration of the day filling her, she smiled and laughed to herself. At this exact moment in her life, everything was perfect, and she was where she wanted to be.

Chapter 19

Drake got back late after lunch from his ride to Reggie's — whose old horse was much better today, and the cut had stopped oozing. It looked as though the old bugger was going to live on and annoy Reggie some more. Reggie had even shed a tear of happiness when Drake had confirmed it.

Drake had ridden over on one of the horses that was going to be picked up in a few days. This mob of horses had all come from the same property, where they had been confiscated from by the authorities. They had apparently been skin and bone when taken, but they were happy and healthy and full of energy when they had arrived at his farm.

Two had managed to put his butt to the ground, but that was it. The horses had mainly been handled well by their original owner. There were no signs of abuse or mistreatment, so he guessed their owner simply had too many horses and couldn't afford to feed them, which was why they had been taken.

No mistreatment meant he had been able to break them in easier without the horses being worried or fearful. Now, when they returned to the animal welfare authorities in the city they could be sold as beginner horses for children to learn to ride on. This was what he loved the most. The horses got a second chance to be something new and gain a fresh life. Something he never could have, so he worked hard to make sure they did.

As he was unsaddling the paint gelding, Sophie wandered over to him. She had not ventured far from the house since Kathryn had been here, but here she was on her way to see him.

Reaching him, she flopped over onto her back, a sad look in her eyes. "What's up, girl?" He bent down and rubbed her belly "Is Kathryn sleeping and you got left outside?" Drake finished rubbing her belly and, grabbing a brush from the bucket nailed to a timber post, started to brush the horse down.

On the ride back, he'd decided that for Kathryn's safety he would take her to the Country Comfort Motel in town, and also follow up with Scott to see what was happening. He would visit her daily to make sure she was safe and had everything she needed for when they got the word, but her time here was over. She couldn't stay.

His temper and frustration had been simmering just under the surface all morning, caused by his actions last night and at himself for who he truly was. Kathryn would be upset, but it was for her own good. He would try to explain, but she would go. He would make sure of it.

Kathryn was not in the house when Drake went in for a very late lunch. What he was preparing himself to do was causing pain in his chest and churning his guts. Wanting to get it over with, his agitation rose at her absence.

After checking her room and his, slamming doors as he did, he went back outside to see if she was there. Nothing. She had left no note, her clothes were still in her room, and she was nowhere to be seen. He called out her name and waited for a reply.

Nothing.

"You can't protect her," the voice echoed through his head and punched a cold chill through his body. Had they found her while he had been away? He'd thought she was safe here, that no one would know where she was. In some far distant part of his mind, he'd been hoping the drug gang would have accepted the media news of her death and lost all interest in trying to recover what Rob had taken from them.

Mind racing with thoughts he never wanted to think, Drake blindly raced through the stables to do another quick check for her before he jogged to the paddocks and other sheds to ensure she was not there before he looked elsewhere or called Richard. Panic was frothing and bubbling below his agitation. His mind filled with images he tried to keep at bay as he searched. His emotions were surging.

Drake was jogging back towards the other side of the stable doors, heading for his Ute, when Sophie whined and barked, bolting off ahead of him.

"Hey, girl." Kathryn rounded the corner of the stables as Sophie did: they nearly collided. She bent and patted her friend on the head. "You missed a great walk."

"Walk!" Drake roared from deep in the stable.

Kathryn jumped. Her eyes not yet adjusted to the dimness of the shed, she put her hand on her brow, and stopped where she was when she saw him.

He glared at her. "Walk? You went for a bloody walk and never thought to leave me a freaking note? For Christ's sake, Kathryn!" Furious, Drake paced the floor, his hand raking through his hair and over his face.

Looking uncertain, Kathryn moved towards him.

He turned and violently kicked a bale of hay sitting on the floor next to one of the stall doors. Bits of hay scattered everywhere. "I was so bloody worried about you. I thought something had happened and those monsters had taken you! But you decided to go for a walk. Don't you understand, I can't keep you safe if you're not here." His temper was climbing and volatility mixing with frustration and relief. Of the fear that had clenched his stomach from the minute he had discovered she was not in the house.

"I'm sorry. I needed a walk. I'm here now," she said placidly, trying to soothe him. She'd stopped coming towards him when he'd kicked the hay bale and growled savagely, unsure of his temper, she stood still.

"Here now?" He was shaking as rage ripped through his body. His intense gaze locked on her eyes. She looked at him confused, and a little lost. He stormed towards her like a bird of prey, she took an involuntary step back but stopped. He should stop, but he didn't. The mix of roaring pain that was slicing through him, drove him forward.

He came onto her before she realised what was going on, her eyes wide as his hands painfully ploughed through her damp hair, his lips crushing onto hers and stealing her breath away. She grabbed at his arms to keep her balance as his forceful momentum pushed her backwards until her back slammed into the wall of the stables, half knocking the wind from her.

He pressed her harder against the wall, his lips crushing hers, taking what little breath she had left. He felt her heart slamming against his chest, felt her struggling against his body that was crushing her to the timber at her back, but he couldn't pull himself away. She was here, she was safe, he hadn't failed her but his anger and fright poured into and dominated his kiss. He needed to know she was real and safe, that she was actually there.

He felt Kathryn digging her nails into his shirt and muscles telling him to pull away, but his mind didn't register, until, freeing her arm and raising her hand, she slapped him hard across the back of the head. He pulled back and let her go. Kathryn dropped to the floor, clasping her chest, tears falling from her eyes.

Drake stood back. He was so overcome with relief when Kathryn walked around the corner that all he wanted was her — to hold her, to feel her pressed up against him, to know that she was safe and in his arms.

But what had he done? He stared down, dazed, at her on the floor of the stables, holding her hand to her chest, tears rolling down her cheeks as she shook with fright, gasping for air. He had done this to her. His body began to tremble, but he locked it down.

Kneeling down in front of her curled up trembling body, he reached for her. She pulled away, recoiling from him. She wasn't ready for him, she needed to get her breathing back and her heart to settle.

"I'm so sorry, Kathryn," he whispered. "Are you okay?"

She shook her head, and a fresh flow of tears spilled over onto her cheeks.

His heart felt like it was dying very slowly, very painfully. Shame and devastation flooded him; he never meant to hurt her. "I'm so sorry.

I ... I ... don't know what came over me." He put his face in his hands, struggling with the churning of his emotions. A soft touch came on his knee and when he looked up, Kathryn mutely held her hands out to him, her eyes filled with pain too.

He tenderly lifted her into his arms and carried her to the house, her head on his shoulder, her tears flowing and wetting his shirt. He whispered apologies and reassurances with every step he took, but still her tears fell and soaked his shirt more. The sensation of the salted wetness slicing into his body tearing him up inside at what he had done.

Drake took the steps two at a time and kicked the door open with his boot, never slowing his stride, he walked directly to her room and sat her on the bed. She was trembling, but the tears had now stopped.

"I'm sorry, Kathryn. I never ever wanted to hurt you." He kissed the top of her head, ready to leave the house and never come near her again, but Kathryn gripped his hand, sensing his intention and pulled him down to squat in front of her.

"Drake. Don't leave me. Not yet." She rested her forehead against his.

He took an unsteady breath and allowed her to take the time she needed. His thoughts were still on that door. He would get Reggie to come and get her and he would never see her again. He couldn't. His actions had just proven that — he could have seriously hurt her with his desire and temper. It had broken free, and now he had to get it back and never let it out around anyone again. He needed to stay solitary and away from others, especially Kathryn.

Chapter 20

Kathryn could feel Drake shaking, even though he tried to hide it. His body hummed with anger and regret at what had happened between them in the stables. He needed to be held as much as she did, but he wasn't going to allow it. If she didn't break through now, she may never get to understand this depth to him that she had just witnessed.

He needed her like she needed him. Sitting up, she took a deep, shaky breath. Drake looked up into her eyes, his emerald ones holding such sadness and despair in them that her heart shattered into a million pieces.

Cupping his unshaven jaw with a trembling hand, she kissed him, tenderly at first, barely a touch. She waited for him to move, but his body was locked in place. Leaning in, she kissed him again, moving her lips over his. His breathing fractured a little and he relaxed just enough for her to slip her tongue into his mouth.

Her hands slid into his hair, she held him to her when he tried to pull away, she wanted him to be as close to her as possible, she needed it as much as she knew he did. Drake tried to pull away gently, but her kisses and hands in his hair made it impossible. She could feel her kisses were starting to heat him, no matter how hard he tried to fight it, she continued to draw him to her. She would make him want her; need her.

"Come to me," she purred against his mouth, drawing him along with her as she moved backwards up the bed so Drake could do nothing but follow. At this moment, she wanted him to follow her to the end of the earth if she asked it.

The end of the bed creaked under his weight as he crawled up and over her where she led him. Kathryn kissed him, wrapping her legs over his hips to stop him from moving anywhere but on top of her. His weight giving her the security she craved.

The kisses eventually started to burn between them. Her fingers found the buttons on his shirt before her hands slipped in and across his chest. His heart pounded wildly against his ribs and his skin was warm and sweaty from his work and the heat of the afternoon.

Feathering her fingers across him, she could feel him tensing with control. He was fully aroused; his manhood pressed intimately against her through his jeans, but he was holding himself back. Locked tight and ridged with control. Tightening her legs in a strong grip she rubbed herself against him. The friction of his hardened jeans chafing against her lace underwear sent chills and shivers all over her body, teasing sounds of pleasure from the back of her throat.

Her moans fired Drake up his hand found her breast and he teased the nipple until she pulled away and moaned. Bucking him onto his back she followed him straddling his thighs unbuckling his jeans, she slid them down, baring him to his knees. Drake's hands were by his sides as he allowed her to do as she wished.

"You will not move your hands. No matter what. Do you hear me?" she ordered. Drake nodded as she intimately stroked him, he pulsated and grew in her hand, moaning as she circled and played with the tip of him with her thumb. His hissing and loud breathing made her smile at the power she had over him.

Being with Drake made her feel stronger and that she could do and be anything she ever wanted. She couldn't fall when he was around, because he would aways catch her. Revelling in that power, Kathryn wanted to taste him, all of him, and she moved down to take him into her mouth.

Drake moved away from her quickly. "No … No. I don't want you to do that. You're never ever to do that. It's not right that any woman be made to do that." He rolled off the bed and zipped up his jeans.

"But I wanted to!" Kathryn jumped off the bed and darted in front, stopping him from going any further. She placed her hands on her hips, standing her ground, he was not leaving this room until she was ready.

"I want you. I want what happened last night. Don't go." She reached out and took his hands from where they were stiffly held by the sides of his body and put them onto her hips. Her hands covering his, Kathryn turned Drake around, stepping backwards to the bed only stopping when she felt the mattress against her legs. Their eyes locked together as his jaw remained tight, seemingly fighting himself.

Eventually losing the internal battle and lowering his head, he hungrily claimed her lips, her throat, all of her. He stripped her clothes from her body and tossed them to the ground along with his shirt, his jeans circled his ankles, stopped by his boots.

Not letting her fall to the bed, Drake picked her up, wrapping her legs around his hips, Kathyrn clung to him as he shuffled her to the wall. Bracing her there with his body, he feasted on her nipples as his fingers slid into her heated wetness. The power had changed, and he took it all. He was consuming her, and she let him. Every inch of her body exploded with sensation as he explored, kissing, licking, biting and touching.

His hands seemed to be everywhere and nowhere but inside her. She was spiralling upwards fast, failing to keep up with his devouring need to consume her.

"Drake please ... please," she begged into his hair as she dug her nails into him. Bracing himself, he lifted her higher, then guided himself deep into her body. Her tightness closed around him, gripping his length, and he frowned in concentration, trying not to lose himself.

She gasped and clenched her walls tighter, making him even harder and he paused to let her adjust and lock his jaw tight, but she shook her head and moved more, trying to take him in all the way, all at once.

Buried deep inside her, groaning, Kathryn could feel Drake pulsating in time with her body. Their bodies locked together as they held onto each other, yearning for more from the other than they could get but taking everything each other had.

She was losing herself to Drake — she could feel it in her body, in her soul and, at that very moment as she sat with him buried so deeply inside her, their heated wet bodies joined together, breathing heavy and ragged, she knew she was losing her whole heart to him.

A part was given years ago but now as he started to move heaven and earth inside her, lifting her body with ease and then thrusting hard and deep, making her cry out with ecstasy, she knew her whole heart now belonged to him.

He drove her hard and fast and when they both came crashing over the peak in a mix of rough words and cries, she held him and let him fill her. She cradled him to her chest when he fell to the floor on his knees, her body still wrapped around him. He was still buried inside of her, yet he did not let her go.

Drake lifted her onto the bed, then removed his boots and jeans. Taking her against the wall was a surprise, perhaps not something he had intended, but he was looking at her with such lust in his emerald eyes that she shivered. He wanted her again already.

She was half dazed from their passion, but taking her nipple into his mouth, he re-aroused her.

It was nearly dark when Kathryn padded back to the bed from her shower. They had spent the afternoon in each other's arms. The pleasures and love he had given her made her legs shaky to walk on.

He had promised her that by the time he was finished she would not be able to walk, at the time she thought it was just a sexually charged threat but now she realised he had meant it. She was tender and a little sore between her thighs. The shower had helped but her legs still shook. He had finally grown tired enough to sleep.

Looking at him now, she smiled. Bubbles of satisfaction filled her stomach, along with knowing she had fallen completely in love with him. Her very soul knew that he would forever hold her heart. She had dreamed of what it would feel like to be with him, to give him that sacred part of her — the reality was way better than any dream.

He was sleeping on his back, one arm under his head, the other resting on his stomach. The sheet, tangled around his hips, did nothing to hide the outline of what lay beneath. Even as he slept, he had a strength about him. She had noticed it when she was in the hospital, it oozed from him. He didn't seem to have a weakness, until this afternoon.

She still didn't understand what had happened in the stables. That person was not the Drake she knew. The horror in his eyes when he realised what he had done then he'd fought to leave her after he had placed her onto the bed — he was not a violent person. Pulling at his shirt she now wore, Kathryn climbed in beside him still confused.

"Where have you been?" he asked sleepily, his hand tangling in her hair at her nape and pulling her to him for a long intimate kiss.

"For a shower. You had yourself imprinted all over my body."

"Good, but if you'd woken me, I could have helped you wash," he said with a sly smile.

"I don't think so." She snuggled against his chest, her leg gingerly draping over the sheet covering his hip. His manhood responded to her nearness.

"Are you okay?" he asked as his arm pulled her closer and he kissed the top of her head.

"Just a little tender, that's all." Heat colouring her cheeks, she realised he now knew her more intimately than she knew herself.

"I'm sorry," he whispered and kissed the top of her head again.

They lay together, comfortable in the silence, lost in their own thoughts. Drake's chest started to shake with laughter. "You know what I was just thinking?" he said a laugh in his voice.

Rising to her elbow to look at him Kathryn shook her head.

"That if your grandmother knew what I had just done to you all afternoon, she would have slapped me harder than she did when I burped at the table."

Kathryn laughed. "She would have taken a knife to this thing..." she grabbed him between the legs, "and cut it off."

Drake sat up and covered her hand that held him so delicately tight. "I believe so," he said in a mock-squeaky voice. Both giggling, they laid back down cuddling.

"You know, I miss her every day," Kathryn said quietly. She had. Her grandmother had been her whole world and now she was gone. A lump formed in her throat, but she fought it down, she didn't want to change the mood of being here with Drake on something she couldn't change.

"I bet you do. I miss my grandfather too." It was a solemn statement, filled with hidden emotions.

Sitting up, Kathryn positioned herself so that she was close enough for them to still touch but she could see into his eyes.

The time had come.

She wanted to know his past. The truth of it. Her grandmother and Brigid had alluded to it and now she wanted to know the truth, to truly understand why he did what he did this afternoon and the reasons behind it. Looking directly into his eyes Kathryn asked, "Drake?"

"Mmm?" he said stroking her face.

"How did you come to be living with your grandfather?"

Chapter 21

He knew it was coming; knew that she would ask. He wasn't sure he was ready for her to know the truth. After what they had just shared, he didn't want her to see him in that light. But the reality of their lives, was now intruding on their afternoon of pleasure and shutting the world out.

Did he trust her with the truth? Would she run?

It didn't matter anymore. He would tell her, then he would make her leave. Once she knew the truth, she would understand why she had to leave and maybe he wouldn't have to force her. Clearing his voice, he wriggled up the bed a little. Not knowing where to start, he just let the words tumble out.

"My grandfather found me after my ... after she was killed, he brought me back here." The release of the words coming out made his voice ragged in his throat. He had never told another soul about what had happened – those who knew anything only knew what his grandfather had told them – and his grandfather had only been informed by what the police had said and pieced together.

Kathryn never said anything, she looked at him, her eyebrows raised to indicate she had heard his words and waited for him to continue.

Suddenly, he wanted her to know it all, to hear it in his own voice. For her to understand why he was about to do what he had to do.

"My father died in a car accident, on his way to see a childish little show that I was in when I was five years old. I had made him promise that he would be there. He died when he ran a red light and was hit by another car. My mum was devastated. My father was the love of her life." He took a breath.

"My father and my grandfather had had a big fight a year before that and stopped talking, but my mother had secretly been sending letters and photos back to Granddad. She believed in family and loving one another. Her own family lived overseas and so having my grandfather as part of our lives, even in that small way, was really important to her." He frowned slightly. Two wrinkles appeared between the centre of his eyes. "I never knew what the fight was about, but after their fight I never saw my grandfather again, till the day he found me. I knew she still wrote after my father's death, but not as often." Drake stopped and worked out his next words.

"My mum got a job at a local café. She loved it and they were really nice to her. I remember they even had us over for a pool party one afternoon." He smiled at the memory and sat up, leaning his back against the headboard. He took Kathryn's hand.

"After about a year, she met a man, they started to date and soon he moved into our house. I never liked him from the start and got the feeling he never liked me. He didn't want another man's child hanging around, but he was clever though, and never let my mum see it." Drake chewed his bottom lip and continued.

"After he moved in, he'd slap me when he would walk past or say nasty things when she couldn't hear. I tried to tell her, but she would say that I had to be better behaved or that I had misunderstood what he'd said." He cleared his throat.

"He made her sell our house and move to a dodgy part of town, saying that if she invested her money then she would be better off. He even convinced her that giving up work to take care of me and him was best. That we could live off what he made." He shook his head. "She did, and that's when things got really bad."

Unconsciously, Drake's grip on Kathryn's hand tightened. "He began to question where she went and with who. He started to isolate her from friends and stopping her contacting her family, saying it was too expansive to call overseas. She wasn't even allowed to shop without him, and anything she wanted, she had to ask permission for." He cleared his voice again and shifted uncomfortably in his spot. Taking a big breath, he continued as calmly as he could.

"I walked in on them one night, because I heard her being sick and him yelling at her." Drake's eyes glazed over as he looked at Kathryn. "He was making her suck him off and she was vomiting from doing it, but he held her there. She was crying and yelling at me to get out." A tear slipped down his cheek unnoticed. "I never entered their room again, no matter what I heard. The horrified look in my mum's eyes is something that will forever be burned into my memory."

He shifted in the bed again. "I remember running to my room, not understanding what was happening, holding my pillow over my ears so I couldn't hear. Then, the next day, he sold her car without her permission and told her she was never to leave the house again without him. She had bruises all over her face and body. She could hardly move without pain. I wanted to stay with her instead of going to school but she forced me to go." He closed his eyes in memory before slowly opening them again.

"I remember walking to school without her and being so afraid. The streets were not safe for someone my age in that neighbourhood. A boy from my class had been kidnapped months before on his way home from school, and he was never found. Mum and I were both so scared."

Her hand shaking in his, Kathryn listened, watching his face carefully. He could feel her gauging and absorbing his emotions. He was too lost in his memories to do anything but let the words keep rolling out, strained but even. He couldn't stop now even if he wanted to.

"The abuse continued and was escalating. He was drinking all the time. He was nice when he wanted something, or when others were around. He was the doting stepfather and husband when we were out in public. When my mother tried to call him out on his behaviour, he would call her crazy or say she was making things up in her head, that she had taken things the wrong way and that his behaviour never changed whether in public or at home. That it was *her* temper and behaviour that changed, and others saw it. People knew she was crazy and had no idea what she was talking about. He was always the victim."

Pausing, Drake slowed his breathing down. The emotions were rolling his stomach over. He continued when he knew he would not lose the contents of it.

"The night before it happened, he came home late from work, my mum and I had eaten, and she'd sent me to bed. He was furious and dragged me back out of bed, his belt around my neck as I crawled along the ground terrified and gasping for air, desperately trying to keep up with him. We were meant to wait for him before we ate. She fought him, and after he let me go, he beat her with the belt so badly she was crumpled on the floor in front of me, coughing up blood and bleeding from her head. I tried to stop him, but he was too big and strong."

Tears begun to flow down his cheeks, but he was still lost in his memories. Kathryn's face was streaked with tears, her hand shaking as she listened, and he saw her, through his tears and the blur of this nightmare memories, holding her breath, fearful of what was coming.

"The next night, when he walked to the pub for his regular Friday night drinking session, mum and I frantically packed a bag each. We were going to leave him for good. As we were backing out, he happened to return in his friend's car. He chased us. My mum did all she could to lose him. Speeding away as fast as possible, we drove up and down streets and even into car parks to lose him. Weaving and even crossing our path trying desperately to lose him. When she thought we had, she headed out of town. Her hands gripping the steering wheel so tight her knuckles were white and she kept looking back in the mirror as she told me she had called my grandfather in the early hours of that morning. He was going to meet us just outside of the city and take us to his farm. My stepfather would never know where to find us as she had burned my grandfather's phone number and all the letters he had sent. We were going to be safe." Drake's voice rose with a sliver of excitement as the taste of what it felt like in that moment long ago had been like. It dropped again to barely a whisper. "We just had to get to the servo to meet granddad."

Drake paused, waiting for his heartbeats to settle. Kathryn waited, her tear-filled eyes fixed on his face, willing him to continue. His hands were cold and shaking, but his breathing was oddly steady. Eventually, he continued.

"It was raining, and I could almost taste the sickly smell of rain on hot bitumen. The lightning was flickering all around us. I was gripping the seat and trying to see through the rain. I could only just see over the dashboard. The windscreen wipers were going so fast, and the sound of the rain was deafening. Mum was speeding down the road. The streetlights were just a blur. I was so scared, I just wanted to be with my grandfather. I hadn't seen him in five years and hoped he'd do as mum said he would and keep us safe." Drake paused and clenched the hand that wasn't holding Kathryn's into a fist. His throat burned with a massive swallow. A deadness and hollow sound came out as his voice when he continued.

"My stepfather caught up and drove into us twice before he managed to push us off the road and into a ditch at high speed."

Kathryn was bracing herself, her fingers were digging into his palm, the pain somehow welcome.

"My mum was trapped by the steering wheel. The force of the impact had pushed it back against her stomach and pinned her legs. Her head was cut and bleeding and she was shaking violently. I tried to get her out. I really tried." He dragged a shaky hand across his dripping nose. "Through the windscreen and pouring rain I saw he'd pulled over up ahead and was walking towards us. I couldn't see what was in his hands, but I knew it was bad. I was screaming and trying to pull her from her seat, pulling and pressing the release in the seatbelt but I couldn't." Drake stopped. Tears flowed heavily down his face and onto his chest. His hands were cold and sweating. The lump in his throat was restricting his voice to barely a whisper.

"Mum turned to me and touched my face, wiping away my tears with her fingers. Her soft beautiful fingers. She was so calm; her smile was just how I remembered it used to be. She kissed my cheek. '*I love you, Drakey, don't you ever forget that. You will be safe and so will I, but you have to run now. You must go and hide. Do not come out till it's safe. Do you understand?*' She kissed my forehead and told me to go." His voice broke as the last words came out. "So ... I ran."

He stopped and didn't speak for a long time. Kathryn didn't move or say anything. She just sat there, tears falling at the pain he'd been through. Perhaps also for the strength of the woman he got to call his mum.

"I ran ..." he said strangulated. "I found a tall tree and hid behind it. I could hear him calling for me to come out, but I waited till it was safe. Some cars had stopped, and people were yelling and running for her. I believed she was going to be rescued. That the other people would stop him before he got to her, then I heard the gun shot. I don't know what happened next. Just that my throat hurt so much from screaming and crying."

Drake turned his face to Kathryn, his mind still faraway in the past. Wiping his face, he pulled his hand from hers and began to brick back up his walls, to contain the pain and horror, push it back into place again.

"A few days later my grandfather, after he was eventually allowed to, came and collected me from a foster home and I came to live with him. We would go to the city when the psych doctors ordered, and we would stay with you and your grandmother, then we would come home."

Drake got up and pulled on his clothes and boots. From the corner of his eye, he saw the horrified look on Kathryn's face. His heart squeezed and he knew — he could see it in her eyes. She saw him for what he truly was. Something cold came over him as his anger threatened to boil over.

Kathryn knew Drake was shutting down and wasn't going to talk anymore. She wasn't sure what to do — let him go and talk later — or talk now. He strode from the room, his shoulders and arms rigid with tension.

At the door, he turned to her. "Pack your bags. Now. You're leaving." Then he slammed the door behind him.

Kathryn sat on the bed momentarily confused at his words before racing after him. He was about to walk out the front door. "Drake! Drake!" she demanded "What the hell are you talking about? I don't understand! Drake, stop right now and talk to me for God's sake!"

Spinning around, he stalked her backwards, his eyes a dark stormy green and looking ready to kill anything that got in his way. Kathryn retraced her steps backwards, heart pounding with fear, until she was stopped by the kitchen bench at her back. She had to stay strong. Standing as tall as she could, she looked him dead in the eyes. Her jaw locked tight; she stared him down.

"What don't you understand? I just told you everything!" he bit at her.

Eyes wide, Kathryn fought to stay strong. He was standing toe to toe with her — the man who made her feel such ecstasy an hour ago was now making her tremble with fear. Gritting her teeth and slowing her breathing, she answered, "You told me how you came to be living with your grandfather. I don't see how that means I have to leave."

A growl roared from deep inside him as he turned, frustrated at her lack of understanding, and kicked the lounge chair. Spinning back to her, his face was filled with anger and hatred — and disappointment. "I know the truth. I heard them when they thought I was sleeping. They all know what I am."

"What truth, Drake? Who said what?" Kathryn was desperately trying to follow and understand what he was saying, but he wasn't making any sense.

"The police. The foster carers they put me with. I heard them, don't you understand? They all knew it straight away. That's why mum said she was going to be safe. She knew what was going to happen. She *knew.* That's why she had to get us to the servo." Fresh tears stung his eyes and he began to pace, racking his hand through his hair and over his face, looking up at the ceiling.

"Drake, please, I don't understand. What did they all know? What did they say?" Kathryn tried to reach out to him, to stop him pacing and calm him so she could understand what the hell he was talking about? His mum knew what? He was so agitated and frustrated. His emotions and memories were clearly swamping him.

He stopped directly in front of her, his face so close to hers she could feel his breath on her face, a coldness in his voice. "That I am *just* like that monster, I was born like it and there is *nothing* anyone can do. They all knew it. Everyone did. Mum knew it. That's why she was taking me to my grandfather."

Drake stepped back away from her and started to yell; spittle flecked on his lips. "I'm just like that bastard of a monster! I ran and she was stuck in the car, I ran from her." Drake was becoming hysterical. "I killed them both. Don't you see? It was *me*. I did this to them and this is my punishment. I have to live with the monster I am. I have to keep everyone away for their own safety."

Despair laced his voice. He began to walk away from her, but his legs wobbled, and he dropped to his knees, fighting for air and gulping.

Kathryn stood frozen, staring down at him. Nothing made sense. He was babbling about monsters and running and 'killing them'. Closing her eyes, she tried to steady her heart and get control of her thoughts. She had to piece things together, and fast, so she could understand.

Drake was hurting, crumbling with such severe emotional pain and destress, hunched over his knees, his head nearly touching the floor as he held his arms across his stomach and rocked, trying to get control of himself as the torturous memories and pain ripped him apart. He needed to be comforted — but she needed space in case she had to run. She should not be scared of him.

Never.

But right now, she was. He was in a volatile state and the wrong move could cause her serious harm. Not going to him and comforting him like she knew he needed was the wrong move also.

Unsure of her choice, Kathryn slid down the wall quietly, her back leaning against the bench and waited for him to settle enough to talk. Her nerves on end, she couldn't help but shake, her whole body trembling with uncertainty of what Drake was about to do.

His emotions calming just a little, Drake turned his head and stared up at her, sitting away from him. She stared back at him and swallowed, trying not to show him how terrified and anxious she was at that moment. But he saw it. Eyes wide, he staggered to his feet, his eyes darkened by hurt, anger and pain. Tears still falling, he silently walked to the door.

Kathryn scrambled to her feet and followed him, making the wrong move of grabbing his arm to stop him. "Drake ..."

Drake threw her hand off him with such force she fell back hard against the wall. Her legs gave way and she slumped to the floor.

Drake ran out the front door.

Chapter 22

Throwing all that she had in her little bag, Kathryn zipped up her dress and listening for any movement in the house, she snuck out the front door.

Her first thoughts were to run through the paddock and cut back across the creek to the main road and walk to town, but then thought he would find her too easily. She would take his Ute and leave it in town. He could collect it later — she'd be gone by the time he arrived. She would find a truckie, or someone leaving town, and catch a lift with them. She was a nobody anyway. She could just disappear and be safe.

It was now dark, and the moon was covered by clouds. It made the perfect cover for her to run to Drake's Ute. As soon as she was in the Ute, she locked the doors and looked back towards the house. Sophie lay cowering under the front steps. There was nothing she could do but leave her friend there.

Turning the ignition, Kathryn sent a silent prayer that she had her licence, something she was proud of. She knew that when she had her own place and café, her next dream was a car. For now, she was grateful for the knowledge as she put the Ute in gear and roared off before he could get to her. She had no idea where he was but if he was close, she needed to get away fast.

Drake stood in the deepest shadows of the stables. Shaking violently. He had never hit or struck out at anyone before, apart from Rob and a couple of dust-ups at school. Like all boys, he'd had to learn about controlling his temper when the male hormones kicked in during his teens, and he had been acutely aware that he needed to control it more than any of the other boys.

Just his look was enough to scare most blokes away. He had never hit a woman and had vowed he never would. Today, he had broken that vow. Self-hatred and loathing flooded him as he watched Kathryn run for her life.

He didn't care if she took his Ute and drove to the ends of the earth — at least she would be away from him and safe. He heard the Ute's turbo as she changed the gears perfectly and disappeared from his life forever.

White hot anger shot through him, and he turned to the solid timber post beside him and punched it again and again. Liquid hot pain exploded in his hand, but he couldn't stop. He punched so hard the sound echoed through the stables and the force rattled the tin on the roof. He kept going. Furious at himself and the world.

At his mother for telling him to run.

He should have stayed and died with her. He should have protected her but the real him, had left her. The monster in him had left her there to die alone. Finally, his anger subsided and the pain in his hands took over along with more tears. He stopped and slid down to the floor against the stable door.

His tears slowed and stopped, replaced by an emptiness that let him feel nothing in the darkness surrounding him both inside and out. He'd lost control of everything, and now Kathryn was running scared of him. He scrubbed his face with his rough, bleeding hands. He had not wanted it to end like this. He had wanted her to understand and leave. The look she gave him when she realised the truth about who he really was — he would remember that horrified look forever.

Kathryn swerved back onto the road as she wiped at the tears blurring her vison. Her heart ached and she was shaking. Her thoughts didn't make sense and she was crying too hard to care. The lights of town glowed into the darkness as she neared the outskirts. She had decided to pull up at the end of the main street, near the park, and leave the keys at the police station, once she had secured a way out of town.

The street was deserted, apart from a few cars parked outside the café. Wiping the remining tears from her face, Kathryn got out and started to walk towards the highway. The sounds of the city had never scared her; she had loved the noises the night brought with it, of people laughing and glasses clinking as they enjoyed their meals. Loud TVs on as she passed the houses near her apartment. Dogs barking and the occasional child crying. The noises had comforted her on her walks home from work.

In this small, quiet, country town it was different. The café was open, but no sounds emanated from it. In the distance a truck was using its exhaust brakes to slow down as it rolled into town. She could even hear the quiet hum of the electricity in the streetlights as they shone to lead her around the corner to the police station. She wasn't even sure it would be open. Stepping up the pebbled stone steps Kathryn pulled on the doors.

"Dammit." They were locked. Retracing her path, she walked back to the Ute. She wasn't going to just leave his Ute locked up with no idea where the keys were, and she couldn't risk leaving a note and letting someone steal it. Not that she thought that was a real threat in the sleepy town, but it was a risk, and she didn't want to do that to Drake.

Looking around, she saw the café again. She could leave the keys there with a note for Richard that they were Drake's.

Grabbing her bag and making sure the Ute was locked, Kathryn walked across the street. The headlights from a car coming up the main street blinded her as she hastened her steps across the road. Her heart leapt when it pulled into a car park behind her. It couldn't be Drake, he wouldn't have been able to get a vehicle and follow in this short amount of time, but she started to run towards the café anyways.

"Kathryn!" The voice had her turning and stopping. It wasn't Drake. It was Richard. "Are you okay?" he asked as he looked around to find what she was running from.

Relief washed over her, and she started to cry again.

Climbing out of his police car in a hurry, he was by her side quickly, taking her bag and leading her back to a seat near his vehicle. "What happened? Is that Drake's Ute? Where is he?"

"I took his Ute. He got mad and so upset that he pushed me away and I fell against the wall. He ran and I panicked. I didn't know where to leave his keys before I got a lift out of town." She could hear herself rambling as she sat on the seat.

Taking a seat right next to her, his arm around her shoulders, Richard let her calm down before quietly asking his next question. "If you want to leave, there's a bus that goes through early in the morning, heading north. You can take that one. I will get his Ute back to him tomorrow. Do you have a place to stay tonight?"

Shaking her head, she started to cry again. She didn't have the money for a bus ticket or for any other place to stay once she arrived in another town. She was either trapped here in town or homeless if she left. Her life was a mess.

"How about I shout you a coffee and something to eat and we can talk about your next step?" Richard offered and stood.

Nodding, she picked up her bag and followed him to the café. It was a small dark place with an odd odour of burnt coffee and oil mixed together. Surely this couldn't be the only café in town? When she asked Richard, he confirmed it was.

"The other one closed a few years ago. It smells odd in here, but the food is good." He smiled as they took their seats in an old booth in the back corner. A few of the other diners watched and gossiped about them openly as they sat. Typical small town. After they received their coffee, Richard asked. "So, are you really okay?"

Swallowing her mouthful of coffee, Kathryn replied, "I just got scared and panicked." She was downplaying it; she had been petrified. Her hands shook even now as she lifted the cup to her lips and let the thick brew burn her mouth.

"Can I ask why he got so mad at you? Do you know?"

"He had just told me about his mother and how he ended up out here with his grandfather."

Astonished, Richard stared at her. "Drake talked to you about his mother? Did he tell you what happened to her?" Surprise was written all over his face.

"Yes? Why?" Kathryn slowly lowered her coffee cup back to the table. There was something in the way he'd asked that made her sure she had just said something he was not sure he could believe.

"He has never spoken to anyone about it, not even his grandfather. When he arrived here, we all tried to help. He never wanted anything to do with me, but that's understandable. He never breathed a word. He suffered nightmares and panic attacks for a long time. His grandfather would take him to the city to see some doctors, but they never helped."

Kathryn nodded. Drake had told her about seeing the doctors. "Why is it 'understandable' that he wanted nothing to do with you? You seemed friends when I first met you."

Their food arrived. A large bowl of chips, and a sandwich that looked like it was made a week ago, filled each plate. Kathryn was so hungry she took a bite. Even if the food looked like it wasn't edible, at this time of night it was better than an empty stomach.

Richard had been watching her, contemplating his next question. "Did he talk about his stepfather?"

"Yes, but by the end he was making no sense, he was raving about monsters and what his foster carers and the police had said that he overheard. I couldn't understand him. I tried, but the more I tried to understand, the more he got upset. I tried to stop him leaving and that's when he pushed me away and I fell. I know it was an accident, but I deserve better than that."

"You do," he replied sternly. "I'm really surprised he did that; it goes against his very nature. If I had any worries, I'd have stopped you from coming out here with him. I was the one Scott called to talk to about Drake. They'd found his file and details of his past and Scott wanted to ensure he was safe for you to be with, given you had only recently met up again. If I'd thought for a second that he'd harm you, I wouldn't have vouched for him."

She could see the disappointment on Richard's face.

"It wasn't like that. Drake is not like that. Well, at least not the Drake I know, or used to know." Kathryn vouched for and defended Drake, but inside she was confused about who he really was. Deep down, she knew the man who had loved her so hard that afternoon was not the same man who had run out the house leaving her on the floor terrified.

Yet, she still didn't understand what was going on and Richard hadn't answered her question. In fact, he had avoided it all together. She wanted answers and wanted them now.

If she was going to get on a bus tomorrow morning and never see Drake again, she had to know it was the right thing to do. That she would never regret it. Calmly but sternly, she asked Richard again. "Why didn't he want much to do with you when he arrived?"

"I think we need to go and see Vicki. Reggie said Drake took you to meet her? That in itself says a lot to me." Richard gulped the last of his coffee and took a large bite of his soggy sandwich, completely ignoring her frown. "Come on, let's get you over there. Are you right to follow me in his Ute?"

Disappointed at his continuing avoidance, she picked up the keys off the table. Vicki seemed straightforward. Perhaps, finally, she would get to the bottom of all the confusion that surrounded Drake and his past and maybe, just maybe, it would help him break free of the pain he was consumed by.

The night nurse was instantly worried when she came to the entry doors of the nursing home and saw them standing there. It was late and many of the residents were asleep. Richard whispered a few words to her, the nurse's gaze going over Kathryn as she listened then nodded. Letting them in, she led the way. The hallways were dark except for a line of tiny lights that were plugged into the walls to give the barest of light for the nurses and any residents that walked the halls of a night.

When Kathryn asked if Vicki would be awake the nurse put her finger to her lips and frowned at her. It was clear they had to remain silent. The hall they walked along was different to the one that she and

Drake had travelled when he brought her here. After a few minutes, the nurse turned and entered another small hall that ended with three doors. All were closed; however, light was visible from under the door to her right. Knocking softly, the nurse stood back and waited.

The door opened and Vicki stood in the doorway, the light spilling from behind her gave her a beautiful silhouette. She was wrapped in her nightgown and when she caught sight of Kathryn and Richard her eyebrows lifted, but she was not as surprised as Kathryn thought she should be by the late-night intrusion of a policeman and someone she had only just met, on her doorstep.

"I guess you had better come in, sweetheart," she said quietly, holding her hand out to take Kathryn's. "I'll handle it from here Richard and thank you. I'll let you know how it goes when we're finished."

With a nod to the nurse and Richard, Vicki closed the door. Then she took Kathryn in her arms and hugged her tight — it was one of those hugs that lasted so long it felt like all the broken pieces of Kathryn's life righted themselves and she was finally safe. Only her grandmother had had the ability to do that, and it wasn't until that moment, she realised how much she'd needed it.

Vicki held her at arm's length and peered into her face. "Would you like a hot drink before you tell me what happened between the two of you?"

While Vicki boiled the kettle, Kathryn took in her surroundings. The room was larger than what she'd seen of the other resident's rooms. It was like a tiny apartment, with a compact kitchen, lounge room and dining area.

Through one door Kathryn could see the bathroom and bedroom. It was a home away from home, and was bigger than the house she and her grandmother had shared when she was growing up. Photos filled the walls and the TV stand. The room smelled just like Vicki. Pulling up one of the chairs near the table, Kathryn sat. Vicki took the one opposite her and offered a plate of biscuits to go with her mug of tea.

"Thank you," Kathryn said quietly taking a sip of the hot brew. "Richard and I just ate at the café downtown."

Vickie's face scrunched up. "That food is horrible." She puffed out her chest with pride. "When I had my cafe a few years ago, people were fed better in this town." Calming down, she touched Kathryn's hand. "But that's a conversation for later, though. Now tell me what happened."

Kathryn repeated her story as she had done with Richard while Vicki just nodded and listened. Kathryn even told her the truth about the city and what had happened — it all came gushing out of her like water out of a tap.

At last, she had told Vicki everything. Exhaustion looming, she finally asked what she was burning to know. "What is Drake not saying? I know I am not wrong about him. I feel we have something special, and that I may even be in love with him," she stated shyly, "but I just don't understand."

Vicki squeezed her hand with a warm, knowing smile. "Drake has never spoken to anyone about what happened to him, or his mother. We all knew how she passed and guessed what may have happened to them in the lead-up, but he never spoke a word. He refused to divulge anything about his past from the moment he arrived here. We tried to give him time, but his nightmares were getting worse, and he wasn't coping at school. He was getting into trouble and a few fights, if you could call them that."

Vicki rolled her eyes at Kathryn and placed her hands in her lap, sitting back in her seat. "The bullies would take one look at him when he stood up for the ones they were picking on and run. The few stupid ones, well, let's just say that the fight never lasted long, and Drake never had a mark on him when they finished. The people who oversaw making sure he was okay from the government suggested that he go to the city and see some doctors."

Vicki leaned over and patted her hand. "From what we heard, Drake never spoke much to the doctors, but he would come home a little better for a few weeks. We guessed it was from the friendship he had struck up with you while his grandfather and he stayed with you and your grandmother. He seemed different. Happier."

Kathryn shifted in her seat as she continued to listen intently.

"His nightmares would always return, though. His grandfather started to write down the things he was saying as he tried to calm him or wake him. It became apparent that Drake had been badly abused, not only physically but mentally and emotionally too."

Kathryn sat sipping her tea, her heart aching as Vicki detailed to her everything that Drake had not said or felt not able to say. As the picture filled in, a lot of his behaviour towards her, being hot and then cold, his panic about her whereabouts and even his protectiveness at the hospital, all made sense. While his mother was married to his stepfather, his childhood was horrific.

Vicki even spoke of how they had tried to help Drake understand it wasn't his fault, but nothing seemed to get through to him. Kathryn knew that abuse wasn't something you could get over quickly, or was easy to understand when you had suffered for so long, especially from childhood. But understanding the whys and hows, and even looking at things in a new light, could maybe ease the pain and help you to live your life in a different way.

Something she herself had struggled to achieve once she learned about her own mother and the reasons why she was being raised by her grandmother. It was her grandmother that taught her to view things differently and to be grateful for what you had.

As the conversation progressed, they shared a second cup of tea together and Kathryn spoke of how she had wanted her life in the city to be, saying sadly that her dream of her own café was now most likely never going to happen.

It was nice to be conversing with someone other than Drake, even though she liked their talks, speaking with another woman, one who was so much like her own grandmother, allowed her to relax and say things that she hadn't been able to say to anyone for years. The conversation lasted for several hours into the night.

Deciding that he needed to get up off his butt and check the damage to his hand, Drake stood and headed towards the house. His arms and hands throbbed from the beating he gave the post. It was he who had come off second best. That post still stood tall and strong, right where it had for the past sixty years.

The sound of gravel crunching up the drive then stopping and the shine of headlights made him hasten his steps to the big doors. His heart thumped wildly. Kathryn was back.

A tidal wave of relief washed over him. Followed by a surge of guilt that she had returned, against all odds, after his stupid and dangerous behaviour. A voice in his head told him that he should be mad that she had returned when he'd told her to leave. But he wasn't.

"Kathryn!" he yelled towards the lights, now in his eyes.

"No, Drake. Its Richard," came the dry reply.

Drake's feet stopped so quickly he slid on the loose gravel just outside the stables. A cold dread washed over him. Something had happened to her. She'd had an accident and been killed. He knew it. He had done it again. Killed the only person left in this world that he loved.

The thought made him pause. He *loved* Kathryn. Always had. Had known it but never wanted it to be true because he couldn't have her and now never would. Anguish tore through him and ripped his heart open like a knife slicing through it. He couldn't breathe.

"Where is she? WHERE IS SHE?" he roared at Richard, resting his hands on his knees and hung his head as he wrestled to get his emotions back under control.

"She is safe and will remain so, but you and I have to have a serious conversation, my boy."

The sternness in Richard's voice and his declaration that Kathryn was safe made Drake lift his head and then stand up as he fought down his rolling stomach and fears.

"She is safe? Not hurt?" Drake asked again as he sucked in deep breaths.

Richard closed the door on the police car, the sound echoing around the buildings in the still of the night and walked to where Drake stood, feeling like a deer caught in headlights. The man walked carefully, watching Drake, like he was approaching a dangerous person and was prepared for anything to happen.

"Yes, my boy. She's safe and unhurt. But very shaken and scared about what you did to her. She'll carry the memory of that with her for a long time."

The words twisted the knife deeper into Drake's chest. He had never wanted to do that to her.

"You want to explain to me what went on here? Because you know we don't take it lightly what you did to her." Richard drew up to his full height, the same height as Drake, but smaller in build.

For the first time since knowing him, Richard looked to be uncertain about who this person was standing in front of him. "I didn't mean to do it," Drake said, disappointment in his actions returning,

"I know you didn't, but what happened?" Richard said quietly and calmly, doing his best to coax an explanation from him.

"Kathryn went for a walk today and she wasn't back when I returned. I panicked, thinking something had happened to her or the gang looking for her had found her ..." He ran his hand over his face and shifted in his boots. "And I'd let it happen, hadn't been able to protect her." He added sadly and took a steadying breath.

"When she walked up the drive, her hair was wet and her clothes were damp. I was so relieved but upset she'd left no note and had been swimming somewhere. I lost control, a little. After I'd calmed down ..." he deliberately left out the afternoon of bliss they had shared, "...she asked me about how I came to live here. Vicki told me that if I cared enough about Kathryn, like she suspected I did, then Kathryn deserved to know the truth. The whole truth."

Rolling his head to ease the tension in his shoulders, he looked back to Richard. "So, it all came tumbling out, but she didn't get it ... didn't understand who I really was ... what I was telling her." Drake clenched his hands. "When I told her to leave, she refused and kept asking why ... and I couldn't explain it anymore. She tried to stop me from walking out, and she grabbed my arm." He swallowed, shame rising like bile.

"I threw my arm back to break her grip." He took in a shaky breath. "She fell against the wall. I didn't even check to see if she was okay. I just ran." His words trailed off.

"And that's when she panicked and drove away," Richard finished for him. "Why did you tell her to leave?"

Drake gave a bewildered smile and shook his head. Was Richard stupid or just making him say what he already knew? "Because of what I am. And don't play dumb with me. You all knew. You, Vicki, Reggie and even my grandfather. You all knew when I arrived what I was. Everyone could see it, even the evil bastards at the city police could see it. I never had any other choice. I have to be alone for the rest of my life, otherwise I will be where that monster is. I will hurt those around me. Don't you get that? Kathryn is far too good for me. I can't keep her safe. I'm the same bloody monster, he was. Born one and then raised by one. What hope do I have?"

Frustration and anguish, topped with pain and desperation, hummed through his body and he paced in a circle while Richard gaped at him with his mouth open.

"Jesus, Drake. That is the biggest load of horseshit I have ever heard!" Richard shot back.

Ceasing pacing, Drake's temper flared and he took a step toward Richard, but the old officer didn't move, just stood his ground and squarely looked him in the eyes, his eyebrows raising.

"Horse shit, my boy," he provoked.

"I ran. I should have stayed and blocked her body with mine. I should have attacked him, stopped him from hurting her. But I ran. I let it happen," Drake hissed through his teeth into Richard's face. Anger at who he was and what he had done storming out of his body.

Richard held his ground. "You were a child, Drake, no more than ten years old. He would have killed you too."

"At least then I wouldn't be living in this hell. Trying to keep it locked up."

"Keep what locked up?" Richard stared at him, a puzzled frown on his face.

Drake turned and paced again, rolling his head and shoulders to relieve some of the burning that was causing him to ache. Were they all stupid? Why could nobody understand? It was clear as day.

"The monster living inside me, like it did in him. Mum knew it. Everyone knew it." He was pacing and kicking the dirt with his boots in aggravation that no one understood.

"I demanded that my father come to see me in the show that day and he died trying to get there in time. I let my stepfather beat and torture my mother until she had no option but to run. I let her die, trapped in that car alone while I ran away to save myself. What type of person is that? A monster."

Richard was still gaping at him, confused.

"I even went to the city to make sure that bastard was actually dead and buried so I knew he couldn't hurt me again. I watched as they lowered the box in the ground and felt happy about it. That in itself shows how messed up I am." He stopped pacing and stepped backwards to lean on the fence post at his back, defeated.

Richard stayed where he was.

"I couldn't even protect Kathryn from being assaulted. By the time I got there she was so badly hurt I had to carry her away." Emotionally drained, Drake hung his head in shame.

Richard walked up to him and placed a hand on his shoulder, squeezing it gently. "Drake, my boy. You need to listen and listen to me good. Got it?"

Drake didn't bother to reply except to gaze off into the night, his soul haunted by the emotions that kept swamping him, trying to crush him to death. In this moment he just wished they would.

"You are nothing like that monster your mother married after your father passed."

Drake huffed in disgust and rolled his eyes. Richard stepped in front of him and waited until he made eye contact. He couldn't see the senior constable's eyes, but with the headlights shining on his face, he bet Richard could see his.

"You will listen to me," Richard said sternly. "You are more like your grandfather and mother than anyone else. You have their kindness and ability to know what other people are needing, most times, without them even knowing themselves." Richard squeezed his shoulder and kept going.

"No one else would have left the comfort of their bed in the middle of the night through a raging storm to go with Reggie and help him with that buggered old horse he loves more than himself, except you. You have been there nearly every day since that thing ran through the fence, helping. And more than anything else, you've kept Reggie calm knowing that you're there with him. Everyone likes you and trusts what you say and do. You do what you say you will and don't promise what you can't. That takes a lot of integrity and moral values that, a lot of people double your age, don't have."

He shifted and tried to keep Drake focused on his words. "And if you say you're going to be somewhere at a certain time, you will be. You look just like your father, but he was always late for everything. Even as a child, he was late." Richard lowered his voice. "You didn't kill him by asking him to go to something that was important to you. You were five years old! Just a child wanting his father to be there to see him do well at something. That's all."

Drake moved away from Richard and started to pace. "Are you going to tell me now that I couldn't save my mum? That nothing I could've done would have saved her?" His voice was rising. "She had no one else. Nowhere else to turn. For God's sake, he was a bloody copper and had everyone believing that he was the perfect husband and father. She couldn't even go to the people who were meant to be there to protect her. To protect *us!*" Trying to calm himself, he rolled his shoulders and neck again.

"I get that. It was a horrible situation that you both found yourselves in." Richard stayed calm, continuing to reason with him. "She knew she had to leave and find somewhere safe. That's why she organised your grandfather to come and get you both. She knew her situation and the serious danger you were both in. She wanted to protect you — the child of the man she had loved. It wasn't about her being safe from you. She knew and loved the person everyone here, including Kathryn, sees. You never were, and never will be, *anything* like your stepfather, Drake. Never."

"How do you know that? I couldn't save her, and I ran. I should have stayed and protected her." Drake couldn't seem to get his thoughts out of the cycle.

"You did as she told you to. She was your mother, she adored you, and to save you, knowing her, she told you to run. Am I right?"

Drake nodded, fighting the sting of tears.

"She wanted you to be safe and survive. And I know you aren't anything like your stepfather because I've watched the man you have become. A man who can take abused and neglected horses and within weeks, sometimes days, have them trusting another human. The patience and love and understanding it takes day in and day out to do that is phenomenal. Your grandfather was good, but he always said you had a true gift."

Richard spoke more firmly. "I see it, Vicki sees it, even Reggie sees that's your true nature. Horses instinctively know you are safe and kind and that's how you get the results you do." Richard moved to stand in front of Drake again and kept driving home his points. "We both know that you get the worst of the worst. The ones so badly beaten that even seeing a person approach has them panicked, but after you've worked your magic, they're the ones that go on to homes that love and cherish them, even allowing children to ride them. Don't you see? No monster could do that. You're not a monster, Drake."

Drake couldn't look at Richard. The things he was saying went against everything Drake believed. He wanted to believe, desperately wanted to believe what Richard was saying, but a voice at his back kept telling him it was all lies.

"But look at what I did to Kathryn today! I can't go back and fix it. Once people, monsters like my stepfather, have lashed out it never stops. I can't do that to anyone, especially not her." He paused for a moment before he whispered, "I couldn't even save her in the city."

"Really? That's not what I was told … You found a woman being beaten by a man who was so mentally affected by drugs that he was more animal then human. You not only protected her while you fought the man, you laid him out cold so you could pick Kathryn up and carry her to safety." Richard shook his head.

"Then you somehow not only stopped her from being killed by a bullet, it only just grazed her head, but you held her till the ambulance got there. You were the *only* one that was able to calm her down when she was scared and confused about where she was and *you* were the only one the police were willing to let her go with, who they trusted to keep her safe, when they felt they couldn't. I think you need to stop believing what that bastard of a stepfather planted in your head and see the real Drake Harrison that we all see. Any person who meets you knows straightaway that you are no monster." Richard patted his shoulder and headed towards his car. "You're not a monster Drake, it's about time you knew that and believed it."

Drake didn't know what to say. His head was spinning so fast he felt light-headed. Richard's words raced around in his mind. "Richard!" He moved to the car window, leaning on it as Richard reached for the ignition. "Is Kathryn coming back?" This was the only thing he had left to ask.

"I don't know. It's her choice. But if she does and you touch her that way again, I will lock you up in my jail faster than you can imagine. She deserves to be taken care of and loved. She's been through enough in her life — you both have." After a moment of staring sternly, Richard's expression softened. "She cares for you a lot." Leaving everything else unsaid, he pulled away and drove back down the driveway.

Drake watched the taillights of the police car until he could see them no more. The night was clear now, and the moon was sitting high in the sky, surrounded by a smattering of stars.

In the distance, he heard an owl hooting. Everything was clear and beautiful. His head had stopped spinning, but his light-headedness was lingering, to the extent his body felt like he was half the weight he was. Like somehow a massive weight had been lifted. He smiled up at the stars, hoping that his parents were looking down at him, that they knew he loved them. He knew what he had to do.

He turned around and tripped over Sophie. He hit the ground and his emotions all bubbled out. He laughed and laughed until he cried, then he lay sprawled out on his back there and let the tears silently flow from the corners of his eyes until there were no more. Sophie licked his face as he truly saw the vastness and potential of the night sky for the first time.

Chapter 23

Kathryn was sitting in the Ute. She had crept up the drive slowly with her lights off and was now watching the house. Everything that Vicki had told her, and the pieces that Drake had said, now gave her a clear picture of exactly what had happened and what demons she believed Drake to be carrying.

The problem was, did she trust him to not lash out at her again? Was she safe and protected with him? Everything in her told her she was, but fear and past experience kept her locked in the Ute watching the dark house.

She kept replaying what Vicki had said and the times Drake and she had shared since that day he'd unexpectedly shown up at the café. They had spent every day since then together, and until that afternoon he had never shown any form of abuse to her.

She had witnessed his true nature with the horses and Reggie. He had way more patience than anyone she ever knew. His behaviour was way out of character, and as Vicki had said when Kathryn had asked her about trusting again, *'refuse to let one person who hurt you define how you see all others, because a real man will tell you the truth and hide nothing about anything you want to know.'*

Drake had done that, even as hard as it had been. He had told her because he knew that if he was a hundred per cent honest with her, then she would trust him no matter what. He had told her something he had never told anyone else. He'd known she could have made the choice of two things: leave or stay. She'd left out of fear, but did she truly want to leave now for good? They still hadn't heard from Scott, although in Vicki's opinion, if the thugs wanted her gone, they would have found her already. She is of no concern to them.

Vicki's words had given her so much hope that they'd talked about her dreams again and how she really was in charge of her own destiny. She could now choose a life that she could be proud of, and with whoever she wanted.

Did she want Drake in that new life? Was having him more important than her own café and home? She had loved him since they were teenagers sitting on the steps of her grandmother's tiny house, surrounded by the sweet smell of white roses. Now, she loved him more than ever. She had felt it that afternoon — he had her heart and soul. But did she have his? Would he really want her to stay if she told him she loved him? He had not mentioned love, or her staying. But Vicki told her that she could see Drake cared very deeply for her.

Taking a deep frustrated breath, she concluded she was getting nowhere with her thoughts going around in circles. She needed answers to her questions. If he wouldn't give them to her, then she would leave — she would only stay if he loved her and wanted her too.

Sophie whined at the Ute door. Lost in her thoughts, Kathryn had not seen her approach. Unclicking her seatbelt and unlocking the door she climbed out and patted the dog. Sophie was glad to see her, wagging her tail happily. Maybe she could sneak back into the house and confront Drake in the morning.

Coward, she thought. She needed to have her answers now. Taking another deep breath, she looked at the house. It was now or never.

Stepping quietly up onto the veranda, she briefly admired the doorknob reflecting the moonlight. Turning it, she pushed open the door. Her heart was beating fast.

Movement out of the corner of one eye made her let out a scream and clutch at her chest. Drake had been sitting quietly on a chair on the veranda watching her sit in his Ute.

"You scared me!" she said, catching her breath.

"I'm sorry. That was not my intention." Standing slowly, he whispered, "Not now and not ever again."

He moved slowly to stand before her, his chest bare, and his jeans hung low on his hips. His hair looked damp in the pale light. He held his arms locked beside him, so he didn't touch her, even though he looked as if he itched to pull her to him and never let her go.

"Kathryn. I am so sorry about what I did this afternoon. I have been hiding from you since you arrived and scared of the dark shadows that have been following me around for far too long. I really am so sorry."

He was so close she could smell the soap he had washed with earlier on his skin. His nearness, and the way he looked, made a low ache start to burn in her stomach.

"You need to know something." She took a step back from him. She needed her words to be clear and precise. "As of this moment, you will never mistreat me, abuse me or lay a hand on me in that manner ever again," she demanded in a voice that even shocked her — she'd never used a tone like it, one that left no room for anything but full agreement.

He nodded and kept his eyes on hers as a way of letting her know she had his full attention. "I'm ..."

She held her hand up to stop him. "You need to know that I spoke to Vicki tonight and she has filled in all the missing pieces that you didn't." She stepped forward to him and let her gaze go over his bare chest before resting her hands on his warm skin, she could feel his heart beating steady and strong. She followed the grooves of carved muscle up and along his collarbone, up his neck to his jaw line and stubbly beard. Her hands cupped his cheeks as her thumbs touched his lips. His eyes closed with the sensation. Kathryn grabbed his jaw hard and made him look at her.

Drake's eyes flew open. She gave him no choice but to look into her eyes.

The moonlight didn't give her much light, but she could see him clearly enough to know that she held his full attention.

"You will never, *ever*, treat me that way again Drake Harrison. Got it?" she emphasised with a painful tug on his stubbly beard.

He nodded and she released her grip. One hand dropped, while the other one rested over his heart. Staring into her eyes, he slowly moved to cover her hand with his. She felt the heat between them flare and pulsate; beneath her palm, his heart began to beat wildly.

"Kathryn," he whispered, so dry-mouthed her name came out ragged.

He took a slow and steady deep breath, moving his other hand to hold her lower back. "You need to know something else … It's you," he whispered hoarsely. "It's all of you. I can't describe it any other way. It is you. You are the only one I will ever want. I have loved you since the first time we met, I just didn't know it."

He took an unsteady breath. Her heart pounding hearing his words "You are my home and my world. I want you here with me until the day I die. You are the only thing that has ever mattered to me, even when I couldn't see it … I love you more than I ever thought I could love someone." He shifted closer "Please stay with me and let me prove to you that no matter what, I will love you forever. That you *are* safe and protected here and you *can* trust me."

Drake watched her for a moment, and she so wished she could see his eyes better. Shocked at hearing the words, Kathryn didn't move or say a thing. Her heart felt like it was going to explode with love and happiness all at once. She just stared at him. Drake didn't move either and she could feel the racing of his heart. Neither knew what to say. Couldn't speak. The world stopped spinning, and everything became clear.

She leaped into his arms, with a little scream, kissing him frantically. "I love you too." She wrapped her legs around him.

Locking his legs to stop himself from falling with her sudden leap, he held her to him and kissed her back, smiling and laughing as relief, happiness and love filled him.

Drake opened the door and walked to his bedroom with her in his arms. He kissed her lips, and his words tumbled around her, "Let me show you how much I love you."

Tumbling to the mattress, she laughed and kissed him hard.

As dawn arrived the next morning, Drake lay awake with Kathryn softly snoring in his arms. They had made tender love to each other, then as she lay on his chest, he told her more about his life. He explained how he'd found it all so confronting and devastating but with his new perspective on the truth of his childhood, he was looking forward to what the future now may hold.

There was still a lot of pain and hurt to process, and as he lay there watching the first streams of light float into their room, he understood his demons would not just go away overnight. It would take time and a lot of effort and mental control to turn his thoughts and actions around from what had been his soul's belief since his step father had entered his world, that of all people, a police officer had told him the truth — had forced him to see it not only for his sake but for Kathryn's as well.

The more he thought about it, the more he realised this truth was there the whole time, but he had been blinded by his stepfather's abuse and fear. He could now have all that he wanted without the fear. He could interact with people more; he could be the man Kathryn needed; he could also be a father if Kathryn wanted.

A thought he hadn't contemplated before, believing he could never be a father or husband, but that was now a wish that could come true. His heart felt light, and he was smiling with happiness. Leaning down, he kissed Kathryn on the top of her head and pulled her closer to him. He would never let her go.

When he next woke, Drake pressed his warm, naked body against Kathryn and her lips twitched into a smile even before her eyes opened. Drake secured her to him with an arm, and his free hand on her breast, fumbling and massaging.

The sun's rays were shining brightly into the room and the birds were chirping loudly. Moving onto her back, Kathryn looked out the window. "What time is it?" Pushing his hand away and rolling over, she rummaged for the alarm clock, which had been knocked to the floor last night. She blinked twice.

"It's lunch time!" She moved to get up.

"I know what time it is," he said sleepily. "You're not leaving this bed. I'm keeping you here." he couldn't help but smile as she rolled back to him and kissed him on the lips. His hand groping her butt, he pulled her so that she straddled his hips, laughing as the fire between them leaped to life.

It was not meant to be.

The sound of gravel crunching as a vehicle drove up the driveway floated through the open windows. Then Sophie was barking as she ran out to greet the person. Groaning, Drake kissed her deeply.

"Nooooo." He kissed her again as she climbed off the bed, their lips still locked together. The curtains were open and when the vehicle got to the fence, the driver would be able to see directly into the room and their naked bodies.

With a disappointed groan, Drake flung back the sheet and searched for his jeans. Kathryn couldn't find her clothes from the night before, except her underwear, so she pulled on one of Drake's shirts and ducked through the house to the bathroom.

Doing up the zipper on his jeans, Drake pushed open the screen door on the veranda to greet the person, his hand rubbing his face as he squinted against the glare of the sunlight.

"Morning, me boy," Richard said as he walked up towards the house with a cheeky, knowing smile on his face. "You just get out of bed?"

"Something like that," Drake replied as straight-faced as he could. Richard was a smart man and he'd already filled in the blanks, as if being shirtless with no boots or socks on with mussed-up bed hair wouldn't have been enough to tell him anyways.

"See you have your Ute back," Richard remarked as he turned to view the object in question.

"Yep, it arrived early hours of this morning. What can I do for you, Richard?" Drake asked. He wanted to help Kathryn in the shower. He could hear the water running and Richard was stopping their fun.

"Is Kathryn able to talk? I've just got off the phone with Scott." Richard's tone went all serious. "We need to talk."

Drake felt his stomach drop. That phone call would determine their future. Holding open the door, he motioned for Richard to come into the house. "You had better come in and have a coffee. She just got in the shower and these city girls can take a while." He grinned, hoping it covered his nerves.

When Kathryn emerged from the bathroom, walking out with Drake's shirt on again and nothing underneath, she froze when she saw Richard sitting at the table with Drake. Colour heated her cheeks. Drake was not helping, his eyes raking over her body and heating it wherever his eyes touched. She knew he knew she was naked underneath the shirt. His smile clearly saying it.

Well, she was not going to turn away now and be rude. Going to the table, she sat in the chair that Drake had stood and pulled out for her, ensuring she was as covered and modest as ever, she sat beside him. Facing Richard, she smiled and said, "Morning."

Drake surprised her by leaning over and kissing her cheek then resting his arm protectively around the back of her chair.

She was nervous, having immediately realised the reason for Richard's visit — he was here to tell her about her situation. He had no other real reason to be there. Maybe to make sure she was okay, but the tension in the air suggested otherwise.

"I can tell you, I am very happy to see you back here, Kathryn, and by the looks of things you've both sorted out your problems. However, that is not why I am here."

She tried to remember to stay calm. Whatever was said, Drake had promised to be with her and keep her safe.

Richard leaned in and rested his elbows on the table. "I had a phone call from Scott this morning. He has heard from their internal source that the leader of the bikie gang has believed the media reports and they are not looking for you — you are a free woman." He smiled at her.

Kathryn let out the breath she had been holding. Drake looked at her and she burst out crying. All modesty lost, she let him pull her into his lap and hold her as she cried tears of relief and happiness. It was over. Finally, the nightmare she had been living was over.

Clearing his throat, Richard said, "There's just one thing Scott suggested, and I agree with him. Extra security, let's call it."

Not sure what to expect, Kathryn turned her eyes to Richard. As did Drake.

"You should change your name. That way we can change everything that's needed here, and no one will ever know. You can start your new life."

"Can I keep my first name?"

"I don't see why not. It's a common enough name. Did you have something in mind for your last name?"

Kathryn looked at Drake, the question in her eyes and he shrugged to tell her it was her choice. Beaming, she turned back to Richard and said proudly, "Harrison."

Richard's eyes widened a touch and he looked between her and Drake, a smile all over his face. "Right then. WOW. Congratulations to you both." He stood up and reached over the table to shake Drake's hand. Still standing, he told them he would sort everything out and they need not worry anymore. They could both start their lives free of the past.

Drake was following Richard to the door when the policeman suddenly stopped, and handed Kathryn an envelope.

"I called in to see Vicki this morning, hoping to find out where you had gone. She said her instincts were never wrong and that you would be here. She also said you would need this, if she was correct."

Taking the envelope and thanking him, Kathryn let him go as she read the letter. Shock made her fall to the couch.

Chapter 24
(6 months later)

The café was busy. People were standing three-deep waiting for their morning coffees; the kitchen was bustling, and Drake was seated in the corner at the coffee bar watching the whole scene.

Kathryn was talking to a group of ladies from the community knitting group who had taken up their usual Friday morning spot in one of the booths near the front of the café. From there they could see who was coming and going and gossip to anyone and everyone who entered.

One of the new girls was cleaning up the table next to them, she had plates piled high on her tray. Kathryn turned and knocked the tray out of the girl's hands with her bulging stomach.

Jumping up from his seat and leaving his conversation with his friend Trevor, Drake moved through the crowd to stop her from bending over and trying to help clean up the mess and broken pieces. She only had her thongs on since her feet were so swollen. Staying still would ensure that she didn't cut her feet.

"Drake, stop, I can do it," Kathryn protested as he bent and helped clear the area.

"Now you let that handsome husband of yours look after you, my dear," said one of the ladies, taking her hand. "You need all the rest and spoiling you deserve while you're growing those precious babes in your belly."

Kathryn smiled down at Drake, who lovingly smiled up at her and rubbed her very large belly. She had made him a promise that she would only do the mornings until the café quietened down, then she would leave the girls to do the rest. He insisted he would sit and watch over her, then take her home. Secretly, she knew he loved the social aspect of being there each day and talking to everyone that walked in.

They had married in a very private ceremony, with only Reggie, Vicki, Gerald and Richard to witness it, a few weeks after they had received the news from Scott. By then she had suspected she was pregnant.

After reading Vicki's letter and very kind offer of her old café at the river end of the main street in town and money to invest in it, Drake had surprised her with her box that she had kept hidden in the laundry shed at her old apartment in the city. She had thought she'd lost it forever. He explained that he had Scott retrieve it, the day Scott had asked Drake to take Kathryn with him back to his farm.

It contained all of her recipes and enough money that she wouldn't have to take Vicki or Drake's offer to invest their money into her café. This café was fully hers and she would do it her way. It had been a thriving success from the very first morning. She had to hire five staff almost immediately to help with the demands of its success. Her blessing was her manager, a daughter of a friend of Vicki's who was Kathryn's saviour, especially when she found out she was having twins.

"You look tired. Let me take you home," Drake whispered in her ear as he now stood in front of her. He had become very doting. At night he would talk to the babies and rub her feet. He had taken over all her household duties and made her rest, sometimes driving her a little crazy. But she loved him with all her heart and knew that he loved her the same.

Nodding, she let him take her home.

Peering out the window as they passed the many properties on their way, Kathryn became lost in her thoughts.

Dreams sometimes have an odd way of coming true. When she thought she had lost it all, she now knew she was getting everything she'd ever wanted. Her café was a success and near a river; she had a family in Vicki, Reggie, Gerald and Richard; she had a home that she loved; she was going to be a mother — and she was married to the man she had dreamed of loving and living the rest of her life with since she had first set eyes on him. A man who had overcome his biggest fear to be more of a man then she could have ever hoped for.

Yes, her life had worked out just as she had dreamed. Drake lifted her hand to his lips as he drove up their driveway. Sophie jumped up from her spot in the sun on the porch and barked in greeting. They were home.

SherylM-author.com

www.ingramcontent.com/pod-product-compliance
Lightning Source LLC
Chambersburg PA
CBHW040525170726
48295CB00012B/340